T0161907

RENEGADE'S WAR

What Reviewers Say About Gun Brooke's Work

Treason

"The adventure was edge-of-your-seat levels of gripping and exciting…I really enjoyed this final addition to the Exodus series and particularly liked the ending. As always it was a very well written book."—Melina Bickard, Librarian, Waterloo Library (UK)

Insult to Injury

"This novel tugged at my heart all the way, much the same way as *Coffee Sonata*. It's a story of new beginnings, of rediscovering oneself, of trusting again (both others and oneself)."—*Jude in the Stars*

"If you love a good, slow-burn romantic novel, then grab this book."—*Rainbow Reflections*

"I was glad to see a disabled lead for a change, and I enjoyed the author's style—the book was written in the first person alternating between the main characters and I felt that gave me more insight into each character and their motivations." —Melina Bickard, Librarian, Waterloo Library (UK)

Wayworn Lovers

"*Wayworn Lovers* is a super dramatic, angsty read, very much in line with Brooke's other contemporary romances. …I'm definitely in the 'love them' camp."—*Lesbian Review*

Thorns of the Past

"I loved the romance between Darcy and Sabrina and the story really carried it well, with each of them learning that they have a safe haven with the other."—*Lesbian Review*

Escape: Exodus Book Three

"I've been a keen follower of the Exodus series for a while now and I was looking forward to the latest installment. It didn't disappoint. The action was edge-of-your-seat thrilling, especially towards the end, with several threats facing the Exodus mission. Some very intriguing subplots were introduced, and I look forward to reading more about these in the next book." —Melina Bickard, Librarian, Waterloo Library, London (UK)

Pathfinder

"I love Gun Brooke. She has successfully merged two of my reading loves: lesfic and sci-fi."—*Inked Rainbow Reads*

Soul Unique

"Yet another success from Gun Brooke. The premise is interesting, the leads are likeable and the supporting characters are well-developed. The first person narrative works well, and I really enjoyed reading about a character with Asperger's." —Melina Bickard, Librarian, Waterloo Library (London)

Advance: Exodus Book One

"*Advance* is an exciting space adventure, hopeful even through times of darkness. The romance and action are balanced perfectly, interesting the audience as much in the fleet's mission as in Dael and Spinner's romance. I'm looking forward to the next book in the series!"—*All Our Worlds: Diverse Fantastic Fiction*

The Blush Factor

"Gun Brooke captures very well the two different 'worlds' the two main characters live in and folds this setting neatly into the story. So, if you are looking for a well-edited, multi-layered romance with engaging characters this is a great read and maybe a re-read for those days when comfort food is a must."—*Lesbians on the Loose*

"That was fantastic. It's so sweet and romantic. Both women had their own 'demons' and they didn't let anyone be close to them. But from the moment they met each other everything felt so natural between them. Their love became so strong in a short time. Addie's thoughts threatened her relationship with Ellie but with her sister's help she managed to avoid a real catastrophe…"
—*Nana's Book Reviews*

The Supreme Constellations Series

"Brooke is an amazing author. Never have I read a book where I started at the top of the page and don't know what will happen two paragraphs later. She keeps the excitement going, and the pages turning."—*Family and Friends Magazine*

Fierce Overture

"Gun Brooke creates memorable characters, and Noelle and Helena are no exception. Each woman is 'more than meets the eye' as each exhibits depth, fears, and longings. And the sexual tension between them is real, hot, and raw."—*Just About Write*

September Canvas

"In this character-driven story, trust is earned and secrets are uncovered. Deanna and Faythe are fully fleshed out and prove to the reader each has much depth, talent, wit and problem-solving abilities. *September Canvas* is a good read with a thoroughly satisfying conclusion."—*Just About Write*

Sheridan's Fate—*Lambda Literary Award Finalist*

"Sheridan's fire and Lark's warm embers are enough to make this book sizzle. Brooke, however, has gone beyond the wonderful emotional explorations of these characters to tell the story of those who, for various reasons, become differently-abled. Whether it is a bullet, an illness, or a problem at birth, many women and men find themselves in Sheridan's situation. Her courage and Lark's gentleness and determination send this romance into a 'must read.'"—*Just About Write*

Coffee Sonata

"In *Coffee Sonata*, the lives of these four women become intertwined. In forming friendships and love, closets and disabilities are discussed, along with differences in age and backgrounds. Love and friendship are areas filled with complexity and nuances. Brooke takes her time to savor the complexities while her main characters savor their excellent cups of coffee. If you enjoy a good love story, a great setting, and wonderful characters, look for Coffee Sonata at your favorite gay and lesbian bookstore."—*Family & Friends Magazine*

"If you enjoy a good love story, a great setting, and wonderful characters, look for *Coffee Sonata* at your favorite gay and lesbian bookstore."—*MegaScene*

"Each of these characters is intriguing, attractive and likeable, but they are heartbreaking, too, as the reader soon learns when their pasts and their deeply buried secrets are slowly and methodically revealed. Brooke does not give the reader predictable plot points, but builds a fascinating set of subplots and surprises around the romances."—*L-word.com Literature*

Course of Action

"Brooke's words capture the intensity of their growing relationship. Her prose throughout the book is breathtaking and heart-stopping. Where have you been hiding, Gun Brooke? I, for one, would like to see more romances from this author."
—*Independent Gay Writer*

"Brooke gets to the core of her characters' emotions and vulnerabilities and points out their strengths and weaknesses in very human terms."—*Just About Write*

"The setting created by Brooke is a glimpse into that fantasy world of celebrity and high rollers, escapist to be sure, but witnessing the relationship develop between Carolyn and Annelie is well worth the trip. As the reader progresses, the trappings become secondary to the characters' desire to reach goals both professional and personal."—*Midwest Book Review*

"The characters are the strength of *Course Of Action* and are the reason why I keep coming back to it again and again. Carolyn and Annelie are smart, strong, successful women who have come up from difficult pasts. Their chemistry builds slowly as they get to know each other, and the book satisfyingly leaves them in an established relationship, each having grown and been enriched by the other. I love every second that the two spend together."
—*Lesbian Review*

Visit us at www.boldstrokesbooks.com

By the Author

Romances:

Course of Action

Coffee Sonata

Sheridan's Fate

September Canvas

Fierce Overture

Speed Demons

The Blush Factor

Soul Unique

A Reluctant Enterprise

Piece of Cake

Thorns of the Past

Wayworn Lovers

Insult to Injury

Science Fiction

Supreme Constellations series:

Protector of the Realm

Rebel's Quest

Warrior's Valor

Pirate's Fortune

Exodus series:

Advance

Pathfinder

Escape

Arrival

Treason

Lunar Eclipse

Renegade's War

Novella Anthology:

Change Horizons

RENEGADE'S WAR

by
Gun Brooke

2020

RENEGADE'S WAR
© 2020 By Gun Brooke. All Rights Reserved.

ISBN 13: 978-1-63555-484-7

This Trade Paperback Original Is Published By
Bold Strokes Books, Inc.
P.O. Box 249
Valley Falls, NY 12185

First Edition: October 2020

CREDITS
Editor: Shelley Thrasher
Production Design: Susan Ramundo
Cover Design By Sheri (hindsightgraphics@gmail.com)
Cover Art By Gun Brooke

Acknowledgments

I want to thank everyone who has been there for me during the writing and editing of *Renegade's War*. Firstly, my children, Malin and Henrik; and my son-in-law, Pentti. You three, together with the grandkids, mean everything to me and I love you all so much. My brother Ove and his wife, Monica, falls into the same category of people I can't do without.

Birgitta, Kamilla, Soli, I love you, my friends. Laura, the way you care about me and understand everything is a miracle. Georgi, Joanne, Sam, Lisa, Rachel F, my online friends, my abroad friends, you are pearls. And those of you who always have something sweet and encouraging to say on Facebook or DM, know that it means so much to me.

The Bold Strokes Books family are an amazing home away from home, and I love being part of it. Shelley, my editor, Sandy, Rad, Cindy, Ruth, Carsen, Toni, and the rest of the staff that are invaluable for us authors. BSB UK's Victoria Villasenor, you have been more supportive than you realize, I just want you to know that.

My first readers, you know who you are, contributed, some reading every syllable, some reading when time allowed. I appreciate all of your efforts so much.

And thank you, Elon. You were a big help as always, with this book, as I had questions about mopeds, off-roaders, and other 70s sort of technology. We will never work on a book together again, but I take some comfort in that you loved the concept and premise of this one, and the upcoming trilogy. After the trilogy, I'm truly on my own when it comes to that first "But what do you think about this…?"

To my readers. Thank you for your patience as my writing schedule got a bit delayed this time. You mean the world to me, and your comments, thoughts, and critique are always welcome. I try to learn from all of it.

Be safe everyone. I mean it.

Gun

Dedication

For Elon
1950–2019
I miss you with every breath I take

PROLOGUE

Sandslot, 1953

The creatures came in the night, all dressed in black. Aurelia knew they were dangerous since her mother and father would not have let these masked monsters in. She looked up at them, silent, tearless, but with so much fear in her heart, she thought it might stop beating. The dark figures seemed to float through the room as they came closer, their feet silent as they met the floor. The leader sat on the edge of her bed and raised a gloved finger to the hole where its mouth should have been. Aurelia knew that gesture. Be quiet.

But how could she? She had to call out for her mother and father. Defiantly, she opened her mouth to scream, but the monster before her again raised his hand, and this time he pointed in the direction of her parents and then dragged his thumb across his neck in a slow, awful way. Aurelia gasped. She was four years old, almost five, but she knew the meaning of that gesture. If she made a sound, they'd hurt her parents. Maybe even kill them dead.

Dizzy from fear now, Aurelia could think only that she was almost a big girl, her mother said, and when she turned five, she could wish for a new bicycle. A blue one with only two wheels, like the one her friend Danny had. Perhaps she would never grow up to be five years old. The creatures looming over her with something white in their hands were probably here to kill her, shoot her dead like in the movies on TV that her parents didn't know Danny's older sister let them watch when she was babysitting.

Now the monster bent closer and pressed the white, damp piece of cloth, perhaps a handkerchief, over her nose and mouth. A strong smell of something strange filled her nostrils and flowed down her lungs, even though she tried to hold her breath. Aurelia's room began to spin and fade around her. She tried to pry her eyes open, but her eyelids were so heavy and seemed glued together.

As the world turned, swirled, and dipped, Aurelia fell into something dark.

Was this death? What else could it be?

CHAPTER ONE

Klowdyn, 1974

"Damn it, Aurelia! That was way too close."

Aurelia turned her head and looked at her friend and next in command, Dacia, who drove up next to her on the narrow path. Dacia's modified off-road bike was nearly as fast as her own, and just as silent. "If it had been too close, we'd be in a Klowdynian cage by now." Aurelia realized she sounded flippant, because Dacia had a point. They had pushed their luck hard this time, but it had paid off. Sixteen family members were now safely past the neutral sector, also known as the dead man's zone.

"Yes, but those damn helicopters weren't far away." Dacia frowned. Her long blond hair poured out from under her knitted cap and fluttered in the wind. "If they'd spotted us, it would have been game over."

"But they didn't. Our camouflage still works." Aurelia didn't want to think about how much longer it would. Whenever they smuggled people across the border toward freedom in Sandslot, their neighboring nation, she feared the Klowdynian authorities would figure out how they deployed their protective, very low-tech shielding, consisting of four rods attached to their off-roaders, with camouflage nets stretched between them like a canopy. She gazed up at her own net. It was beginning to show signs of wear and tear. Time to get a new one fitted.

"So far," Dacia said, shaking her head.

"Come on." Aurelia donned her most confident smile, hoping her friend of almost twenty years would snap out of thinking what could have happened. "Focus on the fact that it was a success, despite the pesky helicopters." Aurelia pulled a face, which indeed made Dacia snort.

"You're looking like that day in first grade when you let loose your frog collection in the classroom." Dacia maneuvered her bike closer. "I'll never forget that sight."

Aurelia grinned, even if the memory still held pain. Yes, the prank was a funny anecdote, but it had been a child's only way to protest the treatment of a friend.

"What are you two going on about?" Milton showed up as if conjured from Aurelia's thoughts. A tall, gangly man, two years older than Aurelia and Dacia's twenty-five, sat like a spider on a fly on his off-roader.

"One word," Dacia called from Aurelia's other side. "Frogs."

Milton chuckled, but Aurelia knew he put up as good a front as she and Dacia did when the subject of The Jeterson Boarding School came up. Having spent fourteen years of her life in the boarding school, from the age of four, Aurelia hated it with every cell in her body, an attitude she shared with her two friends.

Ten more of their team were close behind them on their bikes, some of them pulling small carts, also camouflaged. Aurelia checked her watch. They'd be back in their latest satellite camp in an hour. She was very proud of Milton for scouting the location of the camp, as it was nestled among hills and trees in the Klowdynian wilderness in a way that made it difficult to find, even for those who knew of it. Their base camp was even better hidden. If that was ever compromised, their mission would be over. Tensing at the mere thought, Aurelia begged whatever gods were looking down at them to keep the base camp safe, not to mention the different cells of freedom fighters spread out in various locations and running halfway houses in the cities. So many people needed their help.

"Now you have that look again, Boss," Milton yelled from where he rode his bike close to hers.

"Don't be silly. What look?" Aurelia knew she couldn't fool either him or Dacia but tried to deflect.

"The one where you appear to be carrying the weight of the world on your shoulders. Which you do, in a sense, but you're not alone." Milton motioned to the team behind them.

So typical of Milton to have this conversation shouting on a bike. Any other person would perhaps bring up something so personal while sitting around a campfire drinking wine.

"I know," Aurelia mouthed, not about to continue this line of conversation any longer. She turned the handle of her off-roader and left them behind her. Longing for a shower, albeit cold, Aurelia couldn't wait to get back to the camp.

After about an hour, it was almost dark, which was dangerous. They couldn't afford to use their headlights or a regular flashlight, and if it turned out to be a cloudy night, they'd have to walk and lead the bikes the rest of the way. Some of their headlights had red-tinted glass, which made it possible to switch them on, but not all.

Aurelia turned a corner, one where she always reduced speed as the path was full of roots from the surrounding trees. She kept the bike at fifteen miles per hour, scanning the ground ahead. She blinked. What was that in the middle of the narrow path just before the next bend? Slowing down, she came to a stop while raising her fist. She let the engine idle and stepped off the bike. Dacia and Milton were at her side within seconds.

"What's up, Boss?" Milton's voice held no mirth.

"See it? Over there?" Aurelia pointed.

"An animal or something?" Dacia squinted. She took a step forward, but Aurelia grabbed her arm.

"Wait. We're doing this by the book. No surprises, right?" Aurelia pulled out her gun, a sleek sidearm with a long barrel. She didn't have to look to know the other two had done the same.

Inching closer to the object on the path, Aurelia forced herself not to tense up. Anything along these parts could be a trap. On most days, she was well aware how incredible it was that they hadn't been caught yet.

When she had only ten feet left to go, she stopped, again raising her fist. This was no animal or some garbage. A pale hand protruded from a dark jacket, and the last of the sunlight revealed caramel-blond hair.

"It's a person!" Dacia looked at Aurelia, her eyes huge in her narrow face.

They approached the body on the path with their weapons raised and safeties off. At first, nothing betrayed life in the still form. When Aurelia reached the figure, she saw it had to be the victim of a vicious attack. New bruises and welts on the face, dirt on the clothes, and items strewn across the path told the story of a robbery. It wasn't common in this remote area, but gangs sometimes showed up in the suburbs of Klowdyn's major cities and tried to intimidate the locals and force them to pay for "protection," even attack people who traveled alone.

"He tried to defend himself," Milton said, pointing at the walking stick still in the victim's right hand.

Aurelia crouched next to the man. She tugged her gloves off and pressed her finger at his carotid, scanning him for more injuries. She hadn't been sure of the sex of the unfortunate traveler, but she could tell he was muscular, and the short-cropped hair suggested this was a man. Age or facial features were indistinguishable. She flinched as she felt a steady, if a bit rapid, pulse under her fingertips. Now she saw the faint rising and falling of the man's chest under the thick jacket.

"He's alive," Aurelia said. "Bring Cody over. He's got the biggest cart."

"We're taking him with us?" Dacia gasped. "What if this is a trap?"

"I doubt that." Aurelia studied the bruised features. "He's been beaten into prolonged unconsciousness," she said starkly.

"He won't know where we've taken him, any more than the people we help do. Cover his eyes and secure his hands. Make sure you don't restrict his breathing, and be careful with his neck. He might have internal injuries."

"All right. Mac can take a look when we get to the camp." Dacia pulled out one of the blindfolds they had used on the people they'd just helped across the border to Sandslot and tied it deftly around the man's head. "You do realize he might need a hospital? I mean, Mac's a miracle worker, but the infirmary isn't equipped to do major surgery."

"I know. We'll deal with that if we have to." Aurelia hoped they wouldn't have to risk an unplanned trip to one of the major cities.

Cody came up next to them with his off-roader, and they carefully lifted the injured man onto the cart. They had to fold his long legs, which made the man moan. Clearly his injuries caused him pain.

Taking the lead again, Aurelia, followed by Dacia, kept driving toward the camp. Behind them, Milton rode next to the cart, keeping a close eye on their new acquaintance. Aurelia turned her head back a few times, and each time, Milton gave her the thumbs-up.

They made it back to camp just as the mountain area grew black. Dark clouds hid the stars and the half moon, but the camp had indirect lighting from inside the cave system. Some of the caves were natural, but for the most part, the tunnel system in the mountain was painstakingly manmade—some by smugglers from centuries ago, and some by themselves. They couldn't risk campfires at night being visible from the sky when the authorities of Klowdyn sent their agents up in helicopters to look for them. During the day, they moved around under camouflage nets while in the camp, and at night, they returned to the caves, where they lived in roughly chiseled alcoves.

The camaraderie and passion for their mission kept them, the Tallawens, a close-knit group. Dacia always maintained it was the group's love and complete loyalty to Aurelia that made it possible to live this way for months on end. Aurelia knew her crew was loyal, but also that all of them had an individual reason for putting their lives on the line for the freedom of others. She certainly did.

Tom, this camp's young leader, approached them, relief clearly visible on his face. "That was in the nick of time," he said and smiled. "Everything all right?" He shoved his fingers through his shock of curly red hair.

"For the most part," Aurelia said and dismounted the bike. "We found an injured man by the forest. He's in bad shape. Mac around?"

"She is." Tom looked over his shoulder. "Carla? Get Mac, please."

A young woman merely nodded and stepped back into the cave system. Aurelia walked over to Cody's bike and crouched by the cart. The man lay on his back with his legs bent, covered by a blanket, and someone had also sacrificed their sweater to place around his neck for support.

"Shit." Tom joined her. "Someone did a number on him, didn't they?"

"Yeah. We just have to hope he's not bleeding internally." Aurelia placed her fingertips against the man's neck again. "Pulse is fast but strong. Always something."

"And who do we have here?" a husky female voice asked from behind. "Ah. Another one, eh, Aurelia?" Mac, their medic, knelt by Aurelia's side, pulled out a flashlight, and shone it into the man's eyes. The pupils contracted and revealed blue-green irises. "Good. Equal reactions on both sides. So far, no signs of a subarachnoid bleed." She rose after taking his blood pressure and pulse. "He's stable at least. We better move him into the infirmary."

Aurelia motioned for Cody and Tom to pull the cart toward the cave. The infirmary, which was entirely Mac's domain, was a larger dwelling at the end of the right-hand tunnel. A string of bulbs lit the space as they made their way inside. Several large diesel generators provided power to the cave system, which they could thank Tom's engineering skills for.

Together, they lifted the bruised man up onto the main gurney, where Mac began cutting off his clothes. "I don't need all of you in here. You stay and assist me, Aurelia, and Tom too. The rest of you look like you're starving. Go eat. Bring something back for Aurelia when you're done."

Aurelia knew better than to argue with Mac in her quarters. "You heard her," she said, nodding at her team. Dacia frowned but relented when Aurelia motioned with her thumb toward the exit. "If there's cheese, I'd love some with cucumbers." Sometimes Aurelia felt the Tallawens lived on sandwiches alone.

"Got it," Dacia said and left.

After cutting through the sleeve seams, Mac pulled at the man's jacket. Tom held on to his shoulders as she and Aurelia tugged it off. The plain gray shirt underneath was blood-soaked around the lapels in the front, but otherwise clean.

"Looks like most of the blood came from his nose. Let's check that out first." Mac dampened a washcloth and began washing the blood away, revealing red swellings and bruises that Aurelia knew would darken the next few days and then become multicolored. "Hm."

"What?" Tom leaned in to look.

Mac didn't answer but unbuttoned the shirt and parted it in the front. Aurelia blinked. "He's a she." She lifted her gaze to the bruised face and then looked down at the tank-top-covered chest. The tank top was formfitting and clearly showed that this was indeed a woman lying unconscious before them. Examining the woman's face again, Aurelia now noticed the long, thick, gold-brown lashes that lay in perfect semicircles against the bruised skin under her eyes. It was impossible to judge the shape of her nose, but her narrow lips were curvy.

"She is indeed." Mac gently rolled their mystery guest toward her, allowing Aurelia to pull the shirt off her. "Her back seems unharmed."

"At least she wasn't shot." Tom made a wry face, and Aurelia knew what he meant. When it came to injuries, gunshot wounds were always their main concern, especially if the bullet didn't go straight through.

"Most of the injuries seem to be to her head and face," Mac said, deftly examining the rest of the woman. "Several blows, which individually might not have caused much harm, but this one," she pointed to the woman's temple, "is what worries me the most. The bone here is thin, and that's quite the contusion. I bet she's been attacked from different angles, perhaps by more than one person. She's muscular." Mac pointed at the woman's well-defined arms. "She looks like she'd be able to defend herself."

"Unless they had guns," Tom said.

"Yes. Unless." Aurelia dampened a new washcloth and soaked the dried blood in the woman's short hair. Wiping it off as best she could, she then helped Mac put a clean shirt on her and remove her boots and pants. The three of them lifted her carefully and placed her on one of the cots. Tucking the blankets around the woman, Aurelia looked up at Mac. "Any idea when she'll regain consciousness?"

"No clue, honestly, and her being knocked out this long is worrisome. She's probably concussed, but I don't see any signs of internal bleeding, which is encouraging. Do you have any indication who she may be?"

"None. We all thought she was a guy. I'm going to place a guard at the entrance to the infirmary," Aurelia said, turning to Tom. "We can't rule out anything at this point."

"On it." Tom nodded briskly and left. Within minutes, a tall woman stood by the opening, rifle ready in front of her.

Aurelia rose and looked down at the woman in the bed. The undamaged part of her face suggested she might be a striking individual. What had she been doing alone in the wooded area? Or had her assailants taken her there to settle a score? Perhaps this was a botched attempt to kill her? Unnerved, Aurelia flipped her long hair back over her shoulders. "Let me know when there's a change, Mac." She strode out of the infirmary and walked to the junction of the two tunnels that served as the common area. Chiseled-out benches provided seats along the perimeter. Dacia came up to her, carrying sandwiches and a mug of ale.

"Hey, how's he doing?" Dacia pointed at one of the benches.

"*She* is still unconscious, so pretty much the same as before." Aurelia sat down and bit into one of the sandwiches. "Ugh. No butter, huh?" The bread was dry, and the thin slice of cheese tasted a little stale.

"I know. Cook says his delivery people find it harder and harder to get through the hills. They constantly change their routes, and some of them are damn long. He's getting some supplies tomorrow, though, so lunch should be better."

"Good. It's not just the nutrition. You know that." Aurelia washed the dry piece of bread and cheese down with the cool ale. "If we can't keep our people well fed, morale will start going down the drain, and that's when people start making mistakes."

"I know. I know. So does our cook. He was quite frantic about it tonight. Milton had to reassure him this isn't his fault." Dacia sipped from her own mug. "At least our stockpile of ale is plentiful. We Klowdynians can always go the extra mile for an ale." She bumped Aurelia's arm with her own. "But you, you poor Sandslottish goddess, you're probably doomed." Dacia crinkled her nose.

"Oh, please. I can drink anyone under the table on this stuff." Aurelia grinned and drank some more. Her stomach twitched at the well-meant jibe from her friend. Sandslot, the neighboring country, had been her home until she was four. Whereas Klowdyn kept its people in a strong harness, dictating their lives down to minute details, Sandslot was the opposite. There, people were free to follow their dreams, travel, choose their careers, and have as many children, or none, as they pleased. In Klowdyn, it was mandatory for healthy women to give birth once—no more, no less.

If anyone had more children than that and was found out, all children but the oldest were sent to relocation schools, much like the one Aurelia, Dacia, and Milton had gone to. Unlike most of their schoolmates, they hadn't been adopted. Nobody ever told them why, but Aurelia had gone from missing her parents, to wishing for someone to belong to, to being relieved that she had managed to escape the school with Dacia and Milton when they were eighteen. Now, seven years later, she was the leader of the Tallawens, a renegade group that smuggled Klowdynian refugees and dissidents over the well-guarded border to Sandslot.

Gazing into the foaming ale, Aurelia thought about the mystery woman in the infirmary. Bringing her into their midst might change everything.

CHAPTER TWO

S he had no idea where she was. Staring up at what had to be some sort of ceiling, even if it looked more like bedrock, she blinked several times to clear her vision. Muted lights showed metal shelving and counters to her left. Slowly turning her head, she blinked again and managed to make out two beds, none of them occupied. A figure dressed in dark clothes stood by another counter at the far end of the room with their back to her.

"He-hello?" she managed to mutter and then moaned as her head began to pound.

The figure pivoted and walked up to her. Behind the person, another form appeared, this one carrying something. A rifle?

"Good. You're awake." A woman leaned over her and shone a small flashlight into her eyes. She blinked and moaned again as the light seemed to stab her brain. The woman didn't seem fazed but turned to the person behind her. "Send someone for Aurelia."

The other person nodded and left.

"Can you tell me your name?" the woman asked.

"Um. Sure." Searching her foggy brain and trying to disregard the throbbing pain that seemed to fill her entire head, she shifted restlessly. "I'm...my name's Blue."

"And your last name?"

Blue began to shiver. "Blue, eh..." Everything in her mind seemed to fade back into a gray mist. "Just Blue?" Feeling ridiculously apologetic, Blue looked up at the stern woman.

"Where am I, exactly? And do you know my name?" Her aching body and head suggested she was injured and perhaps the woman had asked her these questions to ascertain if she was concussed.

"No clue, dear." The woman straightened. "Ah. Aurelia. Our guest is conscious, if a bit foggy."

Blue turned her head again and had to grip the side of the thin mattress not to fall off the bed because of the violent vertigo that hit her out of nowhere.

"Hey. Easy." A clear voice spoke as a steadying hand was placed against Blue's shoulder. Another woman, this one appearing much younger, leaned over her, and a mane of long, black hair fell toward Blue and hid her from the world. It caressed her aching cheek, and for an insane second, Blue wanted to turn her head again, despite the threatening vertigo, and hide her face in the silky masses.

"Oh, sorry." The woman flipped the hair back over her shoulders and then sat down on the side of the bed. Now the muted light hit her and revealed an oval face with olive-tinted complexion and black eyes. Her lips were full, and faint dimples added to her beauty.

"I'm Aurelia." The woman patted Blue's shoulders lightly and then let go.

"My name is Blue." Pushing at the bed with her elbows, Blue tried to sit up. Immediately, Aurelia's hands were back against her shoulders, holding her down.

"Just be still for a bit, at least until Mac here has had another chance to examine you. You've taken quite a beating, and we can't be sure about internal injuries yet."

"Someone beat me up?" Blue swallowed, her throat so very dry. "May I have some water?"

"Of course." Aurelia reached for a pitcher on a low stool next to the bed. After pouring some water, she supported Blue's neck as she sipped it. "Better?"

"Yes. Thank you."

"To answer your question, yes. That's what we think must've happened. My friends and I came across you on our way home. You were unconscious, and we brought you with us."

"I see." But Blue really didn't. "And where am I?"

"Somewhere in the Klowdynian mountains." Aurelia shrugged, which made her hair billow around her shoulders. "Sorry, but I can't be more specific right now, as we have no idea who you are."

"Don't I have an ID card on me?" Blue looked down at herself and only now realized she was wearing nothing but a thin shirt and briefs.

"I meant to go through your pockets later." Aurelia motioned toward a counter across the room. "We might as well do that now." She rose, moving lithely. Her surging dark hair shifted around her like it was a separate entity. Blue estimated that Aurelia was about five foot four, but something about her made her seem taller.

Aurelia returned with a muddy bundle of clothes, some cut at the seams. Blue was too fatigued to move and could only watch as Aurelia pushed her hands into the pockets of the trousers and then the jacket. "Nothing," she said as she shoved her hand into the jacket's inner pocket. "Oh, wait. Here's something." She pulled out a small object. "Now we're talking." Glancing at Blue, she held it out for her. It was a wallet. "Up for it?"

"No. You can open it." Blue could hear the husky tremors in her own voice and hated their faintness. Did this stranger loathe any sign of weakness?

Aurelia opened the wallet and pulled out some Klowdynian bills. "You have about forty slaws." She flipped through the wallet. "And here's your ID. Blue AnRaine. Thirty-one years old." Aurelia held up the ID card and obviously compared the photo on it with Blue's face. "I'll be damned if I can identify you with this. The hair's the same, but you're so bruised, we'll have to wait to see what you look like after the injuries begin to fade."

Blue sighed and closed her eyes. She didn't like this predicament at all. Her mind was foggy as hell, and what if the amnesia became permanent? Throbbing, and sometimes stabbing, pain kept her from being able to think straight.

"Don't worry about it. You'll be well taken care of in the meantime." Aurelia stood and leaned over Blue. "You just focus on the healing part, okay?"

"And while I'm focusing, am I to be your prisoner, Aurelia?" Blue somehow knew that her acerbic and slightly disdainful tone was commonplace. It was as if her mouth and vocal cords recognized the sound. Brilliant. Would she ever discover anything pleasant about herself?

"Prisoner?" Aurelia grinned. "Nah. That's taking it a bit far." She tilted her head as she scrutinized Blue. "Though I admit you can't move around freely, as it would put my people in jeopardy."

Blue frowned. "What people?" Where the hell had she ended up?

"Oh, you'll find out soon enough. Once you've healed, we'll send you on your merry way. Mac here says you can't be moved until we know you're not bleeding internally." Aurelia's expression grew somber. "If you turn out to be more seriously hurt than we think right now, we'll try to get you to a hospital, but I can't promise how that'd turn out."

"I don't suppose you have a phone?" Blue sighed as she glanced toward the ceiling. "I can tell we're in some cave, manmade or otherwise."

"Hard to hide that fact," Aurelia said and shrugged. "And you're right. No phones."

Who were these people? And why did a young woman call the shots like this? Blue could tell Aurelia had a commanding persona, no matter her age, but it was a mystery, all of it. Yawning, Blue briefly closed her eyes.

"You need your rest. I'll be back to check on you tomorrow. A medic will be with you during the night, checking your vital signs and stuff. And don't do anything stupid, okay? You'll only jeopardize your health and antagonize our guards."

Of course these people had guards. Too exhausted to be truly curious about what was going on, Blue maneuvered onto her left side. Just as she closed her eyes again, she thought she felt gentle hands pull up the covers around her, but she had no strength to verify what had happened. All she could do was let sleep claim her.

❖

Aurelia cupped her mug of hot-coffee substitute to warm her cold hands. Staring up at the star-filled sky, she tried to focus on the after-action report regarding today's successful mission. Instead, her thoughts kept returning to the injured woman in the infirmary. Something about her, in fact a lot about her, added to her mystery.

"I can tell you're not quite ready to start the meeting." Dacia sat down on the boulder next to Aurelia and drank from her beer bottle. "Let me guess. Our mystery guest that turned out to be a strapping woman instead."

"Too much is weird about her." Aurelia shrugged.

"Tell me about it," Dacia said, snorting. "We find her very conveniently on one of the paths that we take on a regular basis. Still, she's bruised, and her injuries are bad. I mean, who in their right mind would subject themselves to such a treatment if she meant to fool us?"

"Yet she's in very good shape. Muscular. Sinewy, even." Aurelia fell into her usual, and very comfortable, way of bouncing her thoughts off Dacia. "I just realized she must have been trained for hand-to-hand combat. The outsides of her hands looked callused."

"Did you check her feet?" Dacia frowned and drank more of her beer.

"No. I think finding out she's a woman surprised me too much to think that far. I'll be sure to ask Mac, though. But as you say, who would let themselves get beaten within an inch of their lives to infiltrate us?" Aurelia pushed her fingers through her hair, loosening the rubber band holding it back. "Not that we wouldn't be a feather in any law enforcer's cap. That's for sure."

"I wouldn't put it past the BHU to sacrifice a few to achieve something like this situation," Dacia said, her expression darkening as she mentioned the Bounty Hunter Unit. "They recruit only heartless individuals who have no humanity left in their black souls."

Aurelia nearly spit out the mouthful of coffee she'd just taken. Swallowing past her coughing reflex, she bumped her shoulder into Dacia's. "Black souls, eh?" She giggled.

"Do you think I'm exaggerating?" Dacia gave her a haughty look, but her gray eyes sparkled.

"Not at all. I'm just curious which author you're hooked on right now." Aurelia knew her friend went through phases when she voraciously read every book a specific author had written, and now she was clearly hooked on a more dramatic, lyrical one.

"Lisa Stoneheart." Dacia patted one of her pockets and then pulled out a worn paperback. "And she's freaking awesome. You'd like her books."

"If I didn't need a few hours' sleep every night, I might have time to read." That wasn't untrue. Unlike Dacia, who seemed able to substitute reading for sleep, Aurelia found it hard to function if she didn't at least get two to three hours. Perhaps the difference was also that Aurelia was the leader of this pack of freedom fighters and carried the responsibility.

"I know," Dacia said now, resting her head against Aurelia's shoulder. "Hey, I think everyone from today's mission is gathered under the net. If we get this over with quickly, you might even get four or five hours of beauty rest. God knows you need it."

"Oh, great, thanks." Aurelia pinched Dacia's upper arm as she got up. "As if anyone would ever care what I look like."

Dacia also stood, and her expression grew soft for a few moments. "You're beyond beautiful, and the only one who doesn't know it is you."

Taken aback at her friend's unexpected words, Aurelia still chose to ignore them. The after-action debriefing was important, as they could never become complacent. She had no time to consider beauty or even dwell too long on the mystery woman in the infirmary. Sooner or later she would have to deal with the latter, but for now, she needed to make sure they took measures to streamline their operation.

If they didn't keep several steps ahead of the BHU and the Klowdynian authorities, they'd be imprisoned or, worst-case scenario, summarily executed without due process. Aurelia's stomach clenched at the thought of any of the people who had willingly joined her cause losing their lives.

"Okay. Let's do this, and then you can read, and I can sleep." Even as she spoke, she knew she wasn't being entirely truthful. Something she couldn't explain urged her to swing by the infirmary and have another look at the injured woman.

❖

Standing next to Mac, Aurelia studied the bruised woman on the cot. Blue lay very still now, and it was damn near impossible to judge if she was breathing. "What can you tell me about her feet?"

Mac blinked. "Her feet?"

"Yes.

"Well, she has two. Normal set of toes on each. All right, all right." Mac raised her palms in surrender. "What are you thinking of?"

"Any calluses, like the ones on the outside of her hands?"

"Didn't look specifically for that, but now that you mention it…" Mac gently pulled the blanket back from Blue's feet and ran her fingertips along the outside edge of both feet. "Yes. You're right. Damn it, girl. No wonder you're the leader of our merry bunch."

"So, she's trained in hand-to-hand combat at some level." Aurelia sighed. "That poses a problem."

"Sure does."

"Have you given her something, or is she truly out cold because of her injuries?" Stepping closer to examine the black-and-blue face on the pillow, Aurelia spoke quietly.

"She's done for, at least for tonight. She became increasingly slurry and lost all color as soon as she tried to change position on the cot. You can fake being in pain, but not paling into a grayish-white hue on command. She's unconscious."

"Okay." Aurelia motioned for Mac to join her in the area outside the infirmary. "Listen. I can't let her wander around the area unescorted when she comes to—"

"Nor can I. She's badly injured, and I have to figure out a way to keep her immobilized until I know for sure she's not going to die on me." Mac rubbed the back of her neck.

"That should give me time to arrange something. She can't stay here." Aurelia walked back over to the cot and stood there motionless for a moment. Her entire operation in these mountains was about saving people. Even though she was suspicious of Blue, she couldn't disregard the possibility that she might need their help.

As she left the infirmary to finally get some sleep, she knew she would have to come up with a plan that would let her remain true to her promise years ago. It was, as Mac had said earlier, why she was the leader of this merry bunch.

CHAPTER THREE

Three days of staring at the cave ceiling was three days too long. Blue glared at Mac, the medic who was the boss of this part of her unknown location and, it would seem, of her.

"Listen," Blue snarled, her patience so thin now, she was ready to leap off the cot and strangle the woman. "Clearly, I don't have a brain injury or any internal bleeding, or I'd be dead. And I swear, if you come near me with a fucking bedpan again, I'll do something we'll both regret."

"Uh-huh." Mac sounded infuriatingly indifferent. "As if I enjoy waiting on you hand and foot."

"Then let me up, and I won't be your problem any longer." Blue moved and was about to simply get up, when Mac looked over her head toward the opening at the far end of the cave.

"Aurelia. Thank God. You better come and save your latest stray." Pursing her lips, Mac motioned at Blue with a sharp jerk of her chin.

"That bad, eh?" Aurelia approached them. "Good thing I hear you're doing well enough to start moving around."

Blue had already opened her mouth to let both women know how fed up she felt, but now she snapped her jaw shut. Slowly turning her gaze back to Mac, she scowled. "And you could have told me that news right away."

"And missed yet another lovely threat to my life? Why would I do that?" Mac chuckled, and her strict demeanor softened. "I wasn't worried so much about brain injuries or internal bleedings, but rather your neck, as whoever did a number on your face also gave you quite the swelling around the neck vertebrae. As I have no means of x-raying anyone or putting you in a neck brace, I had to keep you immobilized until the swelling went down." Mac shrugged. "Aurelia figured intimidating you might be my best bet."

Slowly Blue turned her attention to the beaming Aurelia. "How about leveling with me?"

"Nah. Wouldn't have worked." Aurelia pulled up a stool. "You were in and out of it for the most part the first twenty-four hours. Do you even remember me sitting with you that first night?"

Blue didn't, and somehow the thought of it made her feel weird and, hell, far too vulnerable. "No."

"Aw, come on. You don't have to look like I was invading your privacy or something. You were really very sick there for a bit." Snorting irreverently, Aurelia then turned serious. "I've looked in on you repeatedly, and only on the third evening did you begin to make sense again. You were pretty lucid when you first came to, but then you got worse." Shrugging, Aurelia flipped her long hair back over her shoulders with a practiced flick of her wrist. "I had to leave camp for a bit, and when I returned last night, Mac told me you'd been doing better with each passing hour since I left. Now you're on day eight here, and Mac says you can start moving about if you promise to keep inside the cave and not wander off. She's going to keep tabs on you for a couple of days more, but you don't have to stay in the infirmary if you don't want to."

"I can? But where would I stay?" Perking up, Blue shifted and sat up on the side of the cot. To her dismay, the room spun violently before she got her bearings. She hoped the other two didn't notice.

"We're a bit cramped here for the moment." Shrugging, Aurelia shot Mac a look. "My part of the dormitory is the most private, and they'll put in a cot there for you if you're okay with sharing."

"You'd share your space with me?" Blue couldn't quite believe it. Aurelia was in charge and no doubt enjoyed whatever privileges that position entailed.

"It's not entirely altruistic. We need to keep an eye on you, not only for medical reasons, but also because of a security issue. So, your choice, really. As we're thankfully short on injured people right now, you can choose to stay here."

No way would Blue become a perpetual guest of the infirmary. Something about the smell of antiseptic and the sight of medical equipment made her heart pick up speed. What was her foggy brain keeping from her? "I'll take you up on your offer," she said quickly, before Aurelia decided to change her mind.

"Super. Once you're dressed in something other than a hospital gown, I'll give you the not-so-grand tour of where you're allowed to go."

"Any chance I can shower?" Blue asked, feeling presumptuous, considering how these people lived.

"Absolutely." Grinning, Aurelia nodded at Mac. "Guess you're off sponge-bath duty."

Aghast, Blue wanted to cover her eyes to block out the image of the hardnosed medic bathing her like a child.

"She's *kidding*," Mac said and motioned for Aurelia to leave. "I'll bring you some clean clothes. We had to cut you out of your own stuff, so you'll have to make do with what we could find for you." She pointed at the chuckling Aurelia, who was making her way past the guard. "I'll show you to the facilities."

Facilities? Blue gazed after Aurelia's disappearing form. So, perhaps this place wasn't entirely primitive. She could literally kill for a shower. Remembering her manners, if a bit belatedly, she thanked Mac. "That'd be amazing."

"Here. Drape the blanket around you. I assume you'd rather put the clothes on after your shower?" Mac helped Blue wrap the coarse blanket around her shoulders.

As she walked next to Mac out the door, she noticed how the guard fell into step behind them.

The shower was short and lukewarm, but wonderful. Blue had to scrub her scalp very carefully, as she was still bruised and had a few stitches. A small mirror showed her bruised face, which oddly enough didn't startle her, but merely annoyed her. She had hoped her reflection would help her recognize herself and kickstart her memory, but she doubted that she'd recognize her features even if her memory was intact. Right now, the top part of her face boasted all the colors of the rainbow, and though Mac assured her the swelling had diminished dramatically over the last twelve hours, she was still puffy around the eyes. She leaned closer to the mirror. Bright *blue* irises. Go figure.

As she carefully pulled on the clothes Mac had brought her—cotton underwear, a worn blue shirt and green military-style pants that were a tad too short—she began to feel better simply for being out of the hospital gown. How did a group of people living in caves even have hospital gowns? Cursing her still-somewhat foggy brain, Blue ran her fingers through her short hair while scrutinizing her face again for signs of anything familiar. She had such a strong feeling that she was on the cusp of knowing everything about herself. If she just could shake that last fog bank that hid the key to her mind, she'd be able to remember who she was and where she belonged.

Clearly, she wasn't part of this diverse crew that seemed seriously armed. She could name the brand of the weapon the guard in the infirmary was holding; she knew she was Klowdynian, and they all spoke with the same Klowdynian accent. President Bowler was the leader of their country, and it bordered against Sandslot in the north and Angley in the south. The capital was Fardicia and…Blue groaned as her suddenly hyper-speed brain tried to summon as much information as possible, which only confused her more. How could she remember all this and not her own background, her parents, her fuckling *life*?

Stepping out of the small area holding three shower stalls made of rough boards, she found Aurelia there instead of the guard. Leaning sideways against the cave wall, one leg crossing the other and with her arms folded, she studied Blue intently.

"Now there's an improvement," Aurelia said, smiling.

"I suppose cleaned and bruised is better than grimy and bruised." Blue shrugged and regretted her move as pain shot along the back of her neck.

"Careful. Mac's still concerned about you." Aurelia pushed off the wall. "Feel like walking a bit? Or did the shower do you in?"

"I'm fine." Blue could tell Aurelia didn't buy into that obvious lie. "For the most part. I need to get my strength, and my memory, back."

"Sure. Well, come on then. I'll show you around a bit and then take you to the dormitory. I don't think I need to place a guard with you, as you're pretty weak still, but don't think we won't notice where you are at all times. We keep tabs on everyone here." Aurelia's smile faded, and her dark eyes grew flat. "We've learned the hard way to not take things at face value."

"Got it." It didn't sit well with Blue to be talked to in this manner, but she had to concede that not even she knew her true agenda or if she presented a security risk to anyone. A faint set of images flickered through her mind so fast at the thought of risking someone else's safety, she couldn't make them out.

"What?" Aurelia took her by the arm. "Feeling dizzy?"

Blue felt more disoriented than dizzy but nodded, not wanting to share any signs of potential improvement. The flashes of blurry faces, if that was what they were, were nothing. "Yeah, a bit. It passed."

Aurelia kept her gentle grip of Blue's arm for a few moments but then let go. "This way." She took the lead out into the larger part of the cave. People stood or sat in groups, some eating, others reading in the light of kerosene lamps. Some seemed deeply engrossed in conversation. To Blue's surprise she saw children playing and a few old people.

"Please don't stare at them, at least not the adults. They've been through enough." Aurelia nudged Blue's arm again.

Blue tore her gaze from the people and tried unsuccessfully to understand what Aurelia could be talking about. "I don't get it. What's happened to them?"

"I may just tell you at one point, unless you get well enough to figure things out on your own first." Aurelia's bright smile was back, but Blue had seen this woman's serious side and knew that pure steel lurked behind the glittering eyes in that stunning face.

"You must realize that this situation makes me very curious, amnesia or not." Blue pushed her hands into the pockets of her pants.

"No doubt, but for now, all you have to focus on is getting better. The sooner you regain your memory, the sooner we can help you get home," Aurelia said. "Speaking of which, whenever you're hungry, you can visit one of the cooking stations. We don't have a shortage of food right now, which means we can all indulge ourselves a bit."

"Thank you." Blue took in the closest food station, which was little more than a cart with some shelves attached to the cave wall behind it. A tall, gangly man in his mid-twenties was handing out what looked like sausages, bread, and glasses of water.

"Hungry?" Aurelia took a step toward the food station.

"Starving," Blue confessed.

"Then by all means." Aurelia motioned for Blue to join her as she walked up to the young man. "Hey, Rory, two sausages, please?"

"Got you, Boss." The freckled man grinned broadly. "I take it this is our newest stray?'"

Blue stared at Rory. "Stray?" She straightened, but before she could tell him off, Aurelia merely laughed.

"What have I told you about comparing our guests to dogs or cats, Rory?" She shook her head, and even if she spoke lightly, Blue saw the steel she perceived in Aurelia grow rigid.

"Sorry, Boss. Welcome to our humble abode." He handed over a sausage wrapped in a bun. "We even have some shandy if you like." Rory was clearly eager to please and get back on his boss's good side.

"Thank you, but water's fine." Blue accepted the sausage and bit into it, finding it surprisingly good considering it had been cooked in a cave.

"Coming up." Rory poured her some water. "Any trimmings for the sausage?"

"No, thank you." Blue had downed half the sausage already. She really wanted one more, but her wounded head still gave her vertigo and nausea, and she knew her stomach might rebel if she pushed it.

They began walking again, finishing their quick meal as they made their way through a narrow part of the cave. Was this all manmade, or did such big cave formations exist naturally? Every now and then someone carrying a rifle or a sidearm passed them, and Blue regarded them warily. Was this some covert military operation, and if it was, where were they located—and why? Who were the civilians with children? To Blue, this seemed like a rescue mission, but she couldn't figure out the circumstances, which was beginning to drive her crazy.

"I can hear the cogs turning, Blue," Aurelia said. "Just take it easy for now, all right? Depending on who you are and what your presence here indicates, you'll no doubt find out more with time. Best-case scenario, you'll wake up and simply be back to your old self again, and then we'll help you get home."

"And until then…I'm not your prisoner, but I'm still placed under severe restrictions?" Blue clenched the empty paper cup.

"Not entirely wrong, but you are also quite safe and among friendly people. Nobody will hurt you. The restrictions are for your safety as well as ours." Aurelia pointed at a wide opening. "There's the dormitory for the senior staff. Come on." She motioned for Blue to follow her.

Walking behind Aurelia, Blue took in the dormitory, quickly counting eighteen cots placed less than one yard apart. Each cot had a small footlocker, and the bedding consisted of pillows and sleeping bags. Raising her gaze, Blue took in the impressive height of the ceiling, estimating it to be at least five meters.

At the far end of the oval-shaped cave, someone had put up a screen. Following Aurelia as she rounded it, she saw two additional cots with footlockers. The one to the left, closest to the screen, contained a sleeping bag and a pillow, while the one to the right was made up with two blankets and a pillow.

"That's yours." Aurelia motioned with her chin. "Judging from your pallor, which is on the grayish side, you need some rest. Why don't you sleep some, and then you can join us outside for some fresh air after dark?"

Blue wanted to get that fresh air right now, but Aurelia was right. Her knees were buckling, and she sat down on the cot with a sigh of relief. It wasn't very comfortable, but she'd slept in worse conditions. The thought startled her, and she gripped the edge of the cot hard. How did she know this? How could she be so sure she'd roughed it worse than this cave and still not know who she was? If they hadn't found her ID card, she wouldn't even know her last name.

"Hey. You better lie down. Perhaps the stroll was too much after all. I'll have Mac look in on you." Aurelia's gentle hand was back on Blue's shoulder. The touch anchored her somehow, and Blue had to resist leaning into it too much. Another tidbit to file for later. She hated to show any sign of weakness.

"No need, really." Blue stretched out on the cot and pulled the extra blanket over her. "I just need some sleep." She yawned and turned onto her side. "Half an hour or so."

Blue thought she heard soft laughter as she sank into a dreamless abyss.

CHAPTER FOUR

When's their ETA?" Two days later, after taking some much-needed time off doing runs herself, Aurelia fell into step with Tom as they walked to the edge of the camp. As the camp leader, he knew every detail about his end of the mission, which made it possible for her to let go and focus on her responsibilities in the missions when she was in these parts of the Klowdynian Mountains.

"Any minute. Dillon's radio clicked half an hour ago." Tom raised his binoculars and scanned the area around them.

The Tallawens had established checkpoints where the leader of the run sent five clicks via their walkie-talkies to let the camps know how far they'd come. It was always nerve-wracking when a team was late checking in, but tonight, Dillon and his team were on time. Five clicks also signified that the mission was going as planned.

"How many are they bringing back to camp?" Aurelia asked, raising her own binoculars to her eyes. It was getting dark, but she was still able to make out the contours of trees and rock formations.

"Four adults and three children. The youngest is only one year old." Tom ran a hand over his face. "It's always bothersome."

Aurelia nodded. It was dangerous to smuggle children under five. Aurelia had found the breaking point to be around that age. Kids older than five could often be reasoned with and were able to understand the logic behind having to be quiet. Younger children or, God forbid, babies, created logistical problems. No amount of explaining the dangers of making a sound at the wrong time could persuade a toddler to stop crying. She'd heard horror stories of smothered and drugged children dying before their families reached Sandslot. Aurelia wasn't happy about using drugs as a method for the people they helped, but she'd had to do it in a few instances. Perhaps she'd been lucky all these years that no panicked parent had accidentally smothered a child she was responsible for.

Shaking off the dread, Aurelia squinted into the binoculars. "I see movement."

"Me too. And I hear them." Tom waved at four people waiting on off-roaders, and they took off down the path.

Aurelia could hear the muffled engines of the approaching bikes. Relieved, she knew they had pulled off yet another mission, and unless something went wrong when they took them toward the border, these seven individuals would live a free, democratic life in Sandslot.

"Ah, and here's our mystery guest." Tom nudged Aurelia's shoulder and nodded toward the entrance of the cave.

Aurelia glanced over her shoulder and saw Blue approach them, her strides long and unhesitating. After resting for an additional two days in the dormitory, only coming outside to get some food and use the facilities, she seemed to have gotten her bearings.

"Good evening, Blue," Tom said. "Good to see you outside."

"Good evening. Actually, I wasn't sure what time it was." Blue stopped at Aurelia's side. "Somehow I thought it might be afternoon."

"It's eight twenty p.m." Aurelia wasn't happy about Blue observing their operation, but she couldn't do much about it unless she locked the woman up, and she wasn't prepared to go that far.

"I heard engines take off just as I came outside." Blue pushed her hands into the pockets of her light jacket.

"We're having new guests," Aurelia said, making sure she sounded like it was no big deal. Given Blue's attentive gaze, she was sure that approach had crashed and burned immediately.

"Anything I can do to help?" Blue squinted into the darkness. "I'm going stir-crazy just trying to follow Mac's orders to keep still."

"Let's see what shape they're in." Aurelia watched as the formation of bikes approached, and since she detected no sign of anything being wrong, she relaxed marginally. They had routines for everything, as they'd learned the hard way over the years to not deviate from their rules. If they did, someone got caught, which meant certain death in Klowdyn. The bounty-hunter units were one thing, but the secret-police headquarters was a nightmare to any freedom fighter. Torture and summary executions happened at the police chief's discretion and without a fair trial. Aurelia pressed her lips together. Hardly any trials went on in Klowdyn where the outcome wasn't a given ahead of time.

Five bikes came into full view, surrounded by the four that had set out to meet and assess them. Usually, that meant the intercepting bike leaders asked the approaching team leader a seemingly random, innocent question, and if they didn't receive the correct answer, they knew the team had been compromised while on their mission. It hadn't happened more than three times, as far as Aurelia knew, but that was three times too many. After the second incident, they put the new rule in place, and when it happened the third time, the interceptors had killed the two bounty-hunter agents sitting in the last cart. That action against the Klowdyns had made Aurelia physically ill, but no less determined to keep doing what she felt was her duty.

The bikes came to a halt, and it was as if that lack of movement woke up the one-year-old. The child started howling, and the blindfolded woman holding it tried to get it quiet, panic in her voice.

"I think that's my cue." Blue stepped forward before Aurelia had time to react and reached for the child. "Let me help you by holding your child, ma'am. You're among friends here." She scooped the bundle up and put it over her shoulder while gently patting the little one's bottom. "You're cold and hungry, aren't you?"

Aurelia gaped until she came to her senses. The team leader was already briefing Tom, and Aurelia didn't want to interfere with his job but helped the woman in the cart remove her blindfold and get out of the cart. She gasped at the woman's large belly.

"Yes. I'm pregnant." The woman wiped at tears that ran down her cheeks. "I'm not due for another three months, though."

"What's your name?" Aurelia assisted her and waved for Blue to follow them.

"Gill. And my son's name is Noah." She held on to Aurelia's arm. "Are we really safe?"

"Yes." Guiding the woman in under the camouflage nets, Aurelia steered Gill toward one of the fur-clad chairs beside an electric heater. "Sit down and stretch out. I know how cramped the carts are, and you've been holding on to that little howler for hours."

"He's been asleep most of the time. I fed him properly like I was instructed so he wouldn't be too hungry during the journey." Gill was trembling. "It seemed the rocking of the cart helped with that as well."

"Are you cold?" Blue asked as she placed the silent child back in his mother's arms. "I think he's happier now. Perhaps the sudden silence and stop set him off." She turned to Aurelia. "Do we have formula or porridge for the little guy?"

We? Aurelia blinked. "Yes. We stock up on formula. Mac has it in her storage."

"I'll be right back then. Can he drink from a cup?"

"I have a bottle with me." Gill pulled one from her small bag.

Blue took it and walked back into the cave. Aurelia looked after her disappearing form, frowning, before she returned her attention to Gill. "I have a few questions. Everyone in your party will answer them, whether you're traveling together or not. All right?"

"I'll answer anything you want," Gill said, pulling the jacket closer around her. "Anything at all as long as I don't have to go back to the Fardicia."

"Good." Aurelia kept her voice even as she asked the routine follow-up questions, also carefully constructed to avoid infiltration as much as possible. If Gill's answers were the same as the information Tom already had about her and her son, they would take them over the border to Sandslot. If something didn't add up, she'd be returned to where they'd picked her up, which was a pain, and burn that particular rendezvous place. If they suspected one of their sites for pickups to be compromised for whatever reason, they couldn't use it again. Their lives, and the lives of the ones they tried to help, depended on that tactic.

Taking her notes to Tom, Aurelia met Blue, who was bringing a blanket and a now-full bottle to Gill and Noah. She wasn't sure what to make of Blue's initiative and readiness to help. Not about to bring it up with Tom, as she'd rather he'd use his own judgment, Aurelia knew she would talk to Dacia and Milton about Blue.

"Got the comparison sheet?" Aurelia asked Tom as she caught him between interviews.

"Gill Sunders, right? And Noah?" Tom gave her a piece of paper from his binder. "Amazing that they made it this far. Now we just have to get them across the border." He scratched the back of his neck. "Tricky."

"Yeah." Walking toward a better-lit area, Aurelia scanned the documents and compared the answers. Everything checked out and she relaxed somewhat. After doing this for years, she had developed a sense of when people were lying to her, or not. She had a good feeling about Gill and her child, but she also knew better than to rely solely on her own intuition. A single mother traveling with a cute child…the secret police or the bounty hunter could easily come up with such a scheme, or even threaten the poor mother and promise her the world if she helped capture the traffickers.

Aurelia knew they'd called people like her traffickers long before she started moving people across the border. Now since the Tallawens had several satellite camps, it was as if the word was even more common. No doubt her success rate had something to do with it.

"That did the trick." Blue showed up at Aurelia's side, making her flinch. "Sorry. Didn't mean to startle you."

Tipping her head back, Aurelia looked up at Blue's bruises, now more green and yellow bruises than black. "No problem. What were you saying?"

"The formula. Noah's eating." Blue motioned with her strong chin in Gill's direction. I grabbed a cheese sandwich for the mother."

"You're good with children." Aurelia studied Blue's expression. "Think you might be a mother yourself?"

Blue clearly hadn't expected that question. "A mother? No." She sounded certain, but something resembling pain traveled over her face.

"You can't be sure." Aurelia felt like an asshole but pressed on. "As you don't remember much."

"True. But I'd like to think I'd know if I ever gave birth. The idea of not…of not knowing is unthinkable." Blue shoved her hands back into her pockets.

Aurelia sighed. "I'm sorry. I could have been more sensitive. Damn it." She flipped her hair back over her shoulder. "Can I make it up to you by getting you some of my secret stash of real coffee? I just have to return the documents to Tom."

"Real coffee? Not that substitute I've had so far? I mean, it keeps your belly warm, but—"

"But that's about the best you can say about it." Aurelia had to smile at Blue's attempt to be polite. "I promise. Real coffee beans. And it's not just mine—it belongs to the camp. We do keep it in a special place, though, so we can use it as a reward or, in this case, an apology."

Blue gave a faint smile, which transformed her bruised face completely. Aurelia realized this woman could be, if not beautiful, then very, very handsome. "Then I accept both."

CHAPTER FIVE

Blue wrapped her cold fingers around the metal mug filled to the brim with real coffee. The taste of the black, hot beverage exploded on her tongue, sending strange flickering images through her mind. She tried to catch them, hold on to them, but like the scenes from dreams fading as soon as you woke up and tried to remember them, these became milky and melted into nothing. This, however, didn't take anything away from the enjoyment of drinking real coffee. Blue knew without a doubt that she must love this beverage, for the pleasantness against her taste buds and the kick her system got from it were immediate.

"Good, huh?" Aurelia grinned at Blue over the rim of her mug. "It's a real morale boost."

"I can imagine you need it at times. A morale boost, I mean." Blue found that she knew the climate of the Klowdynian mountains very well, even if she couldn't remember her own life. "It can be a hard existence to haul people around behind off-roaders."

Her eyes closing halfway, as if Aurelia was measuring Blue's every word, she spoke matter-of-factly. "Yes. It can."

"I'm not blind, Aurelia," Blue said lightly. "I can tell you're part of some group that helps refugees."

"And what's your stand on that activity?" Placing her mug on the flat rock before her, Aurelia became opaque. The difference between her current expression and the sparkling humor from only moments ago was almost tangible.

"I think it's madness to risk yourself like that. I mean, you're all very young people with your life ahead of you." Blue wasn't sure this was her true opinion, but it didn't take a genius to realize what the Klowdynian authorities would do to these people if or when they were caught.

"You have to pick something worth risking your life for, Blue, if you're hell-bent on risking it. Helping people to a life in freedom in a true democracy is worth it, in my book." Aurelia's passion broke through. Clearly this young woman couldn't stay cool and aloof for very long. "And the loyalty and friendship among us helps."

"How many of you are there? Are there more camps than this?" Blue could tell that asking these questions was a mistake as soon as she said the words aloud. "No. Don't answer that. None of my business. I just want you to drop me somewhere tomorrow, or any of the upcoming days, where I can make my way home."

"And where is home?" Aurelia tilted her head, her black hair cascading down her left shoulder like a wild river.

"Eh…Fardicia?" Blue wracked her brain, but hardly any other names of Klowdynian places came up. "Or perhaps I've just learned about the capital. What do I know?"

"If you live in Fardicia, you're either employed by the government or military. Or immensely wealthy. Which one do you think?" Taking her mug again, Aurelia drank the rest of her coffee.

"Paper pusher? No. I don't think so." Blue shook her head.

"I don't think so either. Those calluses on your hands and feet show combat training. Military? Law enforcement?"

"It's such a blur. I'm sorry." For some reason Blue really wanted to be able to give Aurelia the answer. Clearly, Aurelia needed to know Blue's identity to rule her out as the enemy. And from what Blue had witnessed tonight, Aurelia needed every fighter she could find. Not being able to provide the information, Blue rubbed the back of her neck and shrugged. "I really wish I could remember."

Looking remorseful, which oddly made Blue feel worse, Aurelia placed a hand on Blue's. "I realize that. I ought to know better than to push. Your memory will return when it's good and ready."

Blue felt Aurelia's touch, and the strangest sensation built inside, emanating from the area on the back of her hand. She nearly yanked it back, but a weird sense of politeness made her keep it still. "Thank you for understanding. If I were you, I'd be suspicious of someone appearing at your doorstep, well, almost, claiming to not remember anything. At least you and Tom are giving me the benefit of the doubt instead of throwing me in some dungeon."

"Dungeon? Now there's a thought." Aurelia squeezed Blue's hand and then let go.

"Me and my big mouth." Blue finished off the now-lukewarm coffee. "I wish I could persuade you to put me to use, though. Nothing that jeopardizes your missions, naturally, but something useful. Doing the dishes. Whatever."

Aurelia tilted her head again, and Blue began to think this was one of Aurelia's tells. When she pondered something or tried to ascertain the truth, she leaned her head to the left and squinted. Did she have any tells of her own? She felt rigid and rather colorless next to the mercurial young woman before her who commanded all these people—some of them a good deal older than herself and some appearing far too young to do this kind of job. With a lithe, feline body language, Aurelia looked like she could shine or blend into the darkness of the night around them with equal ease. Blue, being fair skinned, muscular, and taller, felt clumsy next to her. Or perhaps that was only until she got over the residual aches and pain—and regained her memory?

"All right. You look like you're good with kids. We have only two really small ones like Noah, him included, but we have six between ages four to ten. They need supervision when we talk through our plans with their parents, as they're too young to be part of our activities. We've found that the eleven-year-olds and up are most often quite capable of taking part in the briefs."

"And you need someone to safeguard and babysit the smaller children?" Surprised, Blue didn't know what to do with her hands, but she settled for clinging to the now-empty mug. No matter how you looked at it, being in charge of children was like guarding someone's lifeblood.

"Exactly. Someone able to defend them and their parents, should it come to that. It would mean being stationary here in the camp."

"Which would also serve the purpose of my not finding out exactly where we are." Blue nodded slowly. That made sense.

"Same as for the rest of our temporary visitors. Nobody can know, or we won't be able to set any more people free." Shrugging, Aurelia stood. "I'm going to check on Tom and his lists. A lot will happen tomorrow. I suggest you stock up on some more rack time."

Blue knew when she was being dismissed, even if the way Aurelia worded her command was polite.

"I will. Thank you. And take your own advice, please."

Aurelia looked surprised at Blue's words. "I know." She tucked her mug into her pocket. "Hold on to it and keep it clean. If everyone is responsible for their own stuff, we don't spread any unnecessary germs."

"All right." Letting the last drops of coffee drop onto the ground, Blue pushed her mug into her jacket pocket. Ridiculously, she felt like she belonged in this camp a tiny bit, all because she had been awarded her own mug.

Aurelia spent an hour with Tom, reviewing the information they had about the dissidents and their children. When they were done, Tom leaned toward her, his elbows resting on his knees.

"Now, I'm dying to know. How was your chat with our amnesia guest?"

Aurelia sighed. "Nothing was wrong with the chat itself, but I can't figure her out. I'm most puzzled by how calm she is, given her precarious situation. She knows her name and has general knowledge of the world, it seems, but that's it. Of course, I can't imagine how I'd react if I couldn't remember who I was, but I'd probably freak out a little bit, anyway." Aurelia stretched her legs out and crossed her ankles. "What about you?"

"If I lost my memory? Well, the paradox about that is, how could I possibly know, as I wouldn't recall my disposition for freaking out or not if I couldn't remember." Shrugging, Tom smiled wryly.

"I don't think that's true." Eager to explain, Aurelia gestured with both hands. "I think our personality is so much a part of who we are that we'll stay calm and collected, if that's what we're like, and vice versa."

"You sure? What if you're a horrible person because you've been mistreated all your life. When you can't remember the abuse, then perhaps your horrible traits go away with the lost memories."

That possibility sounded logical. "I get your point, and sure, abuse can screw us up, but amnesia doesn't scrub us of every single memory. If it did, there'd be no language left, or perhaps even simple understanding of food. You know? So, I think Blue's ability to adapt is ingrained in her. If it wasn't, if her calmness is only skin-deep, we'd have spotted the cracks by now. Instead, it's like she's ready to acclimatize and grab the ball and run."

Tom nodded slowly. "You make a good point. That doesn't mean we can trust her."

"Not for a second. That's why my giving her an assignment might strike you as odd."

"Kitchen duty?" Tom snorted.

"That'd be a waste of talent." Aurelia hid a yawn. She really was exhausted. "She's our new family liaison, sort of. She's clearly good with kids, which is a bit baffling since she has no memory of having children of her own, and clearly being trained in hand-to-hand combat makes that trait even more implausible. But anyway, she's going to assist any families we bring in. That keeps her here, it keeps our runs secret, and she won't go, as she put it, stir-crazy."

"You're joking." Tom stared at Aurelia, and his red eyebrows nearly reached his hairline. "Don't get me wrong. She needs something to do and to pull her weight, but kiddie duty? I didn't see that coming."

Aurelia hadn't either, until she'd witnessed how Blue had handled the child and traumatized mother this evening. The battle-callused hands had held little Noah so tenderly, and her voice had been serene as she talked to Gill.

"You're rarely, if ever, wrong. I trust your judgment. I imagine we'll still have our people keep an eye on her?"

"Absolutely." Yawning openly now, Aurelia stood. "I'm sorry for my rudeness. I need to turn in. Tomorrow is an important day. We have the elderly couple that we're leading down the new path Milton scouted last week. I'm taking him, Dacia, and two of your most seasoned people. We can't risk anything with these older folks. Dacia and I will use the two larger carts, so they'll be reasonably comfortable. Milton will assume the lead, and the other two will bring up the rear."

"I can send more with you," Tom said as they both began to walk back to the cave.

"Not on this new path. We need to be able to hide quickly and effectively, and having too many of us could pose a real problem."

"I understand," Tom said, and she could tell he filed the information away. She relied on him for a lot, especially because he had a nearly eidetic memory.

Aurelia said good night to Tom, and after a quick visit to the lavatories, she entered the cave system. Hurrying to the dormitory, she noticed how cold she was. As long as she'd been engrossed in their conversation, she hadn't paid attention to the chilly evening, but now she was shivering. She had toyed with the idea of a quick shower earlier, but that would have to wait until tomorrow, after their run. Showers at their camps were sometimes lukewarm, but mostly on the cool side, and she would take hours to get warm again if she subjected herself to such conditions tonight.

Tiptoeing through the dormitory where more than half the racks were filled with sleeping Tallawens, she made her way to the screened-off section she now shared with Blue. She rounded it, fully expecting Blue to be asleep, but found her at a small table that hadn't been there earlier in the day. Two small camping stools sat on each side of the table, and Blue was occupying one of them while writing on a piece of paper.

"I hope you don't mind my rearranging a bit," Blue whispered and looked up.

Glancing around their small space, Aurelia noticed that Blue had pushed their cots over more to the right and closer together. She had also gotten rid of the bed sheets on her cot and replaced them with a sleeping bag.

"No problem," Aurelia murmured and opened her footlocker. Pulling out the soft, old clothes she used to sleep in, she turned her back to Blue and began to undress. Her teeth clattered, and she rubbed her arms before sticking them into the shirtsleeves. After donning the pants, she rolled out the sleeping bag and noticed an unfamiliar blanket underneath it. Blue had been issued a blanket to go with the sheets when they readied her cot the other day, but Aurelia was usually fine with just her sleeping bag.

"Temperature has dropped all evening. I talked to Mac, and she said it was a good idea if I brought you one too." Blue shrugged. "You look like you need it."

Aurelia felt silly for wanting to object and not quite sure why she felt she should. "Thank you." Crawling into the sleeping bag and spreading the blanket over it felt wonderful. Had she been so used to roughing it for so long that common sense, like asking for an extra blanket if you were cold, had left her?

"What are you writing?" Aurelia whispered and yawned.

"I'm making notes of my own reactions to everything." She put down the pencil and folded the paper. "Guess I'm a bit nervous that I might wake up one morning and have lost these new memories as well. Silly, I know."

It wasn't. "Not at all. You're handling this situation so well, and if writing everything down helps you feel a bit more secure, then I think it's a smart idea." Aurelia saw that Blue was wearing similar attire as herself. Only when Blue climbed into her own sleeping bag and spread a blanket over herself did Aurelia realize how close they were going to sleep to each other.

"Thank you. I want to be up-front about my experience here and not cause you any extra concern. Your task as leader is hard enough as it is." Blue gave the pillow a few nudges and then lay down.

"You have to stop taking responsibility for being attacked. That's not your fault." Aurelia closed her eyes and began to drift off.

"It's hard not to," Blue murmured. "I feel like I'm to blame, somehow."

"Tomorrow, you'll start really pulling your weight around here. That'll take care of some of this unnecessary guilt." Feeling increasingly warmer, Aurelia was almost asleep when Blue whispered something. "Mm. What?"

"Nothing. Go to sleep, Aurelia."

Aurelia could have sworn she felt a light touch on her shoulder before she lost consciousness.

CHAPTER SIX

Two days later, Blue had created a classroom of sorts, where four children between the ages six and twelve could meet and keep up some idea of school. They turned out to be two sets of siblings, which was forbidden in Klowdyn. It didn't take Blue long to realize that they were refugees because they'd kept their youngest children a secret. Blue knew, as she did with most things that weren't personal to her, that Klowdynian authorities didn't allow more than one child per family. If a younger child was born, it was removed from the family, and eventually a childless family adopted or fostered it. Looking at the two sisters, six and ten, and the brother and sister, seven and twelve, and how cautious they seemed, Blue had to clear her throat before she began talking.

"Hello, and welcome to class. My name's Blue. Why don't you introduce yourselves? First names are fine."

The oldest girl put her arm around the one sitting next to her. "I'm Milly, and this is my sister, Jade." They looked so much alike it was obvious they were related. Both had thick, blond, shoulder-long hair, bright-blue eyes, and slightly upturned noses. Jade had an odd, gaunt expression, which puzzled Blue until she realized that the child had probably not spent much time outdoors because her parents had to hide her.

"Milly and Jade. I'm glad you decided to join me here." Blue sat on a wooden crate, leaving the table and four stools for the kids.

"I'm Ryan." The boy gave a shy smile. "I'm seven."

"My name is Paula." This girl didn't smile. A frown above narrowed eyes showed she either resented being here or simply didn't care for Blue's initiative. Her red hair was kept in a low ponytail, and a multitude of freckles looked almost black against her pale skin. Ryan's hair was a darker shade of red, and he had no freckles. Whereas Paula's eyes were a dark hazel, his were emerald green.

"Ryan and Paula. Welcome." Blue handed out pencils and paper that she'd convinced Tom they needed. "I thought we'd start by getting to know each other a bit in a special way. Instead of talking, please draw something you think is important for the others to know about you. All right? Does that sound like a good idea?"

"I like drawing," Ryan said, grabbing his pencil. "Why's there only one eraser?" He eyed the one sitting in the center of the small table.

"You know supplies are scarce here, right?" Blue made sure she had everyone's attention. "I asked Tom for pencils for all of you, and since you can't all draw and write with the same one, he agreed to that request. I figured you could take turns using the eraser though. Make sense?"

Ryan nodded with enthusiasm and began drawing right away. After a moment, Milly started as well, her pencil strokes hesitant in the beginning. Looking at her sister's paper, Jade soon followed suit. Paula, however, hadn't even picked up her pencil. Blue let her lack of activity go for the moment. Instead, she took her own pencil and began drawing. After a few moments she cast a furtive glance at Paula and saw that the little girl's hands were moving restlessly along the edge of the table.

"Why aren't you drawing, Paula?" Milly asked.

"I don't want to." Paula nudged the pencil and sent it rolling over to Blue. Her chin went up in a clear challenge.

"You don't have to, but I do expect you to take good care of the pencil. It's yours." Blue took it and placed it on top of Paula's paper. "Drawing isn't mandatory."

Paula looked as if she meant to toss the pencil back to Blue, but instead she took it and held it against her chest in an oddly protective gesture.

"What does mandatory mean?" Ryan asked, looking up.

"Mandatory means that you have to do something. It can be by law, or a rule, or an order—or schoolwork, like a test." Blue looked at Ryan to see if her explanation made sense to him, but now he was drawing something that looked like a big, black square with a white circle in the center.

"And what if you don't do what's mandatory?" Paula asked, another clear challenge.

"There are usually consequences. Most rules exist for a good reason. Traffic rules. Rules against crime. That sort of thing," Blue said.

"My brother lived in the basement his entire life because of some mandatory rule that our parents could have only me." Paula spat the words, fury dominating her tone. And perhaps something more, something resembling guilt?

Black square. White circle. Blue stared at Ryan's drawing. A basement with just one lamp…or bulb? Oh, God. "Yes, that's a correct way to put the word in context." Blue met Paula's glare.

"I hate that word," Paula said, her lower lip quivering for a moment. "It's a bad word."

"A word is just a word," Blue said quietly. "It's how people use words and what they let them describe that can be bad. For Ryan to grow up in hiding was bad for him, for you, for your entire family.'"

"When we get to Sandslot, my mom and dad say we can have as many siblings as we like," little Jade suddenly said, making her sister gasp.

"Jade!" Milly covered her eyes.

Ryan giggled. "Maybe you can have a brother. Or a hundred brothers!"

"I don't think Mom wants to have a hundred babies." Jade waved her pencil at Ryan. "Perhaps twenty."

"Oh, my." Blue had to cover her mouth so the smaller children wouldn't see her broad smile. When she turned to check on the two older girls, she saw that Paula had started to draw. Not letting on that she'd noticed, Blue sat with the children as they worked on their pictures. The two youngest ones quieted after a while, and when everyone had put down their pencils, Blue spoke again. "I don't mind sharing my drawing, but it is not... what was the word again, Ryan?"

"It's not mandatory." Ryan beamed.

"Exactly. So, I'm really bad at drawing, but this is what I did." Blue turned her picture around so the children could see.

"Is that...a mug? With something steaming inside?" Milly tilted her head. "Hot chocolate?" She sounded longing.

"It is a mug, yes. And it's coffee." Blue didn't say that it was real coffee. She was pretty sure Aurelia and Tom wanted to keep that stash a secret, only to be used sparingly.

"Why does that describe you?" Paula asked, sounding more curious than angry now.

"Because a person I have come to trust and who saved my life gave me coffee when I was cold and tired, and I got to keep the mug as my own. That made me feel accepted. I must have felt pretty lonely beforehand." Blue wasn't sure how it could feel all right to bare her soul like this to these kids, but it did.

"Like when you gave us our own pencil. And started the classroom for us to use." Milly's blue eyes welled up. "You accept us, even if we have secret siblings and break Klowdyn's mandatory rule."

Blue swallowed. "Yes."

Milly pushed her drawing to the center of the table, nudging the eraser aside. "This is my sketch."

Blue could tell the girl was good at drawing. In the distance she could see a large structure and, next to it animals, probably horses. "Want to tell us about it?"

"We were neighbors with one of the boarding schools for children belonging to governmental officials. They have horseback riding on the schedule, and I love horses. I sometimes sneaked over there with my best friend and gave the horses some grass. My father caught us doing it, and then he made it a strict rule for my friend and me to never go any nearer than in this drawing." Milly pulled the paper back toward her and folded it in half, hiding the sketch.

A strange stirring in Blue's chest made her heart pick up speed. It was as if she truly knew how it felt to sit on a horse. She could smell it—the horse, the leather, and the fresh air. Shaking her head, she nodded at Milly. "I can imagine he was afraid what might happen if the wrong person caught you."

"It could have sent the authorities to our house to do a search. They could have found Jade." Milly sucked her lower lip into her mouth. "And that would have been my fault."

Blue wanted to object and claim that it wasn't Milly's fault, any of the children's fault, that the Klowdynian law was written the way it was, but no matter what words she chose, Milly would still feel this way.

Jade had drawn what looked like a triangle with something growing out of it, but it turned out to be an ice cream cone. "I love ice cream," the little girl said seriously. "I've had it one time, for my birthday. Mom told me that in Sandslot, everyone eats ice cream all the time. Outside. Everyone can be outside and eat ice cream."

How was Blue going to be able to push through this first lesson without crying? The children's history was heartbreaking, and she simply couldn't let any part of herself break. After Ryan explained about his basement and what he called his "pretty light," which was really just a bulb, Blue made fists under the table and shoved her blunt nails into her palms to be able to go on. She glanced at Paula, who hesitated briefly but then placed her drawing in the center like the others had.

Blue braced herself and then studied the detailed sketch. A girl sat in the center of a classroom full of children. Around her were twenty-some desks with one child in each. Behind the girl in the center stood a smaller, faint outline of another child. At least ten other children had these faint images of smaller kids behind them as well.

"That's me," Paula whispered and pointed to the child in the center. "That's Ryan." She placed her finger on the ghost child behind her.

Blue pressed her knuckles against her mouth for a few seconds. "And these?" she asked hoarsely and slid her fingertip along the other children with shadows behind them.

"That's how many in my class who may have secret siblings as well." Paula looked up at Blue with darkening eyes. "I can't tell for sure, but I sort of sensed it. They felt the same as me. Afraid."

Blue had to take Paula's hand. She reached out her other hand to Milly, who sat to her left. The other children did the same, and soon they formed a ring. "Listen," Blue said, once she had her voice under control. "None of us knows what the future holds, but when we are in our classroom, nobody needs to be afraid, and nobody is anyone's secret. How does that sound?"

Four pairs of huge eyes looked at, no, scrutinized her. When Paula suddenly gave the tiniest of smiles, the other three children relaxed and nodded. Blue exhaled. They had a pact.

CHAPTER SEVEN

Y ou've been in here a long time." Milton poked his head into the small room that Tom had set up as his office.

Aurelia looked up from the maps and rubbed the back of her neck. "Hi, there. Did you run the new recruits into the ground?" Milton had taken it upon himself to train three of Tom's recruits, one girl and two, far-too-young boys, in the art of driving the off-roader with a cart behind it. It wasn't as easy as it looked.

"What makes you say that?" Milton sat down on a wobbly stool next to her.

"You have that half grin going on. I saw enough of that at Jeters to recognize it for what it is. You're gloating." Aurelia stuck the pencil into the high ponytail she sported for the day. She'd thought of cutting her hair, as the long, black masses were an inconvenience when roughing it, which was her normal way of existing, and they made her easy to recognize, but each time she made up her mind, she hesitated.

"Jeters." Milton gave an exaggerated shudder, and Aurelia knew the boarding school where she, Milton, and Dacia were kept for years had left marks on all their souls. In Aurelia's case, she had lived at Jeters for fourteen years. Dacia had come two years after her, and Milton one year after Dacia. "It's no wonder we don't mind living in caves day in and day out. Jeters makes this place feel all cozy."

"I hear you." Aurelia pulled her feet up and hugged her knees close to her chest. "When I go into the dormitory here, seeing the cots that aren't very comfortable, I still feel safe and among friends. At Jeters—"

"We hated it with a passion." Dacia came into the room, nudging the maps aside, and jumped up onto the table. "Here. Ran into Mac. She had some shipment come in, and there was one of these for everyone." She handed Milton and Aurelia an orange each.

"Oranges?" Aurelia gaped. "What sorcery is this?" She sniffed the fruit, and the fresh scent nearly made her well up. "I should give this to one of the kids. Two of them could split—"

"No. Uh-uh. Mac has already put away extra for the growing members of our rowdy bunch. And she was going to give some of them to Blue to hand out to her pupils." Dacia crinkled her nose and began peeling her orange. "Speaking of our enigmatic amnesiac, she's really taken to those kids. I might have suspected it was an act, if I hadn't been just as sure the kids would have seen through her if she was being fake. After a week in school with her, they're really starting to relax…even play."

Aurelia rolled the orange between her hands and lowered her feet onto the cave floor. "She's good with them. Even that girl, the one that stares a hole in your head if she finds you lacking in any way, Paula, accepts her."

Milton hadn't bothered to peel his orange but divided it into four parts and bit into them one by one. "Have you two noticed how she sometimes stops in midsentence or midmovement, as if she's about to remember something?"

"I have," Dacia said and placed her peels carefully in a bowl to the side, which Aurelia thought was a good idea. They could be used for tea or cleansing. "That's one thing. What's really hard to see is how defeated she looks when it doesn't happen. I know, I know. I may be reading too much into her body language, but that's what I think."

Dacia was rarely wrong in her estimations. Aurelia took some pride in being a good judge of character, but Dacia had some sixth sense when it came to people, especially the ones that others found hard to figure out.

"And the way she acts around you, Aurelia, is also pretty obvious," Dacia said now, putting an orange wedge into her mouth.

"Wait…what do you mean?" Aurelia was just about to taste her own orange but lowered her hand. "She's perfectly fine around me." She frowned at Dacia, who merely smiled broadly.

"That's what you think because you never notice when someone is being, um, attentive. Like that woman we took across at the south border years ago, before we realized it was too dangerous to get people over to Anglia. She was ready to dig her well-manicured claws into you if you'd paid her a tiny bit of attention."

"Hey, calm down, Dacia," Milton said, chewing his orange slowly. "Perhaps long-distance relationships just aren't Aurelia's thing."

"Oh, you two, you think you're funny." Grabbing the empty mug sitting on the table next to Dacia, Aurelia raised it over her head as if aiming at Milton. "I don't see any of you taking the opportunity with anyone in particular."

"Ha. No comparison," Dacia said and licked her fingertips. "I at least indulge in a one-night stand on occasion, though it's been slim pickings lately. Milton is more like you—saving himself for Ms. Right."

Aurelia saw the shadow that passed over Milton's face at Dacia's words and averted her eyes to not embarrass him. Dacia talked about Aurelia being obtuse, but she'd been completely oblivious to Milton's feelings for her ever since they were at Jeters.

Aurelia put down the mug. Dacia wasn't wrong about her, the brat. Not that Aurelia was saving herself at all, really. Dacia didn't have to sound as if Aurelia was some damn virgin. In fact, they'd all gone through the same phases after leaving Jeters—looking for love and being curious about sex—but Aurelia had been the first one who put that part of life on the back burner once they started the Tallawens. When you risked incarceration or death on nearly a daily basis, it wasn't appealing to expose yourself or anyone else to such danger and heartache.

"Hey. I was only joking." Clearly regretful, Dacia yanked gently at Aurelia's ponytail. "You know me. I'm just messing with you."

"I realize that, and I'm not offended. You know me better than that." Aurelia shook her head and offered a smile. "It just hit close to home. We're pathetic. We won't date any of the Tallawens or any of the people we help. That leaves exactly no one. We can't date anyone who isn't aware of our day job. We'd be risking too much."

"That's what I mean," Milton said laconically. "We're fucked, basically."

"God." Dacia covered her eyes for a moment. "Way to put it in an upbeat fashion, Mil. So, back to Aurelia's Blue."

Aurelia jerked. She'd forgotten how this ridiculous-turned-somber conversation had started. "She's not 'my Blue,' by the way."

"You'd think she was, judging from how her eyes follow you as soon as you're around. Either she's putting on a great act with the amnesia and casing you, or she's into you." Dacia looked pleased with herself as she sat there on the desk, dangling her legs.

"Why don't we change the topic and take a look at the map you're half sitting on, fool," Aurelia said lightly, nudging Dacia, who jumped off the desk and sat down on Milton's left knee.

"Anything wrong?" Milton asked and threw his peels in with Dacia's.

"No. In fact, the opposite." Aurelia took a deep breath and lowered her voice until it was barely above a whisper. "I think

I've found a new path, one we've never used before. It would be perfect for us during Project Maydorian."

Dacia gasped, and Milton leaned forward so fast, he nearly pushed her off his lap. "What?"

"Yes." Aurelia's heart beat harder, making her shiver. "We made a promise that night at Jeters. The Maydorians were the only ones that were decent to us during those years. If it hadn't been for Mrs. Maydorian, we would have starved after all the pranks we pulled on the faculty members." Aurelia gripped the seat of her stool.

They had vowed to one day help Mrs. Maydorian and her husband get out of Klowdyn. Aurelia could still feel her terror when the Maydorians had found the three of them sneaking out of the main dormitory and about to run for their lives. So certain they'd been caught, even if Mrs. Maydorian had been a good person to them, Aurelia had expected to be brought before the headmaster and put in solitary again. When Mrs. Maydorian gave them food packages instead and covered for them as they crawled through the tunnel they'd dug over the last year, Aurelia had promised the woman they'd come back for her and her husband. The housekeeper obviously hadn't believed her, but Aurelia had been totally serious. So were Dacia and Milton.

"This means going back there. To Jeters," Dacia whispered. "To scout it out and prepare them. I mean, if they're ready to leave. If they *want* to." She shook her head. "They might not even be there. Or they could be dead."

"Hey, glass-half-empty." Milton spoke mildly and hugged Dacia to him. "You always knew we had to go back at some point. We—"

"*We* aren't going back." Aurelia stood, placing a hand on her hip. "*I'm* returning to Jeters to talk to them. And don't worry. I'm not an idiot and am not about to enter the school area. If the Maydorians are there, they used to go into the village to fetch mail and order groceries for the school. Mr. Maydorian often worked on the trees outside the wall too. I'll find a way to talk to them without going inside."

"You can't go alone!" Dacia jumped up and took Aurelia by the shoulder. "You'll get caught, and we'll never see you again."

"I'm sorry," a sonorous voice said from the opening behind them. "I couldn't help but overhear. If you need an extra hand, Aurelia, I volunteer."

Aurelia stared at Blue, who looked entirely composed, as usual. How much had she heard of what they were talking about?

"Are you spying on us?" Milton rose, his rigid shoulders, along with his hand that rested on his small holster, betraying his anger. He rarely carried the larger rifles, but his aim with the small sidearm was legendary among the Tallawens.

"Not at all. I merely heard Dacia say she was worried about Aurelia going somewhere alone." Blue didn't move, merely propped her shoulder against the side of the opening and crossed one leg over the other. Her hands were, per usual, shoved into her jacket pockets. "I'm aware that I'm a stranger here, but I don't know who I am either, so that kind of makes us even. But going on a mission entirely alone is rarely a good thing." She held up a hand. "Don't ask me how I understand this concept. I have no idea."

"I don't need company or someone to watch over me," Aurelia said. "You've just started the schoolroom. It's not a good idea for you to leave the camp."

"So, I *am* your prisoner, Aurelia?" Blue's lips thinned.

Frustrated and feeling maneuvered, Aurelia sighed. "No, but you know the rules. If you truly want to leave for good, we'll take you to a place, blindfolded and rendered harmless, and place you somewhere safe but unknown. Considering that your memory isn't back…yet, that'd be tough for you, even dangerous. If you tell anyone you've been in a Tallawen camp for two weeks, you'll attract suspicion, and they would probably keep you in 'protective custody' and interrogate you for the smallest piece of intel. Trust me. That is an unpleasant experience."

Blue blinked, and something seemed to ghost across her strong features. Now that the bruises were barely visible, it was obvious that she was a striking woman. Her short, blond hair lay in precise waves against her scalp, and her blue eyes seemed so light, Aurelia entertained the idea that Blue could see in the dark.

"I can imagine that it must be." Blue commented on Aurelia's words. "I have no interest in revealing anything about the Tallawens or the camps." A faint ember of anger ignited in her eyes. "For heaven's sake, you must really consider me a deplorable person if you think I can bond with traumatized children one day and sell them out the next."

Dacia studied them all, one at a time. "A lot's riding on this decision," she murmured. "Aurelia, you insist that Milton and I remain here, while you initiate what is ultimately your endgame. What if you're lost to us because you refused to take another Tallawen? Please, honey? Take anyone. If something happens, you know that we'll never even get word, and if we do, it'll be too late for us to take action."

"And what makes you think I can fully trust her?" Aurelia pointed at Blue.

"I don't. I mean, not fully. But we take a risk with every recruit. We always have a chance of being compromised." Dacia clasped Aurelia's hand.

"Look at it this way," Blue said laconically. "I'm not really a member of your crew here. I'm expendable. That can be useful." She gave a one-shoulder shrug.

Furious now at how manipulated she felt, Aurelia let go of Dacia's hand and grabbed her mug of deplorably bad coffee. She drank the last of it and grimaced. "Fine. I'll take you." She scowled at Blue. "But you're not going to be with me when I make contact. You'll do what I say, when I say it. I won't risk this mission, and I'll do anything, and I mean *anything* to protect it. Do you understand?"

"I do." Blue's shoulders lowered an inch. Had she been holding her breath?

"Good. You need to find something else to wear, as we're going to ride a bus or a train. And just so you know, you'll be going blindfolded on the back of my bike until we're far enough away from the camp." Challenging Blue to give up and admit defeat, Aurelia instead saw the other woman nod briskly.

"Understood."

God damn it. Would nothing faze Blue? Aurelia studied her closely. "Tell me why."

"Excuse me?" Blue tilted her head.

"Why you're hell-bent on coming along."

Blue smiled, revealing her perfect teeth. "Because it didn't take very long for you to give me my own, personal coffee mug. Whether you realize it or not, that provided me a sense of belonging, even if it is temporary. So, until you kick me out of here, or my memory returns, whichever comes first, I'm a Tallawen and loyal to you."

CHAPTER EIGHT

Blue had nourished some hope that Aurelia had been joking, or at least exaggerated, when she claimed she would be blindfolded on Aurelia's off-roader. She should have known better. Having talked to, and observed, the Tallawen leader, and yes, it hadn't taken a genius to figure out Aurelia was their leader, Blue had noticed that, as giggly and silly as the woman could be with her closest friends, Dacia and Milton, she was also sharp and fierce. Not to mention stubborn as all hell. She had reneged on her agreement to bring Blue with her several times over the last twenty-four hours, questioning what good it would do to include Blue only to report back if Aurelia was caught, hurt, or killed.

"She won't know how to get word back to you. She doesn't know where we are. What the hell's she supposed to do? Take out a fucking ad in the newspaper?" Aurelia flung her hands in the air.

"That wouldn't do much good, no." Milton rubbed his chin. "Mail service around here is deplorable."

"Milton." Aurelia glared at him.

"I have it figured out." Dacia clapped her hands as if she'd just received a birthday present. "At one point, you'll be passing our favorite village. If something happens to you, Blue can leave a message in the pub."

"Which pub?" Blue asked.

"The pub. I can't for the life of me remember the name, but since the entire village consists of only thirty-some houses, it has just one pub."

"What if, instead, she tells the authorities that someone at that pub runs messages for the Tallawens?" Aurelia shook her head.

"I suppose taking her along at all is a risk, but that's our only option. If you won't take one of the Tallawens, Blue's your best chance. You know she can handle herself. She's trained." Dacia stabbed the air with her index finger, pointing at Blue. "If she wants you out of the way, she'll have ample opportunity, I suppose."

"Oh, this sounds better and better." Aurelia flicked her hair back. "I'll be much quicker if I just—"

"Please." Milton stood. "We've been through a lot over the last years. Dacia and I have never asked you for anything, have we? And now we ask this. Please, take Blue, or whoever, and don't go get yourself killed...or caught."

Aurelia had already opened her mouth as if to object again, when Milton's words seemed to hit her. Her shoulders slumping, she sent Blue a quick glance before giving a brisk nod. "Fine. Yes. All right." She stomped away from them but then turned around. "All right," she repeated, and this time her voice sounded softer.

So, here Blue was, blindfolded tight enough to see stars and patterns against her eyelids. She was wearing the supplies and equipment for both of them, as she would be sitting pressed against Aurelia on the off-roader, which made it impossible for Aurelia to wear a backpack.

Milton had lent Blue his leather jacket and a pair of jeans, which fit her well enough to not look strange when they approached populated areas. Aurelia also wore a leather jacket, but her pants were forest green. Milton's boots had been too big for Blue. Luckily, Mac's boots fit her, and, before Mac let her have them, she'd had to promise twice to return them unscathed.

"You bring our girl back now," Mac said firmly. "I mean it."

"I know you do. And I will." Of course it was impossible to make such a promise, but these people had saved her life and kept her around without knowing anything about her. She owed them. Most of all, and she couldn't quite understand how it had happened, this situation was starting to become deeply personal. She couldn't decide whether the kids or this formidable young woman, who fearlessly roughed it in caves to save people and risked her life every single day by doing so, had stolen her heart. Probably both.

"You ready?" Aurelia asked.

"I am." Blue checked the shoulder straps of the backpack, pulling them tighter.

"Then climb on and hold on tight. It's a bumpy ride the first half hour. If you reinjure yourself...not sure your head could take it."

Blue agreed with that assessment. She still got headaches, which only Mac knew about, as Blue had had to ask for an occasional aspirin. "I won't fall off." She felt for the bike, found Aurelia's shoulder, and was just about to swing her leg over the back part of the long saddle when she remembered that the poles holding up the camouflage net above them on the bike were attached there. Plus, two full spare petrol cans had been attached on either side of the back wheel. Carefully sliding her foot between the poles and Aurelia's back, Blue mounted the rear of the bike. She found the back footrests and put one foot up, keeping the other on the ground to help support the bike before they took off.

"You'll find two thermoses of hot tea in the backpack," Milton said. "And sandwiches, some apples. And cash at the bottom."

"I know. I was there when you packed it," Aurelia said, and Blue could hear a smile in her voice. "When we get far enough away from here for you to lose the blindfold, Blue, I'll fill you in on what else we have."

"That would be good." Aurelia moved, jerked, and then Blue heard the off-roader roar to life. After that, Aurelia engaged some innovation of Tom's that muffled the engine somewhat. It was by no means quiet, but it didn't sound like an antagonized sewing machine anymore. This was obviously required when they went through areas within earshot of people.

"Bye, good people. We'll be back in a few days. If it's more than a week, check in with the pub." Aurelia moved again, and now the bike took off.

Blue had already placed her arms around Aurelia, and now she circled her waist, gluing herself against her back. She was starting to think Aurelia never exaggerated about anything, as the ride was indeed bumpy. Closing her jaw tight, to not accidentally bite her tongue, Blue focused on trying to become one with the woman driving this hellish machine. Above them she could hear the camouflage flutter in the wind. It had seen better days, but it would keep them from being spotted by helicopters or small planes that patrolled the mountains.

Just when Blue thought she couldn't manage the sharp turns and the painfully bumpy paths they rode on, Aurelia stopped the bike and let the engine idle. "You can remove your blindfold."

Grateful, Blue tore off the offending fabric and tucked it into her pocket. Better save it in case Aurelia decided she had to wear it again on the way home. *Back. On the way back.* Glancing around them, she noticed that the scenery looked a lot like it did near the camp. Green hills and small mountains, gnarly trees, wildflowers, and even a brook. They had made so many twists and turns, Blue had no idea where they were.

"We're going to follow this wider path until we reach the forest down there." Aurelia pointed ahead of them. "We have to take down the camo net and the poles then, or they'll snag. The path in the forest is pretty narrow, but apart from a few roots, it's not as bad as what we just rode through."

"Sounds reassuring."

"Once we're at the other end of the forest, we'll make camp by a small lake and be able to clean up. From there, we're on foot for a bit."

Blue wasn't privy to many of the details, another of Aurelia's conditions. Clearly, their mission would be conducted on a need-to-know basis. This didn't sit well with Blue, but she understood the terms for her presence here. If she had to shut up and do as she was told, that was what she was going to do, unless Aurelia got herself into a dangerous situation.

The forest was dark and dense and seemed to go on forever, and as they drove the bike among the trees, Blue inhaled the clean, fresh scent of pine. She had eased her grip around Aurelia, but when roots did show up on the path intermittently, she had to hold on harder again.

"We'll stay for a break and have some tea and a sandwich in an hour or so. That okay with you?" Aurelia yelled to drown out the off-roader's engine.

"Yes!" Thank God. She could use a cup of tea, even if she'd always preferred coffee. It took a little while before Blue realized what had just gone through her head. Had always? How could she possibly know what she "always" had or hadn't liked? Was this another sign that her memory was returning?

As Aurelia skillfully maneuvered the large off-roader among the trees, Blue turned her head over her shoulder every now and then to make sure nobody was behind them. They'd be hard-pressed to hear anyone over the noise the bike made. She figured she should tell Aurelia about her reasoning, or she might wonder what Blue was up to. "Path is empty behind us!"

"What?" Aurelia leaned back a little, almost putting the back of her head onto Blue's shoulder.

Blue repeated what she'd just said.

"Empty? Oh. Oh! Good." Nodding vigorously, Aurelia patted Blue's right thigh. "Good thinking."

Blue's brain nearly stalled at Aurelia's unexpected touch and at her praise. Feeling ridiculously pleased with herself, she shook off her reaction and focused on holding onto Aurelia. It was impressive how Aurelia managed to steer the bike in this terrain, considering it was huge compared to some of the others Blue had seen around the camp.

Aurelia drove for yet another hour and then pulled off to the side. "Jump off. We need to lead the bike into the clearing with us. In there," she pointed, "we won't be seen from the path. And if we keep our voices down, they won't even know we're here."

"Got it." Blue was relieved to dismount the bike and help Aurelia move it into the forest. Farther in was a pretty clearing with an abundance of autumn wildflowers and fallen trees that made it look quite idyllic. "I guess this is one of the stops you use when passing through here."

"You guess correctly." Leaning the bike against the sturdy trunk of a tree, Aurelia then helped pull the backpack off Blue. "Were you all right to carry this? I mean, you were still quite bruised only days ago."

"I'm fine. My bruises are only a faint yellow in some places. I can't feel them." Blue stretched and then rolled her shoulders. "How about you? I know you're used to riding all over the place on those things, but that one's a monster."

"I can feel it some." Aurelia shrugged and then grimaced. "Well, that just proved my point."

"I can drive some if you want."

"No. Thank you, but no. We have another six hours to go, and then it'll be too dark to drive. As you might have seen, our bikes don't have headlights. They used to, as we figured we might need them at one point. Then we had several incidents when people put them on by mistake or forgot to switch them off. We can drive in the dark on familiar roads, or in open terrain, but not in the woods. This bike has a red-tinted headlight, though, so we can get some guide light at least."

"I understand. Makes sense." It did, but it also presented another kind of danger. Driving in near-dark conditions, despite knowing the area well, had to still be dangerous. Foxes or rabbits weren't big animals, but if they ran out in front of an off-roader at the last moment, someone could break their neck.

Aurelia had opened the backpack and pulled out a thermos. "I hope you brought your mug," she said, raising her eyebrows.

"Never leave home without it," Blue said without thinking. Her cheeks warmed as she pulled the mug out of her pocket.

"Neither do I," Aurelia said after staring at Blue for a few, odd moments. She poured some tea into their containers. "Powdered milk?" She wiggled a small plastic bag.

"No, thank you." Blue sipped the tea, which wasn't bad at all. Whoever provided tea for the Tallawens had managed to score something decent. Oddly, this fact made Blue happy. The Tallawens sacrificed a lot by living the way they did. They deserved, at the very least, a good cup of tea. She accepted a sandwich from Aurelia and bit into the homemade bread with butter and cheese. "Thank you."

They ate in silence until their sandwiches were gone, Blue furtively watching Aurelia, who sat on her discarded leather jacket on the ground, leaning against another fallen trunk. She was looking up at the crowns of the trees around them—less fir and more birch and beech. How the hell did she know how to recognize trees? Perhaps she'd been a botanist? Blue snorted to herself. Not likely.

"What's so funny?" Aurelia had redirected her focus onto Blue.

"I just realized I know the names of the trees." Blue relayed her silly thoughts. "Figured I might have a secret past as a botanist."

Aurelia smiled broadly. "A botanist with martial-art skills? Now there's a thought."

Blue chuckled. "Sounds like a winning combination to me."

"I suppose. I can picture you pruning some poor tree with your bare hands." Aurelia covered her mouth with her free hand as more giggles broke free, holding onto her mug with the other.

Blue grinned, somehow knowing that Aurelia didn't share this type of obvious mirth with just anyone. The glitter in Aurelia's eyes and the way she flushed as she obviously tried to not laugh aloud was mesmerizing. With her straight, dark eyebrows and her black eyes, it was as if everything about Aurelia lent more mystique to the clearing.

They sat in companionable silence while finishing their tea. Then Aurelia jumped up and donned her jacket. "Time to get going again. This was nice, though." She gave Blue a quick glance, her eyes still smiling.

"I couldn't agree more. Some tea, a sandwich, and ridiculing my winning combination of a career choice. Of course, it's nice."

Again, Aurelia pressed a hand against her mouth. Above it, her eyes seemed transfixed as she looked at Blue. After removing her hand, she tilted her head and flicked her hair back. "I'm starting to think you may have quite a lot to offer, Blue," she said softly.

Before Blue had time to react, Aurelia closed the backpack and gave it to Blue. She then pulled the bike off the tree. "Ready?"

Blue donned the backpack and gripped the back of the bike. "Always."

CHAPTER NINE

As they neared the edge of the forest, Aurelia turned off the broader path and onto one less traveled. This would be harder on both them and the bike, but they'd lucked out and not met anyone in the woods, and as they neared more densely populated areas, they had to be increasingly careful.

When they reached a clearing she recognized from earlier missions, Aurelia pulled off the small path, wincing as she bounced over roots and shrubs. Blue's arms wrapped harder against her waist. She felt the outline of Blue's body pressed against her own, but she was grateful that the other woman knew how to ride as a passenger. Beginners didn't always understand that you had to ride as one and not lean the opposite way as the driver when rounding curves. Blue had been glued to Aurelia's back the entire time, which had made for a less cumbersome ride.

Slowing down even more, Aurelia let the bike make a ninety-degree turn. After traveling about fifty yards into the denser forest, she came to a stop. Around them stood four large beeches, and with the shrubbery between them and the trail, this was a good place to spend the night.

"This it?" Blue swung her leg back over the bike and stepped off. She took off the backpack and rolled her shoulder.

"Mm." Aurelia had turned off the engine and was standing still, listening intently. She heard some birds, but no voices and no other engines. "Seems we're alone, but keep your guard up. This area may feel like the wilderness to city people, but we're only a few hours' walk from civilization. We'll hide the bike and spend the night here. Tomorrow we're going to walk down to the main road and catch a bus."

Blue looked at Aurelia in disbelief. "The bus?"

Having braced against pushing the bike into the shrubs, Aurelia stopped. "Yes? It's the most inconspicuous and definitely the most common way for regular people to travel in Klowdyn. Surely you must know that. Or is that part of what you've forgotten?" She meant the questions honestly and without malice.

"I can honestly say I don't remember ever having ridden in a bus." Frowning, Blue let go of the backpack and helped Aurelia push the vehicle where it was barely visible. Aurelia fetched some dead branches she had used before and used them to cover the part of the bike still sticking out.

"Are we spending the night under the sky?" Blue looked around them and then up at the tree crowns. "What if it rains?"

"Trust me, we're all set, even if our conditions won't be luxurious." Aurelia had to smile at Blue, who looked at her as if she'd lost her mind. "Can you remember camping?"

"The concept, yes. Personal experience, no."

Aurelia opened the backpack and removed a thin tarp with eyelets around the edges. A thin rope was threaded through them, and now Aurelia pulled it out in the corners, giving two of the ends to Blue. "Here. Tie them around the two trees on your side, about two feet off the ground. I'll do the same. This will be our ceiling. I'll attach my end four feet off the ground. That'll create a bivouac where potential rain will drain at the back. If it rains hard, we might get a little damp, but not wet."

Blue nodded. "Okay."

Aurelia watched Blue tie her first rope, and whether she had been camping before or not, she knew how to make knots that wouldn't unravel. After they adjusted the tarp to keep it taut, Aurelia opened the backpack again. This time she pulled out two rolls made from a foam material. "Our mats." She handed them to Blue and found the sleeping bags. As she'd had to bring two, she'd had to settle for the thinner ones, and she hoped the night wouldn't be too cold.

Blue took the sleeping bags and rolled them out on the mats. "We may be damp and cold, if we're unlucky," she said matter-of-factly.

"We'll live." Aurelia took out the two thermoses. "We'll have to replenish again. The tea's probably not very hot anymore, but we need to keep up our strength. Good thing we have plenty of sandwiches." Pushing the backpack in under the tarp with her, she sat down on one of the sleeping bags and pulled her legs up. After checking her watch, she nodded to herself. "We made good time, considering two of us were on the bike. If we go to sleep after we eat, we'll get enough hours of rest."

Blue checked her watch. "I take it we'll be up as soon as it's light enough." She crawled in under the tarp and sat down on the other sleeping bag, holding her thermos and sandwich.

"Yes. We have to. I have some makeup and a few accessories to help us look the part even more." Aurelia bit into her sandwich and nearly choked on it at Blue's look of disbelief.

"You're joking. Makeup?" Blue had raised her sandwich but now lowered her hand again.

"Clearly just for me, judging from your expression." Aurelia had to laugh. "I promise I won't force you to put on mascara or lipstick."

"That'd be smart." Blue took a bite of her sandwich and then poured some tea into the mug that served as a lid for the thermos. "Ew. Pretty cold."

"And still full of good stuff all the same." Aurelia drank from her mug. "But, I agree, still ew."

That was when Blue gave one of her rare smiles, broad and bright. She even chuckled. "Told you."

Aurelia had to stop herself from sticking her tongue out at Blue, who was obviously teasing her, but she crinkled her nose in a way that Dacia or Milton would have recognized as her way of teasing back.

"Can I ask you a personal question?" Blue asked after swallowing another bite of her sandwich.

"You can. I can't promise I'll answer, though. It depends."

"Fair enough." Blue finished the sandwich before she continued. "How do you know Dacia and Milton? I can tell you go way back."

"That obvious, huh?" Relaxing some, Aurelia smiled. "We're old schoolmates."

"From childhood?" Holding onto the mug, Blue wrapped her arms around her pulled-up legs.

"Yes. I was six years old when I met Dacia, and Milton came to our school a year later. We found each other right away and have been each other's family ever since." Aurelia didn't volunteer how excruciating the two years she'd been alone had seemed, being only a little girl, but she could hear how her voice grew soft and wistful. It was bittersweet to think of those early years when the three of them had been far too young, but also so feisty together. The risks they had taken at Jeters had only increased with age. She guessed their escape had been the ultimate gamble.

Blue studied Aurelia for a moment. "Are you talking about one of the boarding schools?"

Clearly, Blue's fractured memories still made it possible for her to remember the boarding-school system in Klowdyn. "Yes," Aurelia said. She kept calm, refusing to acknowledge the pent-up rage that always simmered just beneath her skin when she thought of all the children that were taken, no *stolen*, in Klowdyn and, in her case, Sandslot, to fit in with some political agenda. "I was four when I was enrolled." That tidbit was ambiguous enough.

"Four?" Blue frowned. "You were sent to a boarding school at four?"

Aurelia knew it wasn't smart to give away any details, but the four-year-old Aurelia had protected her parents during her kidnapping and wasn't about to have Blue think her parents didn't care about her. "I was removed from my home and taken to one of the state-owned facilities." Her voice stark, Aurelia then downed the last of her cold tea and shoved the thermos back into the backpack. "My parents had no say in the matter."

"Ah, so you were a secret sibling." Shaking her head, Blue sighed. "I'm sorry that happened to you."

"That makes it sound like I accidentally contracted a disease." Aurelia raised her chin. "It didn't happen to me. It was done to me." What if she did have siblings? What if her parents had had more children after her abduction? A tiny voice she had struggled with many times over the years taunted her by suggesting that her parents had moved on and found new happiness with new children.

"Please. I'm sorry for asking. I didn't mean to be insensitive," Blue said and took Aurelia's free hand. "I've learned so much in such a short time from the kids back ho—at the camp."

Had Blue nearly said "home" and cut herself off? Her heart softening again, Aurelia began to feel as if her emotions insisted on tossing her around lately. Hearing Blue nearly say the word home and then stop herself was shaking Aurelia up considerably. She would have to keep tabs on herself so she wouldn't give any of her reactions away. Opening the backpack farther, she pulled out a toilet roll and a small garden shovel. "I'll go shock the deer that roam the woods. Back in a bit."

Hurrying to another little clearing, Aurelia did her business and dealt with it to cover any traces. This was truly roughing it, and she hoped she wouldn't have to explain this part in detail to

Blue. After all, there were some limits. As she made her way back, she could tell the temperature had gone down and wasn't tempted to bathe in the nearby lake. Not for the first time, she wished they could make a fire, but it was simply too dangerous. Some of the helicopters patrolling the mountains and the woods around them could detect smoke and heat. It was new technology, but it hadn't taken the Tallawens long to get the information. Their survival depended on them being one step ahead of the bounty-hunter units. The day the Klowdynian authorities had access to even more fine-tuned cameras that could differentiate between the body heat of a human being and that of an animal, they might be forced to work simply from an urban setting, which was infinitely more dangerous in many ways.

Aurelia walked back to the bivouac and handed the shovel and toilet paper to Blue. "Don't leave any traces," she said, feeling stupid.

Merely nodding, Blue bowed out of the shelter and walked in the same direction Aurelia had.

Aurelia removed her boots, climbed into her sleeping bag, and pulled the zipper up to her chin. Placing the boots under the mat, she used the elevation as a pillow of sorts. This was the part of going on missions she loathed. Never spoiled by the finer things in life, since no regular person in Klowdyn was, she admitted to loving the feeling of a soft pillow under her head. Using boots under a mat simply wasn't enough, but it would have to do. Shivering, Aurelia tugged the sleeping bag closer around her. It was going to be an uncomfortable, miserable night.

Blue slipped in under the tarp, mindful not to step on Aurelia, who had crawled into her sleeping bag. Dusk was upon them, and it seemed to hit faster than anywhere Blue had ever been. Halting just as she was about to move past Aurelia's still form, she barely stopped a whimper from breaking free. How the hell could she know about dusk in any other place?

"You all right?" Aurelia murmured from her side of the bivouac.

"Yes. I'm fine. Trying not to step on you. It's damn dark." She knew she sounded too animated, but she had to mask this new glimpse of her previous existence. Or were these automatic comparisons merely an echo of how people in general thought and spoke?

Managing to not dig a knee into Aurelia, Blue reached her sleeping bag. She pushed off Mac's boots and was about to place them at the foot end of the mat, when she felt Aurelia's hand on her arm.

"Put them under your mat as a pillow. It's not a perfect solution, but it beats getting a kink in your neck from lying on a hard, flat surface." Aurelia yawned. "God, that was a long ride."

"Good idea, and yes, it was." Blue followed Aurelia's advice and unzipped her sleeping bag. Crawling inside, she kept all her clothes on, as it felt as if it was getting colder by the minute. "You warm enough?" Blue asked casually.

"I will be." Aurelia's voice shivered.

"It's colder now. I could actually feel the temperature drop as I was heading back from the latrine." Blue didn't hesitate. She extended a hand and felt Aurelia's cheek. "You're really cold. Did you bring a hat?"

"I thought I did. I'm no fool. It gets cold at night, even at this time of year, and I normally wear a knitted hat when camping." Aurelia sighed. "I remembered to pack everything for us but that. Are you very cold?" She sounded apologetic.

"Not as cold as you, but that can work to our favor. This type of sleeping bag can be zipped together, right?" Blue sat up and pulled the backpack closer. "Can you dig out the flashlight? Unless you forgot that too."

"I didn't." Aurelia propped herself up on her left elbow and stuck her hand into the large bag. She found the flashlight and gave it to Blue. "What are you thinking?" Sounding cautious, she blinked when Blue turned on the flashlight.

"We have to get warm or we won't sleep, and if we don't sleep, we'll end up being careless from sheer fatigue and jeopardize the mission." Blue pushed the backpack out of the way and examined the zippers. "As I thought. We should zip our sleeping bags together and share. And before you ask, I have no idea how I know this, but it sounds like common sense and survival 101."

Aurelia was quiet for a moment, and Blue was certain the stubborn girl would refuse. Getting ready to argue further, she was taken aback as Aurelia merely said, "All right, then." When she heard Aurelia's teeth clatter, it took only another second for Blue to realize why. At least she was still shivering.

Unzipping her sleeping bag completely, Blue then did the same with Aurelia's. "Just stay covered." Blue worked fast. Finding the ends of the zippers, she managed to merge them and close them almost all the way. She switched off the flashlight, pushed her now-quite-cold feet into the double sleeping bag, and closed the last of the zipper. "There we go. We'll feel much warmer in a little bit."

"I t-take your word for it," Aurelia said. Blue could feel her shiver.

"Come here." Not giving Aurelia a chance to object, Blue pulled her close with one arm and nudged the lumpy boots in farther under the mat. Aurelia ended up with her head on Blue's shoulder. Blue wrapped her arms around Aurelia and held her close. An unexpected twitch in the center of her chest made her close her eyes. She loathed the idea that Aurelia was suffering so much from the cold. What if she had insisted on going alone after all? What would have happened here in the forest? If alone and suffering from increasing hypothermia, a person could succumb to the cold.

"Getting a little warmer," Aurelia whispered. "It's never been this cold in September before. Usually we get really mild weather this time of year."

"Feels more like December, if you ask me." Blue tucked the sleeping bags tighter around them and scooted them both farther down. Now she could pull the top of the sleeping bags over their heads, leaving only their faces exposed. Breathing was good, after all.

"I agree," Aurelia said and yawned again.

"Go to sleep. We'll be all right like this." Blue murmured the words against Aurelia's hair.

"I'll try." Hiding her face against Blue's neck, Aurelia shifted back and forth, her hands restless.

"What's wrong?" Blue frowned.

"I want to be on my side, but I can't get comfortable. My arms are in the way."

"Ah." Blue took Aurelia's right arm and tucked it against her own waist under her jacket. "Can you tuck the other between us?"

Aurelia shifted again and wormed her right arm between them. "Yes. Like this. Much better."

"May I tuck my hands under your jacket?" Blue asked cautiously. Even if they were clinging to each other to keep warm, they were crossing some unspoken boundaries. She didn't doubt that Aurelia had been in the same situation before, perhaps with Dacia and Milton. Nobody survived in this part of Klowdyn unless they possessed some serious survival skills. This didn't just entail a tactical and strategic mind, courage, and perseverance, but also being willing to do what it took. In such a situation nobody allowed feelings of awkwardness to get in the way. Right now, when Blue should focus only on keeping them warm, forbidden thoughts kept surfacing of how amazingly soft Aurelia felt against her and how the slender arm around her waist made Blue feel safer.

"Sure," Aurelia murmured and pressed her cold nose against the area just below Blue's right earlobe. "I don't mind."

Closing her eyes as she tucked her hands in under Aurelia's jacket, Blue found enough warmth to start to relax. She pressed her cheeks to the top of Aurelia's head. Perhaps she'd be able to sleep too.

"You're so warm." Aurelia's voice was barely audible. "I'm glad Dacia told me to take you." She held on tighter to Blue. "I can be a stubborn idiot at times."

"I'm glad I'm here too." Swallowing to combat the surge of emotions that ricocheted like stray bullets in her mind, Blue pressed her lips to Aurelia's temple. "Just relax and go to sleep."

As Blue felt herself drift off as well, she wished she knew more about the mission they were on. Perhaps Aurelia would share more details tomorrow.

Aurelia sighed and Blue held her closer, gently rubbing her back under her jacket. Either way, Blue was committed to making sure this woman returned to her friends in one piece. As she closed her eyes, she began to nod off, and faded images floated to the surface. Blue tried to wake up again, but the images mixed with her dream. Unable to assemble any potential clues, she saw a line of men in uniform. They were standing at attention, and she thought she could hear her own voice saying something.

The more she tried to capture the elusive memories, if that was what they were, the more cryptic they became. Before Blue fell asleep, she remembered how she merely stood still and saw something long and narrow rush toward her face. Before it landed, other hands were there, tugging at her. Voices called out, and Blue wanted to respond, but she couldn't speak.

Somehow, she realized she was dreaming, but that didn't stop the faces from parading in front of her. When the image of a middle-aged man with white hair and a neatly trimmed mustache appeared, Blue whimpered. She wanted to wake up, but the dream had her in a tight grip. The man was familiar, but she had no idea who he was. She should know, for his name wasn't buried very deep. His eyes were a pale blue, his hair thick and kept very short. His lapels were adorned with some sort of insignia.

"Who are you?" Blue whispered. "Can't you tell me? I'm begging you."

The man merely glared at her and made a dismissive gesture with his gloved hand. At that moment Blue recognized the insignia on them and managed to speak. "Father?"

CHAPTER TEN

Aurelia knew something was wrong as soon as they boarded the bus. Per usual in Klowdyn, people rarely looked each other in the eyes, but kept to themselves. You never knew who might be an informant, or even an agent for the BHU. The bounty-hunter unit consisted of two branches: the ones in uniform who worked alongside the police and the undercover operatives that could be...anyone. People were so used to moving only within their known circles, they never struck up a conversation with a stranger.

As soon as she and Blue had stepped onto the bus and paid the driver, they'd taken a double seat in the middle of the bus, near the exit door. On the way two men smiled at them, and one even said hello. That just wasn't done.

"The men," Blue whispered now, "what was that about? Granted, you're the most beautiful woman I've ever seen, but even so..."

"Had it been at night, I would've surmised they're drunk," Aurelia said, shaking her head. "We may have to get off this bus in the next village and take the next one. We'll be delayed."

"Or we could distract them." Blue had scooted forward in her seat, which put her on the same level as Aurelia. "The way they dress is strange also. Aren't people around here mostly farmers or factory workers?"

"Yes. At least the ones that take the bus are." Did Blue realize she'd called Aurelia "the most beautiful woman she'd ever seen"? Amid everything, those words still lingered.

They had woken up in the same position they'd fallen asleep in the joined sleeping bags, stiff and aching, but warm and reasonably well rested. After a quick breakfast with more tepid tea and sandwiches, Aurelia had repacked the backpack. The weapons fit in a padded compartment that wouldn't fool anyone who knew what to look for, but the rest of the backpack was filled with the rest of their food, some money, and their first-aid kit. They rolled up the tarp, camping mats, and sleeping bags and hid them along with the off-roader. Aurelia wasn't sure if their proximity during the night had embarrassed Blue, which would be strange since it was her idea, but they hadn't spoken much as they began walking across the fields to the main road.

"What do you mean by distracting them?" Turning her head to whisper into Blue's ear, Aurelia found herself closer to her companion than she realized.

"They're either agents who think we look suspicious or simply guys who aren't above flirting with a woman this early in the morning, so you should be able to—Shh. Here they come. That didn't take long."

Aurelia looked up as the two men sauntered down the aisle, the younger one with his eyes locked on her. "I want to kick them in the shins," she said through gritted teeth.

"But you won't." Blue nudged her. "Smile at the young one as he passes and then turn your attention fully at me."

Without a clue as to what Blue had in mind, Aurelia fired off a fake, blinding smile as the young man stood by her seat. She then, quite thankfully, looked back at Blue, who suddenly appeared annoyed.

"You can't help yourself, can you?" she said, sounding frustrated.

"What?" Aurelia flinched.

"I saw it. It's like you can't help yourself." Blue pushed her fingers through her hair and huffed. "Pathetic."

"I have no idea what you mean." Aurelia truly didn't, but by now she'd caught on to the fact that Blue was putting on an act. It had taken her a few bewildering moments, but her own confusion was evidently the right response.

"Oh, please. You always do this." Blue shifted her gaze to something above Aurelia's head. "Do you mind? If you think you're going to pick up my friend on a bus when she's on her way to work and at an ungodly hour, think again."

Aurelia couldn't believe that Blue was challenging these men, whether they were agents, informants, or mere workers. Klowdynians kept a low profile and would never dare to risk anything by—oh. Eventually, Aurelia's brain caught on to Blue's unorthodox plan, or at least part of it. She covered her eyes with her right hand. "Oh, this is so embarrassing. Don't you realize you're the one causing a scene?"

"Excuse me, ladies." The older of the two men said as he walked back to stand right beside Aurelia. "I apologize for my young friend. He's never met a pretty girl he didn't like, and you're a very beautiful young lady." He bowed politely. "We're stepping off at the next village, and he won't bother you again."

The men did indeed get off the bus, and just as Aurelia thought they must've been who they said they were, she saw through the window how the older man punched the younger one in the shoulder before pulling out what looked like a walkie-talkie.

"Shit," Blue hissed. "Nobody but officials would pull out a radio in public. Well, at least now we know. But I really don't think that's about us. I think he's reporting the young guy for breaking character."

"You think? We shouldn't get off at the next stop?" Aurelia had never been in this situation and wasn't sure why she was certain that Blue had.

"No. Let's keep going. We're not far from the village where we change busses, right?"

Aurelia had decided that Blue needed to know their route if they became separated and had shown her on the map before they broke camp. "Correct. We have two changes before we reach our goal." Aurelia thought quickly. "Why don't we take one bus later when we get there?"

"My thoughts exactly." Blue grinned. "The look on your face before you caught on, though."

Aurelia glanced toward the ceiling. "It's not like I had a lot of time to think. Talk about being tossed off the deep end. And you took a gamble." Leaning closer to Blue, Aurelia whispered the words with emphasis.

"It was a good way to put them off our scent."

Blue was right. Who in their right mind would cause a scene on a bus when two potential agents approached them? It had been a gamble, but a smart one. Did she feel a bit off her game because this mission concerned the Maydorians? Pinching her thigh hard to snap herself out of her doubts, Aurelia straightened in the seat.

The rest of the first leg of their journey was uneventful. Aurelia found herself nearly nodding off, which wouldn't do. She was in charge on this mission and refused to put that burden on Blue, no matter how much she was starting to trust her. It had felt so good to wake up in Blue's arms this morning, so safe and warm it had hurt physically to free herself and get up.

In the village where they meant to take another bus, they walked into the waiting room and sat down. When nobody seemed to pay them any attention, Aurelia stood and headed toward the restroom. Blue joined her, and after they turned the corner in the dingy old station, they instead exited the side entrance. Not a soul was in sight outside. Hurrying down the street with Blue taking up the rear, Aurelia stopped by an overgrown hedge. She pushed through it, nearly getting her backpack stuck, but Blue shoved it, propelling her through. After joining Aurelia, Blue looked around. "That house has seen better days."

An abandoned house sat in the middle of the tall grass. No windows, and with half the roof gone, it looked like the next storm would easily level it. "Sure does," Aurelia said. "The bus to our next stop leaves in an hour. Unless we see something amiss when we return to the station, we can probably be certain we've dodged any potential agents."

"Agreed." Blue looked around. "It's not very tempting to try for indoors. What about the far-left corner? I think the sun's going to come out. We might catch a few rays over there."

Aurelia nodded, and they walked through the tall grass. She kept her hand on the sidearm tucked into the back of her pants. Milton had painstakingly sewn holders into the back of several of their clothes, and new recruits trained how to draw the gun and take aim until the response was committed to muscle memory. Once they had that move down, it was time for their shooting range.

Aurelia was a good shot, but the best one they had was Dacia, hands down. The woman could hit her target with such speed and accuracy, it was eerie. It also made Dacia annoyingly happy to always beat Milton and Aurelia. Milton could at least say he was the fastest runner and strongest climber. Aurelia knew she was a well-rounded freedom fighter, but she excelled in tactics and reading the people she met and bestowing her enthusiasm upon them.

"Isn't it time you trusted me with a gun?" Blue's alto voice broke Aurelia's train of thought.

"I don't know. Is it?" Aurelia pushed some tall weeds aside and poked her head inside the doorless opening. It was dark and smelled of wild animals, most likely from the neighborhood's stray cats and dogs.

"I think so, but you're the boss." Blue shook her head at the abandoned house. "I'm not going in there. The smell will linger on our clothes and cause suspicion. And besides, the roof looks like it's ready to cave in."

"I agree. Let's sit here. The weeds are tall enough to hide us." Aurelia moved sideways along the wall, careful not to bend any of the weeds. Some old boards were stacked against the wall under what used to be a window, and she carefully sat down. The boards squeaked but held up all right. Blue took a seat next to her, sighing.

"I suppose you don't trust me yet. Can't say I blame you." She sounded matter-of-fact, but as Aurelia glanced up, she detected signs of distress in how the skin around Blue's eyes tensed.

"It's not a question of trust." Aurelia tried to explain. "I know you're trained in hand-to-hand combat. Your calluses prove it, and you move in a way that says you're either that...or a dancer."

Blue snorted. "A dancer. I think not."

"My point exactly. And even if having combat training suggests that you've trained in using firearms, I don't know that. Hell, *you* don't know that. If I give you a weapon, and you either end up hurting yourself or someone innocent, it's on me. As much as I loathe the people we fight against, I'd rather not have bullets flying."

Blue relaxed marginally next to her. "Fair enough. But if we wind up in a situation where bullets are already flying and we're in danger, you will have to trust me. Please." She pulled her knees up and hooked an arm around them.

Aurelia nodded slowly. "If that happens, I will."

Now Blue smiled, which stirred something deep in Aurelia's stomach. What was it about this woman that made it impossible to remain collected? They were on a mission, no, not just a mission. *The* mission. The one she'd vowed to carry out to settle an unpayable debt.

"All right." Blue leaned back against the wall. "Can you tell me anything about the mission? I mean, you don't have to tell me names, places, or dates. I realize you have to keep that stuff confidential. But why this is out of the ordinary."

"That obvious, huh?" Aurelia sighed. "I don't know how much you've picked up around the Tallawens these last few weeks."

"Some. Some I've deduced on my own. Like the bond between you, Dacia, and Milton. You're like siblings. Well, you're like a sister to them, but those two...I'd say they're tiptoeing around each other, both afraid to take the first step."

Aurelia gasped. "That's very perceptive. I know Milton worships Dacia, but she's oblivious...and as much as I'd love to see them happy, I've never interfered. I know Dacia is as apprehensive about relationships as I am."

"Perhaps it's easier for me to see, being an outsider." Shrugging, Blue tugged at a long grass straw. "Milton is easier to read, but the way I see it, Dacia puts on a good act to throw everyone else off the scent."

Aurelia conjured up images of Dacia and Milton. She tried to think of the last few years without the "childhood filter" she normally put on them. The constant teasing, Milton's protectiveness, and Dacia's growing competitiveness. Aurelia didn't have a problem with this, or, rather, she did have issues, but if Dacia and Milton ever figured it out, she'd be happy for them. The Tallawens had several couples among their operatives, but having relationships was always tricky. How could a person watch their partner in life take such risks to save others without being tempted to risk the mission by trying to keep their loved one safe? How could their feelings ever be as impersonal as they sometimes had to be? "When we grew up together at the boarding school, we were like musketeers, and as none of us was adopted, we formed a bond. It was pretty obvious that the principal and the security staff kept a close eye on us in general and me in particular."

"Why do you think that was?"

Reaching into a side pocket on the backpack, Aurelia pulled out two bottles of water and handed one to Blue. "I always knew they treated me very differently than the other kids. They attempted to give me a new name, but I refused to use it, ever since I woke up on the bed where I'd spend most of my nights. I knew I was Aurelia and that I'd been stolen." It had taken a lot of energy to keep fighting them regarding something that symbolized who she had been and who she was becoming. She had refused to be the person they tried to mold her into.

"I bet that didn't go over well with the people in charge of the school." Blue shook her head. "The kids back at camp are all horribly afraid of ending up at one of the boarding schools. I don't remember ever having discussed the places with anyone, let alone visited one, but I suppose I could have."

"Do you have any memories at all?" Aurelia asked softly.

"I'm not sure. In my dreams I see a man in his late sixties who keeps talking to me, but for all I know, he could be a fictitious person. Whoever he is, he's always displeased." Blue rubbed the back of her neck.

Aurelia studied Blue. No, she didn't think the man in her dreams was someone her brain had conjured up. The tension had increased and turned her features into sharper planes and angles. Aurelia ached even more for Blue, but if she was being completely honest with herself, she had never seen Blue more beautiful than she was now, sitting back against the old house.

Checking her watch, Aurelia stalled so she could gather her thoughts. "Our school, Jeters, is one of the largest. When I was in my late teens, before we escaped, four hundred kids were there. Some were as young as I was when I ended up on the third floor, where they have employed nannies."

Blue's eyes darkened to a threatening, stormy blue-gray. "How old were you?"

"Four. Almost five." Speaking casually helped relieve the feelings of resentment, even hate, toward the ones who had separated her from her family. "They said my name was Emily Bright. Over and over, they acted as if I was simply a fanciful child who took fantasy games to the extreme. No matter what, I knew my name was Aurelia DeCallum, even if they forced me to write the name Emily Bright on my school papers, drawings, and so on. But I refused to be Emily in my heart. With Dacia and Milton, who went through the same ordeal about names, I always used my real one, and in return they shared theirs with me.

"That was the start of our rebellion, and we became masterminds at tormenting the staff. As kids, we knew we weren't mature enough to survive on the outside, so we bided our time. Instead we pranked every staff member…well, except for the two people I'm going to see. They were different—warm, caring, and clearly unhappy with the way the rest of the staff treated the children. The only kids that thrived at Jeters were the ones who were legitimately there, sent by their parents, going home on weekends, holidays, and so on. That was about two thirds of us. I wouldn't say the staff members were overly kind to them, but they showed a certain respect. You know—they knew there'd be hell to pay if the parents of those kids received complaints." Aurelia stopped talking for a moment. "God. Look at me. You probably regret ever asking about my past." She sipped from her water bottle.

"Not for a second." Blue bumped Aurelia's shoulder with her own. "And I want to hear more."

Checking her watch again, Aurelia saw they had to return to the station in ten minutes. "Okay. It was thanks to the people I'm about to meet that we managed to escape when I turned eighteen. Milton, being two years older, had already been put to work at the school, working ten- to twelve-hour days in the garden or the fields. You'd think we weren't living in the sixties at the time, but before the industrial revolution, the way they made him and other young men and women that were of age work wasn't unusual. He didn't complain, not once, but instead provided all the information he could about the outside world."

"Did you ever get to leave the school grounds?" Blue placed a gentle hand on Aurelia's knee.

"No. I was their prisoner for fourteen years." Jittery now, Aurelia glanced at her watch. "I'll have to tell you more later. Time to go."

Blue stood, extended a hand to Aurelia, and pulled her up. She found herself well within Blue's personal space, which made her lose focus for a millisecond. "All right," she said huskily. "We better get a move on." She donned the backpack, and suddenly Blue's hands were in her ponytail.

"Grass." Blue pulled the offending straws from Aurelia's hair and then turned and began walking along the faint path they'd created when they crossed the deserted lot.

Aurelia followed right behind Blue, feeling the other woman's hands in her hair, on her knee, and how it had been to wake up entirely engulfed in someone else's arms this morning. Shaking her head, Aurelia flipped the mental switch in her brain and focused on what might be waiting for them as they stepped onto the street and into the station.

The next phase of their mission had truly begun.

CHAPTER ELEVEN

Six hours and two uneventful bus rides later, Blue stepped off at a stop just inside the perimeter of a small city called Jeterson. She vaguely remembered the name, but of course, she had no idea if she had ever been there. For all she knew, it looked like any other city of its size. Judging from tall chimneys in the distance, a lot of Jeterson's residents made a living from industrial work.

"Stealth 101," Aurelia said quietly as they walked along the main road toward the center of Jeterson. "Go find a public place where nobody thinks it's strange if you hang out. Like a library. I'll go locate the person I need to talk to. I plan to be back here in two hours."

"Here as in at the bus stop?" Blue didn't like the sound of this plan.

"Yes. According to the schedule, they run at a quarter past, every hour." Aurelia hoisted the backpack and tightened the shoulder straps.

"I think you have to decide here and now whether you plan to trust me or not." Blue refused to back down. "If something happens to you, I'm supposed to just abandon you and go to that pub in one of the villages we passed and let everyone know? How about being a little more proactive? And besides, what if I'm apprehended? You have no idea who I am, you won't be able to find me—you can't even attempt without risking your own safety. That means you jeopardize your important mission. It's illogical, Aurelia." Frustration rose within her, making Blue want to grab Aurelia's shoulders and shake her.

"You have some nerve." Aurelia's eyes burned with anger. She tugged Blue off the sidewalk and into a narrow alley. "You can't just demand trust."

"And you can't go in on your own, half-cocked, and rely on your street smarts to see you through. Let me come with you. When you find your contact, I'll make myself scarce, and you can have your meeting. Then we'll find our way back here and suffer through the lovely bus rides all over again. Please. Milton and Dacia rely on my helping to keep you safe." Blue knew the last part was a dirty trick, using the people Aurelia loved most in the world as leverage.

"Oh, God, you're infuriating." Aurelia clamped one hand against her forehead. "All right!" Then she seemed a little calmer. "All right." She cast a glance around the corner, both ways, before stepping out on the sidewalk again. "But we need to get a few other things straight."

"No problem."

"I do the talking. The person I'm seeing has no reason to trust you. So, none of this…this arguing in front of him."

"Of course not."

"And if I decide that you need to watch from a certain distance instead, or leave during the meeting, I don't want to hear any objections." Aurelia sighed.

"Goes without saying," Blue said.

Aurelia growled under her breath. "For the love of…can you stop being so damn agreeable all of a sudden?"

Blue frowned. "You want me to object after all?"

"What do you mean?" Aurelia glared at her.

"You said you don't want to hear any objections." Blue rubbed the back of her head, feeling a headache coming on. This had happened on and off after her concussion.

"I don't mind opinions, just no objections to what I say to the person we're going to help. This mission means everything to me. And not just to me. You know that by now."

"I don't plan to wreck it for you—or anyone. I'm here to help you ensure it will pan out the way you planned it." Blue hoped Aurelia was able to hear the honesty in her words.

Aurelia nudged Blue's hand. "I can be such a bitch when I'm focused and nervous at the same time. Usually I'm not nervous at all. Ask Dacia. She calls me a reckless adrenaline junkie most of the time." Clearing her throat, Aurelia colored faintly. "There's some truth to that, but this time, as I said, it's personal."

"And making sure you succeed and that you're safe is personal to me." Blue hadn't planned to be so up-front about her own motives, but Aurelia deserved the truth if she was going to start trusting Blue at all.

"Yeah?" Smiling now, Aurelia's eyes glittered. "Then I think we have a deal we both can live with." She lengthened her stride to match Blue's. We'll be at the inn where he told me he always tries to sneak in and have a beer while on errands. Unless he's changed his habits, he'll be there in half an hour. Come on, Blue. You're about to meet the man who saved my life."

❖

The last seven years had not been kind to Ellis Maydorian. His hands looked painful as he paid the innkeeper for the beer before looking around the outdoor area for an available seat. Seeing her chance, Aurelia walked over to the man who had helped save her and her friends' lives and smiled cautiously. "We have an empty seat at our table, sir," she said quietly.

"Oh, that's lovely of you, dear," Ellis said. Even his voice had changed. Aurelia remembered it being much more forceful and resonant. What were they doing to this man at Jeters? A horrible thought struck her. Was this her fault? Had they realized who'd helped the trio escape and punished the Maydorians?

As Ellis sat down at the worn wooden table, he sipped his beer and sighed with contentment.

"Do you remember me, Mr. Maydorian?" Aurelia asked in a whisper as she leaned closer to him.

"Excuse me?" Ellis glanced up and frowned. "Should I know you, young lady?"

"It's been seven years." Aurelia shrugged and made sure nobody at the tables surrounding them could overhear. "I've changed, of course. You were the only one at Jeters who called me by my real name. Only in private, of course. I'm Aurelia DeCallum. My friends at Jeters were Dacia and Milton."

Ellis was perhaps a husk of the man he used to be, but clearly nothing was wrong with his mind. His eyes grew sharp. "Are you crazy, girl? You can't approach me in a public place like this and talk about a time in my life where a lot nearly went very wrong." He glared at them. "And who's this?" He flicked his callused fingers at Blue.

"This is my friend Blue." Aurelia patted Ellis's left hand. "Seven years ago, I made your wife Martha a promise. I'm here to make good on it."

"A promise?" Clearly taken aback, Ellis blinked. "I have no idea what you're—" He gripped the edge of the table. "Oh, that. A little girl's gratitude and eagerness to repay a perceived debt." He shook his head dismissively. "No need for any grand gestures, girl."

"Listen. I often doubted I'd be in a position to fulfill my promise to you. You saved our lives that day, Mr. Maydorian. We owe you and your wife everything."

"And just what do you think you can do, young Aurelia?" Ellis took another mouthful of beer.

"What I've done for countless other people. I can get you to Sandslot." Aurelia checked the tables around them, but nobody seemed the least bit interested in their conversation.

"What are you talking about?" He was starting to sound not annoyed, but very tired.

Putting everything on the line, and with her heart sinking deep into the recesses of her belly, Aurelia pushed on. "You have heard of the Tallawens, I would imagine."

"I have." Squaring his shoulders, Ellis clung to his pint and his knuckles whitened.

"Then you know I'm being truthful. We've saved a lot of people. Dacia and Milton and I agree that we need to put things into motion with you and Mrs. Maydorian before our luck runs out."

"You're implying that you're part of the Tallawen? Does that entail you too, young lady?" This time it was Blue's turn to be on the receiving end of the man's attention.

"Yes," Blue said immediately. "I'm a fairly new member, but they saved my life, and I can vouch for them, if that means anything at all."

"It doesn't." Maybe he realized he sounded quite gruff, because he softened his tone. "I don't mean to be dismissive. I know you girls mean well, but leaving Klowdyn was never an option for Martha and me." Ellis's eyes filled with sorrow. "So, whether you're legitimate or if this is a Klowdynian trap doesn't matter. We would never leave."

Aurelia wanted to cry but didn't allow any tears. She hadn't expected Ellis to jump at the chance to live the rest of his life in a free, democratic country, but she hadn't expected him to be so dismissive. "You don't want to discuss it with your wife, sir?"

"I don't have to. I know she won't want to leave. Ever." Placing his hands on the surface of the table, Ellis shuffled his feet. "Now it's time for me to go collect the mail and the groceries—"

"There's someone you can't leave behind—you and your wife. Someone Aurelia doesn't know about. Someone who will be punished if you defect." Blue's gentle, yet firm, voice stopped Ellis, and he slumped back into the chair. "That's why you've never attempted to leave Klowdyn, even if you find what goes on at Jeters abhorrent."

"How do you know?" Ellis whispered hoarsely.

"It's the only thing that makes sense." Blue took Aurelia's hand under the table and squeezed it.

Aurelia allowed the encouraging touch for a few moments. Inwardly, she chastised herself for not figuring this possibility out. "Is Blue right, Ellis?" she whispered mildly. "Do you have someone like that? A child perhaps? Or a sibling?"

Ellis blinked at the tears that gathered in the corners of his eyes. "Our daughter, Lorna, and her two children. She was once married to a government official, and as long as Martha and I played our part at Jeters, she lived in relative luxury and was even allowed an extra child. After her husband died four years ago, her life has become increasingly difficult and closely monitored. She's even had criticism and veiled threats regarding her youngest child. I think they fear that her husband shared things with her. She's a loose end, if you will."

"Did he?" Aurelia asked.

"She hasn't confirmed anything either way, not to us, but I think he might have. He was truly in love with her, and they actually eloped. If he hadn't held the position he did, and he was very well connected, that alone would have been grounds for punishment." Ellis scratched his chin. "So, you see, we could never leave her."

Aurelia's mind raced. She glanced at Blue, who nodded discreetly. Catching Ellis's gaze and trying her best to sound convincing, she spoke quietly and fast. "I have only one solution. We bring Lorna and her children along as well."

Ellis paled. "This is nothing to be cavalier about."

"I've never been more serious." Aurelia knew it would take some doing to convince the startled man, but she had made a promise and was certain she spoke for Dacia and Milton as well.

"It can be done." Blue drank from her teacup.

Ellis looked so tormented and anguished, Aurelia almost regretted putting him in this situation. He had shown her so much kindness and been a beacon through the fourteen years she'd been a prisoner at Jeters. He'd sometimes snuck her and her friends some fruits or carved them wooden toys. One time, he and his wife had wrapped presents for Christmas, a day that normally wasn't celebrated in Klowdyn.

"How can you be so sure?" Ellis's voice barely carried across the table.

"Because it's been done before. Many times," Aurelia said. "We'll have to get you to safety simultaneously, of course."

"Of course," Ellis echoed faintly. He ran his hand over his face. "Are you really this confident, Aurelia?"

"I'm confident but also realistic," Aurelia said firmly. "How many children does your daughter have?"

"Two girls. Charlotte is seven and Pippa is five," Ellis said. "Lorna is thirty-nine, and her husband Ian died four years ago. Charlotte remembers some things about her father, even if I think she learned of the things from looking at old photos. Pippa is too young to remember Ian at all."

"And they live here in Jeterson?" Blue asked.

Ellis shook his head. "No. They live in Fardicia."

Aurelia was torn about that piece of information, which was both a blessing and a curse. It made for a greater anonymity since almost a million people lived in the capital, but it would be harder to extract them. Aurelia would have to come up with some creative plans with Dacia, Milton, and Blue. It didn't escape her that she automatically thought of using Blue's clear sense for tactics.

"Are you *sure*?" Ellis asked pointedly. "There's no way in hell I'm taking this plan to Martha if you're not absolutely sure."

"I'm as sure as it's humanly possible. Just as sure as you were when you relied on us kids not ratting you out for helping us, within the walls and outside of them. You took such a chance. As did Martha."

"How will it happen?" Ellis asked, and Aurelia thought she could spot a new expression in his eyes.

"I'll confer with Dacia, Milton, and Blue," Aurelia said. "Once we figure out a plan, one of our people will contact you using a phrase I'll teach you before you have to go. I need you to be my eyes and ears here and deliver information back to me through them. You'll provide us with your daughter's address and help us find a way to convince her this can be done—and then it is up to you, Martha, and Lorna, to make the final decision." Wanting to take Ellis's hands in hers, Aurelia still didn't, knowing full well that such a clear demonstration of affection would make people take notice, and you never knew when someone would find something worth reporting.

Aurelia instructed Ellis about the exact wording their operative would use when contacting him and Martha. Then she had him quietly repeat it to her several times until she was satisfied that he knew it by heart.

"God bless you, girl," Ellis said as he stood. "No matter what comes from this, God bless you."

Her chest hurting at his amazed tone, Aurelia shook her head. "You and Martha saved us. This is the right thing to do." She stood as he left the inn's backyard, wondering if she'd taken on more than she could deliver. She told herself this was no different from any other rescue she'd carried out with the Tallawens, but it wasn't entirely true. This was personal, and that made it all the more complicated.

"Aurelia?" Blue murmured and nudged her arm. "Time to head back."

Suppressing a shiver, Aurelia nodded. "Yes, it is. We have work to do."

CHAPTER TWELVE

Blue noticed the two people shadowing them first. For the last block, two women were keeping the same pace as Aurelia and she were. "Isn't that the type of coat you wanted?" To make sure, Blue stopped by a shop window and pretended to look at some clothes.

"What?" Aurelia took a few more steps but then returned to Blue. "What's wrong?"

Blue was glad Aurelia was astute enough to catch on immediately. "Look at the reflection in the glass. Two women, one blonde, one brunette, to the left. One's pretending to tie a damn shoestring."

"I see them. For how long?" Aurelia's lips tensed.

"Three blocks."

"They can't be their best people. Her shoes don't even have laces." Aurelia sighed. "I'm sorry. I let myself get preoccupied and didn't notice."

"That's why it's good to have two of us on a mission like this." Blue kept her gaze on the women even as she pointed at the clothes in the window.

"Oh, great. Rub my nose in it." Aurelia snorted. "Should we move on? We can't stay looking at that ugly coat for much longer."

"Yes. We should use one of this city's narrow lanes to lose them." Blue kept an eye on the women wherever possible in the passing windows. Clearly the woman had tied the nonexistent shoelaces, and they were now walking at the same distance from them as before. "Sooner or later they'll cross the street, and then it'll be more difficult to follow us without attracting too much attention."

"My thoughts exactly. There's a lane over there that I remember from when we walked here earlier, mainly because the shop this side of it had bras the size of parachutes in the window."

"Really?" It was Blue's time to laugh. Sometimes when Aurelia's sense of humor poked through, she was delightfully funny. "Nothing I should get, you mean?"

"Only if you plan to dive off a cliff."

They walked at the same pace until they passed the bra shop. There, they took a step around the corner and began to run as fast as they could. Blue hadn't had the chance to run very much after her attack in the mountains, which meant she had no idea if she was fast. Next to her, Aurelia clearly was. To her relief, Blue's longer legs and generally good form compensated for her recent concussion.

They didn't have time to turn their heads to see if the women had rounded the corner as well. Blue was just going to assume they had. "To the left over there." She pointed.

"Left? That's the wrong direction."

"If they're behind us, we have to throw them off." Blue kept up the pace up but could tell she wouldn't be able to run this fast much longer.

"All right."

When they reached the end of the alley, they threw themselves to the left, and Blue prayed it wouldn't be a dead end. It was. She was about to turn around when Aurelia yanked her arm. Gasping, she pointed at a half-open door. "Back door."

Blue understood and jumped up the three steps, with Aurelia right behind her, and pulled the door closed behind them. "Think it's the bra store?"

"Aurelia!" Blue whispered. She didn't have enough air left in her lungs to laugh.

They stood silently, and Blue half expected some well-endowed woman to appear to chase them out the way they came in.

"What do we do now?" Aurelia tossed her ponytail back over her shoulder. "I can't keep running with the backpack on. It also sets me apart."

Opening a door to their left, Blue peered inside. "A locker room. And where there are lockers, there are—"

"Clothes." Aurelia beamed. She stepped past Blue and examined the lockers. "No keys. Either they're empty or, no, here we go. She started pulling out a coat from the first one and held it up. "I can make that work. And look. A hat. Even better."

Blue followed suit, and after her third attempt, she found a jacket completely unlike the one she was wearing. It had a masculine cut, making her broad shoulders even more so. She transferred the content of her pockets into the new jacket. She didn't see a hat, but in the fourth locker, she found a plaid cap. She pulled it down to cover most of her forehead.

"Yeah. That's awesome. How do I look?" Aurelia asked.

Blue turned and blinked. "Please tell me you didn't find any scissors."

"Scissors?" Aurelia stared at Blue in confusion but then crinkled her nose. "No. I didn't cut off my ponytail. It's under the hat." She pointed at her head. Good enough?"

"You look very different."

"Then we have to find a way to get out through some other door."

"Or window." Blue walked up to the door and opened it a crack. "Still nobody in the corridor. I hear faint voices farther up."

"Okay. Hang on, though. Here you go." Aurelia held out a sidearm to Blue. Extra rounds." She handed Blue two clips.

Now Blue knew that Aurelia trusted her. The enormity of that revelation was so significant, she could barely process it. She was going to have to try to sort out her reaction later, when she had time to think.

Aurelia pocketed several more clips in her own pockets and then pushed the backpack with the rifle and the rest of their equipment into the locker. "Let me just make sure I have what's important." She pulled her wallet from the inner pocket of the coat. "Yup. Got it."

They inched into the corridor and walked heel-to-toe past several closed doors until they reached the other end. The voices grew in intensity, but when Blue opened it a fraction, she saw it was indeed a store, but not the one they'd joked about. This was one of the state-owned grocery stores, where the ones high up in the hierarchy could buy premium food and items for their families. Everyone inside seemed completely focused on getting their prime steaks and fine wines.

"Just walk like you own the place," Aurelia said. "Put your arm around my shoulders."

Blue automatically did as Aurelia said and couldn't help but pull her closer than strictly necessary. She was going to protect Aurelia and get her out of the city where she'd been kept prisoner for so many years, if it killed her.

When everyone's eyes seemed turned away from the door, they stepped through and sauntered through the store. Aurelia even paused at a shelf holding baby food, which made Blue think of little Noah, who had arrived at the Tallawen camp a couple of weeks ago. What she wouldn't give to be able to provide something like this for the little guy. However, soon enough he was going to have a new and better future in Sandslot with his mother, and he and the baby Gill carried would be fed the right things.

They slowly made their way through the store, hoping nobody would think it too odd that they hadn't bought anything.

As they were only steps from the door, Blue's heart sped up. A guard stood to the right of it, or maybe he was some sort of doorman.

"Keep walking," Aurelia whispered and nudged Blue, who realized she had slowed down.

"Did nothing we have to offer suit you today, Madam?" a female voice said from behind them.

Blue gripped Aurelia's shoulders harder as they stopped and turned around. A petite blond woman stood holding a clipboard and a pen. Her nametag said MISS HARROW.

"Ah, Miss Harrow. How nice to see you again," Aurelia said and smiled broadly. "We made all our purchases the other day, thank you. We were so pleased with your charcuterie that we had to come back to order two of your party platters." She leaned closer to Miss Harrow. "We're having some *very* important people for lunch Sunday, and everyone knows your grocery store provides nothing but the best."

"Why, thank you, Mrs. er…I'm sorry. I meet so many people I can't recall your name." Poor Miss Harrow's cheeks turned a bright pink.

"Oh, I completely understand. I'm Sarah Graham, and this is my husband Paul. We've lived in Jeterson for only a few months."

"Then I hope you'll continue to find us your best choice," Miss Harrow said merrily.

"Most definitely," Aurelia said and gave Blue such a loving smile, it made her tremble. "Right, darling?"

"Of course. But now we have to go, Sarah."

"I won't keep you a moment longer," Miss Harrow chirped and hurried on with her clipboard.

The man at the door held it open for them, and they slipped out and onto the street. Not about to let go of Aurelia just yet, Blue turned them back on the same route they'd taken before she spotted the women shadowing them. To her horror, the same women stood at the entrance of the lane where they'd veered off.

"I see them," Aurelia murmured. "Let's just go straight past them. They won't expect that, and we don't look anything like we did just before, remember."

Blue was certain they were caught. She wouldn't hesitate to shoot to allow Aurelia to get away, but the idea of Aurelia being trapped and perhaps not able to get on the bus out of this godforsaken place hurt her. She began walking toward the female agents and kept her focus on them even if she looked down at Aurelia, who now wound her arm around Blue's waist.

The two women didn't offer them a second glance. Blue and Aurelia walked less than a yard away from them, but the women were so busy looking up and down the street and back into the alley, they weren't at all interested in the young couple that strode past them.

When they'd gone enough blocks to feel safe, Blue turned her head and couldn't see the women or anyone else following them. She finally relaxed but kept her arm around Aurelia anyway. Aurelia didn't seem to mind, as her arm remained around Blue's waist the entire distance back to the bus stop.

CHAPTER THIRTEEN

They made no mention of blindfolds on the way back to the camp, nor did Aurelia ask for the gun back. She had taken yet another step forward in placing her trust in this stranger. In fact, when you thought about it, Blue was a stranger even to herself. Yet once Blue knew where the camp was located, she could choose to leave any day, make her way to the closest village, and look up any police station and ask for help to identify herself. She knew her name and date of birth, and that was all it took, really. The idea of Blue leaving was enough to jolt Aurelia back into focusing on driving the off-roader through the last of the forest.

"Need a break?" Aurelia hollered back at Blue, who had her arms wound around her waist, holding on tight.

"That'd be nice. When we get home, I don't think I ever want to sit down again in my life. These saddles look really smart, but after a certain number of hours…"

"Okay. We'll stop just short of the tree line. We need to assess the open fields anyway. You never know when the helicopters will sweep in." They had to be certain that no aircraft was in sight before they sped across the exposed area, even after donning their camouflage.

"I don't suppose starting a small fire is a good idea." Blue sounded wistful as they dismounted the bike after leaving the path and going into the woods about thirty yards.

"You suppose correctly." Aurelia was also cold after having walked back to the camp in the early morning. They'd taken the last bus out of Jeterson and then several different night buses until they reached their original bus stop at dawn. After taking turns nodding off and keeping watch, they were hungry and exhausted when they reached the clearing where they'd left the bike. Now, having ridden for hours through the woods, Aurelia realized her arms were aching from maneuvering roots and boulders.

"At least we still have some food. I was afraid animals might have gotten into the bigger bag." Blue pulled out some sandwiches. "Some more cold tea won't kill me, but I might actually strangle anyone who stands between me and some substitute coffee when we get back."

Aurelia accepted one of the sandwiches and sat down on a boulder, grimacing at the cold, damp surface. "It must've rained when we were away. I'll enjoy a lukewarm shower more than usual, that's for sure."

"Agreed."

Blue ate the sandwich in four big bites, making Aurelia chuckle.

"Pity we couldn't actually buy any of the fancy food in that grocery store. Even the baby food I browsed was better quality than the stuff regular people have access to in Klowdyn."

"The price tags suggested that you're right." Blue regarded her evenly where she sat on another, taller, boulder. "I was impressed at how quickly you read that woman, Miss Harrow, at the store. You knew she'd be tremendously flattered at your praise and impressed by your connections. I was ready to bolt out of there and keep running, but if we had, we'd have run straight into the agents at the corner."

"Instead, they didn't even look at us." Smiling broadly, Aurelia then ate the last of her food. "I hope the people whose clothes we stole didn't mind what we left instead."

"Either way, we made it out of there, and now we have a chance at getting Mr. Maydorian and his family out. Do you have a plan already?"

"Parts of a plan." Aurelia tapped her lips, thinking about all the work she faced when they got back. "After we've had a decent night's sleep, I need the four of us—you, me, Dacia, and Milton—to sit down and work out the details. I have a new route for us to take before we cross the border with the Maydorians. It's one I've contemplated before, but I have to admit, I've saved it for this purpose. Ever since we escaped Jeters, I've known this day would come, when I'd be ready to carry out my promise."

"How did you escape, exactly?" Blue leaned her forearms against her knees and stared at Aurelia intently. Aurelia, in turn, found it easy to share the events that had changed her life a second time.

"We spent the better part of a year digging a tunnel under the wall surrounding the grounds around Jeters."

"Why did it take a year?"

"The wall's three feet thick and goes deep. Maybe because the ground contains a lot of clay, but I don't know. The fact that it does contain so much clay made it hard and heavy to dig, and we only had large spoons and a stolen ladle to work with and not a lot of time. Some nights we snuck out, and two of us would dig while the third kept a lookout. Guards patrolled the outside of the wall, but sometimes they'd do an unscheduled round on the inside. We chose the part of the grounds where the gardeners' compost piles were kept. Ellis Maydorian caught us in the act one day when we weren't paying as much attention as we should, and we thought we were toast. We honestly did. Instead, he just placed his finger against his lips and made a shushing sound—and let us be." Aurelia wiped at a tear that dislodged from her lashes and ran down her cheek. "After that, he saw us several times, and the last month before we made it out of there, we found small shovels waiting for us when we came to dig. That made the last part go a lot faster."

"How did you prepare for the outside?" Blue moved to a boulder right next to Aurelia and took her hand, warming it between hers.

"We were always good students. That gave us at least a few privileges, even if we were nowhere near as well treated as kids at private schools. I mean, kids whose parents actually sent them there. So, we studied everything we could get our hands on about Klowdyn and Klowdynian law, culture, history, and social science. We were allowed to watch some television, so we knew how people dressed."

"What do you mean, how they dressed?" Blue looked confused.

"We were always in school uniforms. If we'd been seen wearing those on the outside, we'd have been caught within hours, at best." Shrugging, Aurelia found she was actually leaning into Blue, hoping for some shared warmth. "We did what you and I did yesterday. We nicked some clothes, one piece at a time so it wouldn't set off any alarm bells, and those were the clothes we escaped in. We'd stocked up on some food, flashlights, batteries, water bottles, that sort of thing, because we knew we were heading for the woods. We'd be sitting ducks in the open."

"You must've been nervous, afraid, even."

Aurelia shook her head slowly. "No. Not really. What we truly feared was being kept in that school indefinitely. We broke into the principal's office and stole our records the night before. It was a gamble. If they'd found out, we'd have been locked up in one of those cells in the basement." Aurelia both saw and felt how Blue flinched.

"Cells? Are you serious? They locked children in cells at that place?"

"Only the students that were kidnapped were subjected to that particular type of punishment. The last two years, the three of us went from being relentless pranksters that were hardly ever caught, to very serious students on a mission."

Blue unbuttoned her long jacket, put her arm around Aurelia's shoulders, and pulled her close, wrapping the jacket around her. "You're shivering."

"Not sure if I'm freezing because of this cold September, or because of the memories of Jeters." Aurelia pressed her face into Blue's neck, marveling how warm the other woman was. "Mm. Better."

"You don't have to talk about it anymore if it upsets you." Blue pressed her lips against Aurelia's temple.

"I don't mind. Dacia claims it's good for the three of us to vent about it."

"Were you ever locked up in the basement?" Blue asked.

"I was. Several times. The first time, I thought they'd keep me there forever, but then again, I was only seven years old at the time." Aurelia shuddered.

"Seven?" Blue hissed the word. "What horrible, barbarian people can do something like that to a child?"

"People taking their orders from the Klowdynian authorities. People who think it's okay to kidnap a four-year-old and keep her from her parents for fourteen years. People like that."

"And why haven't you taken yourself, and your friends, over the border and stayed there?" Blue shook Aurelia gently, and it wasn't hard to detect the frustration in her voice. "Why?"

"I've been across the border many times—and always returned." Aurelia knew they had to keep moving, but she was reluctant to stand up and lose the warmth inside Blue's jacket. "We should get going."

"Shh. Give it another two minutes. All right?" Blue still held on tight to Aurelia. "Just soak up some more warmth. Did your escape go smoothly or…?"

"It did go like clockwork to begin with. Martha Maydorian had made us extra food, and Mr. Maydorian had managed to get his hands on an old used backpack. We were ready, but then the guards came five inches from finding us among the compost piles.

That's when Mr. Maydorian saved us from being discovered. He wasn't supposed to be outside in the middle of the night, but he made up some story about foxes getting in on the grounds by the main gate and asked if the guards hadn't closed it properly. That sent them scurrying."

"And that's when you promised him you'd be back to help him and his wife." Blue murmured the words against Aurelia's temple.

"Yes." Breathless, Aurelia allowed herself a few minutes to calm down. "And now we need to mount the camo nets and get out of here."

"Agreed. And please, will you let me drive? I can tell how stiff you are." Blue stood with Aurelia still wrapped up in her jacket against her.

Aurelia hesitated. "All right," she said slowly. "Just pay attention to the sky. If we spot a helicopter, we have to stop and be very still. They won't be able to see us unless they hover right beside us and get a side view."

"Got it." Blue let go of Aurelia, and they removed any trace that they had ever been in this small clearing before Aurelia donned the large backpack that now weighed a lot less since they had lost their smaller backpack, and their rifles, in Jeterson.

"I hate losing the rifle and extra ammo," Aurelia muttered. "Tom won't say anything, but he's very particular about our inventory list, no matter what items are on there. Or not."

"It was that or fail the mission." Blue ran her bent index finger along Aurelia's cheek. "Okay. Time to get going." She pulled the rods free from where they were attached to the bike, and together, they mounted them and the camouflage net. Blue straddled the off-roader and kickstarted it with ease.

Aurelia carefully stuck her leg between Blue and the back rods and wrapped her arms around Blue's waist. It wasn't as warm as it had been inside Blue's jacket, but she would be more protected against the wind than before. She patted Blue on the shoulder to let her know she was ready, and Blue let the bike roll back to the path.

Relieved that Blue turned out to somehow remember how to drive a bike like this, Aurelia relaxed marginally. Then she turned her head and rested her cheek against Blue's back. The fabric of the jacket was coarse against her skin, but she didn't care. She kept her eye on the sky, looking for helicopters, but also finding herself admiring the crisp blue sky that peeked through the dense, gray clouds. Winter would be upon them in a few months, and that always worried her. People had to stay inside the caves much more, and they had to seal them if the winters got too bad. Teams had to go out to get food for their people, and each run entailed yet another risk of being detected or betrayed.

They raced the bike across the open terrain, and Aurelia found she wasn't quite ready to breathe normally before they were among the hills that quickly turned to mountains. Whenever they reached a fork in the narrow paths, she patted either Blue's right hip or the left. Nearing the area where she needed to alert the camp about their approach, she called out for Blue to stop.

"What? What's wrong?" Blue turned her head around, obviously looking for potential trouble.

"I have to send the clicks. Hang tight." Pulling out her walkie-talkie from a side pocket on the backpack, Aurelia switched it on and clicked five times, waited three beats, and clicked five more. That was her personal signal, and when she received the same back, she pressed her forehead against Blue's back, sighing in relief. "Just follow this path until you see the camp, Blue," she said, raising her voice to be heard over the idling engine. "We'll be home in just a little while."

"Sounds good to me. Hold on." Blue gunned the engine, and the bike took off again. This time, Aurelia felt a smile spread over her face. Yes, they'd soon be among friends and would plan how to keep the promise to Ellis and Martha's family.

CHAPTER FOURTEEN

Entering the camp, Blue smiled as she saw several people, including her pupils, run toward them. They flocked around her and Aurelia, and the warm, seductive feeling of coming home made her smile. After Aurelia stepped off the bike, Blue did the same and let one of the women in charge of the off-roaders lead it away. Blue merely stood there when several pairs of small, slender arms wrapped around her hips, and one set actually hugged her left leg tight. She glanced down at the smiling faces of her students, and the little one hugging her thigh and actually standing on her boot-clad foot had to be a young sibling. The little girl was three years old at the most.

Blue's heart went from being a mere blood pump to a molten mess of too many feelings at once. She crouched and put her arm around the little girl. "Hey, there. You my new student?"

"I'm Molly." The little blond girl looked at her with big green eyes.

"Hello, Molly. I'm Blue."

Molly's eyes grew bigger. "You're not blue. You're blond." She pointed at Blue's hair sticking out from under her cap.

"There you are, child." A woman hurried over and took the girl by the hand. "I'm sorry. This one can't stop talking about going to school, like her siblings. She knows you're the teacher."

Milly and Jade had joined the woman and the girl, and only now did Blue realize that the woman before her had dared to set three children into the world. Either she was incredibly brave or equally careless. Perhaps both. "You have lovely girls," Blue said, and meant it. "Milly and Jade are very bright, and this little one seems to take after them."

"Thank you. I'm Cheryl." The impossibly young-looking mother smiled shyly.

"And I'm Blue."

"Good job, Blue, getting our captain back in one piece and not missing any teeth." Milton came over and slapped Blue on the back. "However, she says that after rattling around on the bike that the roots in the southern woods are worse than ever and made her teeth nearly break."

Nodding good-bye to Cheryl, Blue accompanied Milton over to Aurelia, where she stood between Tom and Dacia. "In my case I was afraid my kidney would come out."

Snorting, Milton nudged Blue with his elbow. "I hear you. We need to find more new paths, or the authorities can just follow our tracks by looking for all the body parts strewn along our usual ones."

"What morbid stuff are you going on about now?" Dacia groaned but accepted Milton's arm around her shoulder. "Body parts?"

"Never mind. Dinner's almost ready. If I tell you, you won't be able to eat."

"I believe you." Dacia returned her attention to Aurelia. "So, did you make contact?"

"Yes." Aurelia drew a trembling breath. "We're on. First thing tomorrow morning, we'll review the plan and make some alterations. I'll need you two and Blue with me to brainstorm. You too, Tom, as you're the camp leader here."

"All right." Tom looked intrigued. "I know you've always had a special mission in mind and that the three of you were just biding your time." He looked over at Blue. "And with your obvious tactical prowess, we should be able to hatch a good plan."

Aurelia beamed, but Blue could tell she was exhausted. "Aurelia and I need some proper food, some decent coffee, and a good night's sleep."

"But we want to hear everything!" Dacia said.

"And you will," Aurelia said. "Let's go grab some food and sit outside under the nets. I can tell from here that someone's fired up a few of the gas heaters under there. I can see myself cozying up to one of them."

Blue used the latrine and washed her hands twice, enjoying the feeling of having them clean. A shower after dinner was next on her agenda. The five of them were joined by Mac, who looked every bit as weary as Aurelia did.

"You all right, Mac?" Blue asked as they sat in a circle, balancing the bowls of rabbit stew on their laps.

"I spent all afternoon cleaning wounds on one of the new recruits who had an accident with one of the off-roaders. He'll be fine, but he scraped his arms and legs pretty bad. Gravel's hard to get out." Mac rolled her shoulders, and Blue imagined that their medic had been hunched over, picking small rocks and gravel from the boy's wounds.

Blue and Aurelia took turns relaying the details of their mission. When Aurelia described their meeting with Ellis Maydorian, both Milton and Dacia became teary-eyed.

"I can't believe they have a daughter. And grandchildren." Dacia's chin trembled. "We have to figure out a way to time it properly so we can get them all out at the same time."

"That's the plan." Aurelia yawned. "Or it will be."

"Time for showers and bed," Blue said quietly. She saw Dacia and Milton exchange looks, as it did sound as if she was trying to tell Aurelia what to do.

"I know. I'm fading fast." Aurelia stood, and it was obvious to Blue how rigid she was. As she rose as well, she realized she wasn't much better.

"Let me get that for you." Blue took Aurelia's bowl and walked over to where everyone was responsible for cleaning their own utensils, plates, and mugs. She quickly took care of her own things and Aurelia's and then returned. "Let's go."

❖

Aurelia gave a little wave to her friends and then walked next to Blue as they went into the cave system. They made a quick stop at their alcove for clean clothes, and it was cute to see Blue's surprise when she found her footlocker outfitted with the basics in her size. The tall, powerful woman who had been with Aurelia every step of the way during their mission cleared her throat twice before she managed to say, "Well, would you look at that. Thank you."

"That's Dacia for you."

"Dacia?" Looking surprised but pleased, Blue took her soap and toothbrush from the inside lid of the locker. "I'll remember to thank her."

In the shower, the water was cool rather than lukewarm, but that didn't matter. Aurelia was grateful to clean the dust off her skin and hair and feel like herself again. She donned soft, well-worn sweats and thick socks, then brushed her hair and clipped it back, used to the fact that it normally took hours upon hours to dry. When she stepped out of her stall, Blue was already done and waiting for her.

"The water woke you up again," she said and smiled. "Somewhat."

"Yeah. It wasn't freezing, but close enough." Feeling jittery, Aurelia wasn't sure her reaction was just because of the cool water. Back in the alcove, Aurelia was shivering so hard, she could barely unzip her sleeping bag.

"You're too cold. Can we get a heater in here for you?" Blue frowned. "You'll catch your death if you—"

"I'll be fine, Blue. I just need to get into the fucking sleeping bag." Hearing how harsh she sounded, Aurelia stopped. "I'm sorry. I didn't mean to snap."

"I know." Her voice soft, Blue came over and unzipped her bag. "Get in. If you want, we can hook up to my bag and share the warmth like we did in the woods. Unless you feel awkward about it, I mean, being back here." She stood and shoved her hands into her pockets.

Aurelia's heart fluttered and her cheeks warmed. "Keep saying things like that, and I'll be warm all on my own," she said and chuckled. "Yes. Let's do the hook-up. I'm too cold to worry about what anyone else thinks. Honestly, I never concern myself about anyone's opinion anyway."

"Somehow that has occurred to me." Blue pushed their cots together. "This won't work. My cot has hard edges. One of us will end up on the edge if we connect the sleeping bags."

"Hm. Can we manage on my cot? It's wider than yours." Aurelia stepped closer to Blue. "Or just scrap the whole idea."

"No scrapping. Here's what we'll do. We take your cot. Go lie down before you fall over. We'll unzip both sleeping bags and use them as a double duvet." Blue quickly opened both sleeping bags fully. "Like so."

Aurelia climbed into her cot and turned, facing the cave wall. Someone had clicked off the light from the dormitory side, and she could barely make out her own hand as she held it up before her face. "You coming?"

"I am. Was just fetching my pillow when it got pitch-black." The cot shifted some when Blue lay down. She arranged the sleeping bags over them and then wrapped her arm around Aurelia from behind. "Lift your head."

Aurelia raised her head off her pillow and felt Blue shove her free arm under both her and the pillow. She settled down again, and now Blue pulled Aurelia back against her. "Warmer?"

"Yes. Hm. Getting there." Aurelia took Blue's hand and intertwined it with hers. She pushed it in under her shirt and thought of the time in the tent when they were in a very similar position. Squirming, she felt her system slowly igniting, and her breathing labored.

"Aurelia?" Blue shook her a little. "I didn't realize your hair's still damp. Let's move up and off the bed as much as possible."

"Oh, okay." Aurelia moved her hands to accommodate Blue but was too slow. Blue moved her hair with such a gentle hand and then returned it under the covers and back to where it was before.

"Just relax," Blue murmured, and her breath caressed Aurelia's now-bare neck. All the small hairs stood at attention, and Aurelia couldn't help but moan softly.

"You're trying to warm me up in all sorts of ways." Aurelia tried to sound as if she took offense, which wasn't true at all, and failed gloriously.

"And how am I doing?"

"Getting warmer."

Chuckling deep in her chest, Blue pressed her lips against Aurelia's neck. "And now?"

"Do you expect me to be able to think, let alone speak, when you do that?" Aurelia whispered, afraid someone would overhear them.

"You're a smart, capable woman. I'm sure you can do it." Blue's low voice reverberated against Aurelia's skin. "You're an amazing person. I knew that from the moment you hovered over me in the infirmary."

"Ahem. Thank you." Aurelia groaned inwardly. Thank you? What a pitiful phrase to use right now.

"You're welcome." Blue nuzzled the back of Aurelia's neck, and her hand moved upward after caressing her stomach. "May I?" Blue asked as she reached the area just below Aurelia's right breast.

"Yes." Aurelia whimpered quietly. "Yes."

Blue reached farther up and cupped the small mound. Aurelia's nipple met the touch by pebbling, which made it so sensitive, she was about to beg for Blue to engulf it with her mouth.

"You feel so good," Blue murmured. "I should be ashamed of myself for doing this now, when you're cold and tired, but I'm completely past that point. The only thing that can stop me now is one word from you."

"Let me turn around." Aurelia shifted awkwardly, and the soft laughter from Blue defused the tension but did nothing to slow her heartbeat. Aurelia found she had even less space now that they weren't spooning, but she wanted to pretend she could see Blue's features, even if it was too dark. Truth be told, she wanted to kiss Blue properly—so she did.

Blue gasped and pulled Aurelia tight with her strong arms. She slid one hand in under the waistband of Aurelia's sweatpants and cupped her ass. Aurelia couldn't wait. She parted her lips, inviting Blue in. Tongues met, swirled, caressed, as they explored each other's mouths. Blue's short, wavy hair was soft to the touch and already dry. Aurelia pushed the fingers of her left hand into it and tugged gently.

"Mm?" Blue tried to prolong the kiss.

"I want you so much." Aurelia was well beyond any awkwardness or doubt at this point. "You have no idea."

"I think I do." Rolling Aurelia onto her back, Blue moved half on top of her. She pushed Aurelia's shirt up, baring her in the cool cave where people slept on the other side of the curtain. Not even that part fazed Aurelia. When Blue closed her lips around one of her nipples, she could have howled, but instead she merely drew a deep breath between clenched teeth. Whatever Blue did with her tongue felt beyond good. Not wanting to be selfish, and, yes, who was she kidding, fueled by a desire to reciprocate, Aurelia slipped a hand down the front of Blue's too-big pants. She found undergarments but merely wiggled her fingers in under them. "This okay?"

"Oh, God. Yes." Blue whispered the words hotly in her ear. "I had no idea…"

"About what?" Aurelia cupped the damp curls between Blue's legs, and Blue in turn raised one leg and hooked it over Aurelia's hip.

"About how much you want me…I know I've wanted you for some time now." Blue pressed her lips to Aurelia's before she could answer and kissed her so long and deep, they were both gasping for air when she finally let go.

"Oh, I want you all right," Aurelia murmured. She found it easy to part Blue's folds with her fingers, the hard clitoris ready to be touched. Aurelia pressed her thumb gently against it and searched lower with her other fingers.

"Go…inside…" Blue was shaking now, but her free hand was working its way under Aurelia's baggy sweatpants. Glad she hadn't put on any briefs, Aurelia spread her legs as wide as the narrow cot would allow. Blue didn't hesitate. She mimicked Aurelia's caress, and it felt so good, so hot, and so damn right, Aurelia had to press her mouth against Blue's neck to remain quiet. Then she remembered Blue's plea and found her entrance, circling it with two fingers while her thumb did the same with Blue's clit. She slowly pressed two fingers inside and found Blue so wet that her index and middle fingers slipped into place without effort.

"Oh…" Aurelia couldn't believe how hard Blue squeezed her fingers. She curled them, wishing she was a bit more experienced, but it had been such a long time. Deciding she would simply try what she liked herself, she began massaging the rough patch of tissue firmly.

Shivers ran through Blue, Aurelia could feel them, and she tried pressing harder with her fingertips.

Blue groaned quietly and then entered Aurelia with her fingers. "Damn…you're so hot." She kissed Aurelia again. "And I can't get enough of you."

"I don't want you to, either. I want you to want this—and me—again. Soon." She started moving her fingers in and out, slow and deep, making sure she never lost touch with Blue's clit or the patch inside her that gave her so much pleasure.

Blue let her fingers flank Aurelia's clit, then move into her, all the way, and out to coat the clit with all the moisture pooling between Aurelia's legs. Her breathing became labored, and she picked up speed. Aurelia guessed Blue was getting close to orgasm, and she wouldn't be far behind.

"It's like fire." Blue whispered huskily in Aurelia's ear. "Everything about you is like fire."

"And it's all because of you." Aurelia spoke the words before she had time to edit herself.

"Oh, Aurelia. You're the one. The only one." Blue kissed her, more for emphasis, it felt, than for anything else. "I'm going to come."

The ridiculous politeness in Blue's voice nearly made Aurelia giggle, but she was also going headfirst as she careened toward her own bliss and instantly lost interest in giggling. Then Blue's inner muscles began squeezing Aurelia's fingers rhythmically, while Blue arched against her. "Ohh…"

"Shh." Aurelia kissed Blue and captured the moan that was building inside her. This was fortunate, because when Aurelia's orgasm hit, she nearly screamed. Blue had probably guessed she might and kissed her through it.

The release was almost painful, but oh, such sweet agony. Aurelia still had her fingers buried within Blue, and when her orgasm hit its peak, she gripped her harder, which sent more tremors through Blue.

Descent was bliss but also sorrow. Aurelia pulled her hand free and instantly wanted to push it back, to continue what they'd just discovered, but sleep was her enemy. Her mind was growing foggy, and she barely registered how Blue managed to slip in behind her again. All Aurelia knew was that she felt safer and happier than she ever had. "You're amazing," she managed to whisper while she was still semi-awake. "I adore you."

Blue snuggled closer and, with some effort, resumed their original position. "Sleep, Aurelia. We'll have time to talk tomorrow. And yes, I adore you too."

Smiling to herself, Aurelia reached back and patted Blue's hip. "You sleep too."

"Oh, I will." Blue held her close, and the double sleeping bags kept them warm.

Aurelia allowed herself to be selfish and not toss and turn while planning missions, like she did on most nights. This night, while held by the woman she had come to rely on and, yes, love, she slept.

Blue woke up, startled and on edge, in the middle of the night. Her heart was pounding, and she was completely disoriented. A woman slept in her arms, and it took her ten good seconds before she remembered. Yes. Aurelia. The cave. The Tallawens. A mission to Jeterson. The even bigger mission coming up. So much to do.

Images began to flicker through Blue's mind. Her, as a child in a library, no, a study, being small enough to barely be able to look over the edge of the large desk. A gray-haired man she was afraid of. Snap! Father. Yes. Her father. In uniform. Snap! Over to a boarding school. A lot like Jeters, but also entirely different, she surmised. Strict rules and uniforms. Pre-military? So, not like Jeters after all. Snap! There, a horse. She, on its back, a polo club raised as she charged among her teammates and the opposing team. Snap! Her in uniform, a BHU uniform. Promotion after promotion. Snap! Bringing in terrorists, deserters, and...ordinary people trying to leave Klowdyn illegally. Snap! Pitching her new plan to a group of generals. Infiltrating the Tallawens to learn more about their enigmatic leader, a woman known only as Aurelia. Snap! Ordering her closest men to make the assault look convincing.

Blue pressed her face into the black masses of hair that belonged to the woman she was meant to learn about and ultimately bring to justice. This woman, who held her heart in her courageous hands. Blue's memories kept flooding back, but she knew only that she was duty bound to betray everyone in this camp in order to carry out the mission she had given herself. Yet how could she? Other images, of newer memories, warred with the old. The children in her makeshift classroom. The little girl dreaming of having ice cream. Of being allowed to be outside with her sibling. The angry girl who finally began to let others in. Then there were the faces of their parents, frightened and hopeful in a strange concoction.

And there were Dacia, Milton, Tom, Mac…and Aurelia. People who nursed her back to health, who began to trust her, just like Blue hoped they might when she had planned the mission, but now she felt nothing but gratitude and loyalty to them once she'd learned about the Tallawen. These people weren't terrorists or human traffickers. They were heroes, every single one of them.

Hiding tears of panic against Aurelia, Blue struggled with her old self, the career soldier who led the Bounty Hunter Unit with such finesse that even her father was reluctantly impressed. Her new self, the person who had learned about the Tallawen without any prejudice against them, had been watching them work from a pure angle that now made her able to see the truth.

And still, it was her duty to betray every single one of them—including the woman she loved.

CHAPTER FIFTEEN

The morning meeting in Tom's "office" was surreal on so many levels, Blue could barely think, let alone help plot the rescue of the Maydorian family. She sat next to Aurelia, who had gotten up before Blue awoke. Blue had fallen asleep very late, and after she finally got a few hours' rest, it had been almost morning. Clutching her mug of real coffee, normally such a treat, she tried to keep calm and not yell at the other four to stop talking.

Dacia, Milton, and Tom sat on one side of the rustic table, while Blue and Aurelia sat on the other. Aurelia had her hand on Blue's knee, and the touch scorched her as if she were drenched in kerosene and Aurelia's hand was an open flame. She wanted to withdraw, to tell Aurelia to let go, but of course she didn't. She sat there, listened, took mental notes. Dutybound to deliver all intel to her commanding officers, Blue found she knew more than enough to take this entire branch of the Tallawens out. She could surrender names of operatives and fugitives, of illegal children—Blue's stomach clenched so fast, she dropped her mug. It clattered to the floor, and the coveted coffee splashed over the others' feet.

"Blue?" Aurelia snapped her head around and stared at Blue with huge eyes. "Are you all right?"

"I'm fine. Just…perhaps a bit tired." It was all Blue could do not to allow tears to fall at the thought of the children she'd taught, children who dreamed of freedom and ice cream, of being allowed to go outside without fear of being detected, punished, and taken from their families, like Aurelia had been.

"Why were you at Jeters?" Blue heard herself ask, looking at Milton and Dacia.

Dacia's eyes grew wide, and she cast a questioning glance at Aurelia.

"Why do you want to know?" Milton asked kindly. "I mean, does it matter?"

"I suppose not, but I know some of Aurelia's past, and…" She thought fast. "Since I work with the kids, I thought it might help me to know what such schools are up to. But if it's too painful…"

"Ah. That's all right." Dacia leaned forward, placing her elbows against the table and her chin in her hands. "I'm number three out of four children in my family. You can imagine what happened. My parents were incarcerated when I was four, and my older siblings were sent to different schools. I went to Jeters, and there I met this one." Dacia pointed at Aurelia. "She was the same age, and while I was a scared little rabbit, she was a mini tiger. She didn't give those fuckers an inch. The following year, Milton showed up, two years older than us, and we followed him like puppies. He was very flattered." She batted her eyelids at Milton, who demonstratively rolled his eyes.

"I was a wreck. You took care of *me*." Milton shrugged. "I have no siblings. My parents were also sent to prison, but for espionage. You could say that they did the same thing as Aurelia's parents, but from inside Klowdyn. They held illegal meetings, organized protests, and were quite famous. Or infamous, perhaps."

Blue could barely take in their situations. She'd gone to the best schools, brought up by a man who enjoyed a high position within the military and later also politically. She knew what she knew—what she'd learned about the outside world's unfair treatment of Klowdyn, of the sanctions that were meant to blackmail the Klowdynian government into submission but only induced more fighting spirit among the population. Those who opposed the regime were traitors who had allowed foreign ideas and values to erase their patriotism. Blue had dedicated her life to serving her country, doing what was right, and yet, here were people she'd come to know, to trust, that also believed they fought the good fight.

"How do you know all this, if you were four and six at the time?" Blue asked, realizing she sounded harsh.

If Dacia noticed Blue's tone, she didn't let on. "We stole our files before we fled Jeters. I still have mine. One day, when Klowdyn is a free country and President Bowler has stepped down, I will find my parents and my siblings." Large tears flooded Dacia's eyes. "Every time we get to help new dissidents or refugees, I have this hope…this *dream*, that one of them will be my sister or brother, that they've made it and are heading for a new life in Sandslot. So far, it hasn't happened, but it can. Right, Milton?" She looked up at the gangly man beside her.

"Sure, it can," he answered instantly. "One of these days, you'll see someone familiar, and it'll be one of them." He pulled her into his chest with one arm, while sending Blue a clear warning with his steely gray eyes. *Don't contradict me.*

"And you, Milton?" Blue spoke quietly. "What do you dream of?"

Milton was obviously not prepared for that question but didn't seem to have to think for very long. "I want to do what I do—help innocent people who are at the mercy of an unjust government that uses oppression to govern. This is what I want, and these are the people I want to do it with." He gazed around him. "That includes you, unless you've had second thoughts."

Aurelia gasped. "Why would you say that?" She stood, and Blue put a hand against the small of Aurelia's back to calm her.

"Because of the sudden third degree," Milton answered calmly. "Something's up."

Aurelia turned and studied Blue. "You're very pale. Are you not feeling well?"

"I didn't sleep well. I apologize for coming on too strong." Blue wasn't lying. She was sorry for upsetting Dacia and challenging Milton. "I worry sometimes that I'll accidentally do something to put any of you in jeopardy, simply because I haven't informed myself enough. And now..." She took Aurelia's hand and tugged at her to sit down again. "Now, especially, I'm just..." Blue sighed. "I can be an idiot at times."

This statement brought an unexpected smile to Milton's handsome face. "Can't we all? I wish I had a penny for every time these two, including you, Tom, have called me even worse things."

"So true." Dacia straightened and kissed his bearded chin. "But we love you anyway."

Milton's eyes took on a completely different gray hue as he hugged Dacia.

"Not that anyone's asked me about my past," Tom said lightly, "but I'm a former teacher from the suburbs of Fardicia. I was pretty clueless for quite some time, but when I started working at one of the capital's boarding schools, I soon picked up on the system that these three have described."

So, she wasn't the only one who had lived in both worlds, clueless or not. Blue willed herself to relax. No matter the outcome of this mission, she had to find some time to think how she should proceed. She couldn't go against direct orders; that was just not possible. Pressing a hand against her aching stomach, she knew she could never let any of the refugees still in the camp, or the Maydorians that she and Aurelia already had risked their lives for, be captured. The mere idea that Aurelia, the woman she had made love with last night...wait...last night. Was the passionate lovemaking what had triggered her memory to return? Realizing the futility in trying to guess, Blue tried to focus on what the other four were saying.

"We need a double mission to take place simultaneously," Aurelia said. Clearly, they were back into the planning stage.

Blue gave herself a mental shrug, using every part of her military training to push the errant thoughts to the back of her head. She needed to pay attention. "I agree," she said calmly. "One team to take care of the older Maydorians, and a smaller team, perhaps just one person, to extract their daughter and her children."

"We could use the network to get Lorna and the kids to a smaller town, but not too small. We don't want to attract a lot of attention." Aurelia pointed at the map they had tacked to the table. "What about Cerdynia? Its population is about fifty thousand, isn't it?"

"Thereabout." Milton nodded. "We've all been there a few times though. We need to use a fresh face—" He blinked and then turned to Blue. "Like you."

Blue hadn't seen that coming, but now Milton was jotting down notes on a pad. "We should have a team of four, with two backups, when it comes to Ellis and Martha. They're older, and not very fast, and I would imagine they're frailer than when we knew them. You two met Ellis. Would you agree?"

"Yes," Aurelia said. "So, who do we send with Blue to fetch Lorna in Cerdynia?"

"Nobody. I'll go alone. I'll prepare here, and you'll show me the alternative routes."

"But how will you get them here?" Dacia began chewing the back of a very short pencil.

"She doesn't," Milton said and snapped his fingers. "Blue takes them to a rendezvous place where we'll be waiting with off-roaders and carts. She just needs the correct password for our contact in the urban part of the underground."

No, oh, God, no. They had to stop giving her information she would end up using against them. Blue wanted to bolt so badly, but she remained next to Aurelia as she and the other three drew up the plans that would bring all the Maydorians to the Tallawen satellite camp. She was going to do this last thing for them, to help Aurelia fulfill her promise to Ellis and Martha, and then she would have to return to Fardicia and report to her superiors.

As soon as they had chiseled out the last bit of their plan, with two contingency plans for both extractions, Blue got up and walked outside. Because of a thick fog, no sun cast its pattern through the camouflage nets, but the air was just what she needed, crisp and cool. She greedily inhaled it, and just as she exhaled for the second time, she felt slender arms around her waist. "Blue?"

"I'm a bit out of it," Blue tried to explain. "But I'll be sharp and ready to go in four days. As for the car, we need to make sure the one we steal is a common one. Nothing fancy." She thought of her father's foreign-brand car that had felt like bragging as soon as she rode in it.

"All those details are on paper, remember?" Aurelia hugged Blue. "Why don't we go round up your students? I'd like to meet them, and they've missed you, so I'm told."

"W-what?" The unexpected words from Aurelia nearly made Blue back up, but instead she held Aurelia closer. "The kids?"

"Yes. Come on." She dragged Blue with her toward the cave entrance. "I like to see you in action," she said and giggled that typical Aurelia-giggle that was so damn contagious.

"All right," Blue said, knowing she'd regret losing her clear sight of her goal, which she would by seeing the kids that had stolen a piece of her treacherous heart. Every time she was faced with the truth that was evident here in the Tallawen camp, her mission faded into something not only distant, but also something so *wrong.* Blue's head ached. She wished she could tell Aurelia that her memory was back, but the idea of watching the love, affection, and passion die in Aurelia's eyes when she learned the truth about Blue ignited a fear that was like an excruciating physical pain, and Blue began to breathe faster again. Reeling herself in, using every technique she'd come across as a soldier and BHU leader, Blue knew she had to do what felt right.

CHAPTER SIXTEEN

The children stood next to Blue and regarded Aurelia with a guarded expression. Their roles were reversed. Whereas Aurelia was the leader of the Tallawens and Blue still very much the outsider, here in the classroom, Aurelia was the outsider and Blue the familiar face. Aurelia could tell the kids were in awe of her. She was aware that her reputation as the Tallawen leader preceded her and that some idolized her. Aurelia always claimed that people found the idea of the Tallawen leader, not necessarily the person, awe inspiring, but when Dacia and Milton heard her explain that theory to most people, they just went "pft" and shook their heads. Dacia would even go so far as to say, "We know who gets second billing here, and it's not you, Aurelia."

Now, looking at the children, Aurelia knew they'd listened to their parents and how much their hopes and dreams for the future rested on her. Not for the first time, the pressure built inside her. Not just for these kids, or the Maydorians, but for all the souls that passed through any of her camps. She had started this movement. And no, she wasn't the first to help smuggle refugees to Sandslot, but she was the first who did on this scale and for free. Whereas some ruthless people would charge the refugees and dissidents a fortune, and still abandon them sometimes,

Aurelia and her Tallawen survived because of secret benefactors in both Klowdyn and Sandslot.

"You're so pretty," the youngest girl, Jade, said.

"Thank you. That's sweet of you to say." Aurelia could tell they were intrigued by her visit but seemed to love having Blue back. "Blue and I just returned from a mission, and I don't know how much time we'll have for more lessons. I do have special assignments for you, if you want to help us with the next phase of our operations."

The children straightened, and Blue looked at her quizzically.

"What can we do to help?" asked Paula, the stone-faced young girl who stood behind the only boy in the room with her hands on his shoulders.

"Once we start our journey toward Sandslot, we're going to need to make the carts extra comfortable, as we have several very young children going this time. You could help by gathering tall grass, heather, anything to help make the carts softer."

"They weren't very comfy when we rode them here," the boy, Ryan, said. "Better be careful with the babies."

"Right?" Aurelia smiled. "I think Paula, being the oldest, will be in charge of this part of our mission. Paula, you report directly to Blue, and if she isn't available, go find Tom. You know who that is?"

"Of course." The twelve-year-old girl nodded curtly.

Aurelia and Blue sat among the children and talked with them, and that was when Aurelia noticed something different about the woman who was now her lover. It didn't surprise Aurelia that she gave every child her total attention, as that was her way, but in this instant, it was as if Blue absorbed every syllable the children uttered, no matter how silly or unimportant it was. When the youngest girl, Jade, leaned against Blue, looking adoringly up at her, Aurelia saw how Blue had to swallow several times. She obviously cared deeply for these children.

Once the kids got ready to go gather grass and heather, Aurelia and Blue walked over to the camouflage nets that covered the sheds where they kept the bikes. A young woman, Iris, and two men were in charge of the maintenance, and Aurelia knew their runs kept these three very busy.

"Hey," Iris said and grinned at them. She had several smudges on her face, and her white-blond hair was haphazardly tucked in under her cap. "Were you trying to kill my best bike while you were gone?" She tried for a scowl, but Aurelia could see the sparkles in her eyes.

"Not us. Blame it on that damn forest. I swear the root system is out to get us. Or at least my kidneys," Aurelia said, expecting Blue to chime in and say something similar, but she merely greeted Iris and the man with a polite nod.

"Ha. And of course, you didn't slow down much to help the suspension survive?" Wagging her finger, Iris then let out a raucous laugh. "And before you try to weasel your way out of it, Aurelia, I know you have only one setting on your bike—full speed ahead."

"Is there any other way?" Aurelia tried her best innocent expression. "Now, in all seriousness, Tom and I need your report regarding the condition of the entire inventory of bikes and carts as soon as you can manage it."

"I hear you. Don't worry. You'll have it this afternoon." Iris saluted. "*Ma capitaine.*"

"Thank you." Aurelia exchanged a few words with the two men working with Iris and then started walking back toward the room where they'd left Tom, Dacia, and Milton. She hesitated for a moment, suddenly feeling self-conscious. "Blue? Are you all right? Or should I ask, are *we* all right?" She tucked her hands behind her back while she walked, or she might make a fool of herself and take Blue's hand when perhaps that was the last thing Blue wanted.

"Yes." Blue answered quickly. "Yes. Of course we are."

"You didn't say a word in there. You didn't say a lot to the kids either, come to think of it, although they seemed quite content with you just being there." Aurelia stopped and caught Blue's eyes. "Do you regret last night?"

That sparked more life in Blue. "No! Not at all. Never." She ran her fingers through her hair. "I just have a lot on my mind."

"New memories?" Aurelia flinched.

"Not per se. Scattered images." Blue averted her eyes. "And I'm preoccupied with how we'll coordinate the rescue of the Maydorians."

"Me too." Aurelia took a step closer. "But I know that, together, we'll figure it out. We have to." Cautiously, as they were in the middle of the camp, she extended her hand.

Blue regarded it as though uncertain what to do, but then her shoulders seemed to lose their tension, and she took Aurelia's hand and raised it to her lips. "We'll figure it out," she said, echoing Aurelia's words.

Relieved, Aurelia tugged Blue closer, and they continued hand in hand.

As long as they were studying maps, identifying weaknesses when it came to their plans, and estimating risks, Blue was all right. But when they had a lull in their intense discussions, her conscience created problems. She lost focus and could hear her father's voice as he berated her for not being the son he'd expected. Not even when she graduated summa cum laude from the military academy did he entirely acknowledge her achievement. No wonder she was eager to swallow everything he stood for, which was the same as what Klowdyn's government preached, as she had always been desperate to win his love. But now, having lived another life for weeks, without any interference from a man who had never fully accepted her, Blue knew her inner axis had shifted.

"What do you think? Blue?" Dacia bumped her fist against Blue's shoulder.

"Um. Sorry. I lost track for a moment." Blue's cheeks warmed. "You were saying?"

"Never mind that. You're clearly exhausted." Dacia looked accusingly at the others. "Are you aware of the time? We've missed dinner."

"No, you haven't." Mac's voice interrupted them as she poked her head in, carrying a tray. "Here. Some stew, courtesy of our best hunters. And one glass of beer each, just because I'm such a pushover." Tom yanked his maps aside, and she put down the tray. "There you go."

Tom got up from his chair and offered it to her. "Join us, Mac, please."

"Thank you, I already ate, but I'll have a beer, if you insist."

"We do." Aurelia grinned. "And we're almost done. We just have to go over everything once more, and then we'll put our plan in motion tomorrow. We'll have the Maydorians here in four days, unless we hit a snag." She raised her gaze to the others. "And there will be no snag."

"Of course not." Milton lifted his mug after filling it from the pitcher holding the beer. "Here's to a snag-less mission."

"Snag-less," Dacia, Tom, and Mac echoed, and even if Blue didn't say anything, she raised her mug as well. She wasn't hungry but ate some of the stew anyway. She'd need every ounce of her strength when she carried out her part of the mission, and that meant she couldn't skip any meals, no matter what.

"I've finished my exams of our remaining refugees. They're all in reasonably good health, and the children that have been in hiding are already showing signs of improvement. The fresh air, being allowed to play and attend the makeshift school, combined with a more protein-rich diet—it all helps."

"All those rabbit stews have a plus side to them," Milton said, and peered into his bowl. "Though I admit that can get a little old. I don't mean the rabbit in person—what?"

"The way you explain things," Dacia said, snorting. "We all have the same constant rabbit diet. We know what you mean, cutie."

Milton shrugged. "Well then, I can't be the only one who's ready to try something else."

"I remember having a hamburger once when I was really little," Aurelia said and sighed. "With long potato sticks. French fries."

"Potatoes. Remember when we used to be sick and tired of potatoes. Now they're a rare treat." Dacia placed her chin in her hand. "What about you, Blue? What do you long for?"

Clarity of mind. Blue nearly spoke the words out loud. "I love fish." She caught herself, but it was too late.

"Fish?" Aurelia gaped. "When did you remember them?"

"No idea," Blue said with a calm that was entirely false. "The answer just popped up right as Dacia asked me."

"Amazing." Dacia beamed. "Mr. Maydorian used to go fishing in a local river sometimes, and he'd catch salmon and cook it for the principal and his family. On very rare occasions, Mrs. Maydorian would save us a tiny little cube. You're right, Blue. It was very good."

Blue saw the big pieces of fish her father's housekeeper had cooked for them, with potatoes, bechamel sauce, and peas. She could also envision how far the distance between her father and her at the dinner table in the dark old house. No wonder she would focus more on how the food tasted than on her father's disdain.

"All right. Let's go over it one last time," Tom said after they'd finished their rabbit stew. "Good that you're here, Mac. It's important for you to be in the loop when it comes to the older couple."

"No problem." Mac leaned against the cave wall. "Fill me in."

As Tom reviewed the plan again, Blue felt Aurelia's hand on her knee under the table, and it was as if that touch, paired with the memories of how her father had manipulated her thirst for love and acceptance throughout her life, made her thought process crystal clear. She now realized what she must do and why. She understood her duty and how to carry it out, no matter what. For the first time since her memory had returned, Blue could relax.

CHAPTER SEVENTEEN

Blue stepped out of the small car and scanned the street. As did so many other neighborhoods in Cerdynia, it held mainly two- and three-story stone buildings lined up on both sides, some containing shops with apartments above them, and others purely residential. The café she was looking for was located two buildings down, and she casually made her way over there, stealthily scanning the people she passed and who walked on the other side of the street.

A bell chimed as she pushed the door open, but nobody paid her any obvious attention at first glance. This was how things were in Klowdyn. Outwardly you minded your own business and went about your day as if everything was all right. When Blue stealthily gazed around the café, she could tell that nobody was unaware of her arrival.

Eight wooden tables with candles in the center next to some salt and pepper shakers provided seating for the patrons. The scent of coffee, pastries, and pies filled the air, and if Blue had been hungry and not here on a mission, she would have enjoyed browsing the menu written in chalk on the black wall behind the presently unmanned counter. It always amazed her how people in Klowdyn could vary the limited range of groceries and produce available to ordinary people.

As she waited for the café owner to return, she rested her hip against the counter, feigning boredom. It wasn't hard to spot the two government agents. Tucked away into the far-right corner, they sat dressed in flat caps, plaid flannel shirts, and jeans. This attire told Blue they were new at their jobs, as they had chosen clothes right out of the agent handbook. When training her own agents, she had always advised against this choice. Blue could tell from the rigidity in the locals' shoulders that they knew who the strangers were. Granted, because the agents were green, it wouldn't be hard to lose them if need be. Still, she knew better than to get too cocky. For all she knew, more seasoned agents could be lurking in the streets or back alleys. Either way, the Tallawen wouldn't be thrilled to hear that this place couldn't be used for quite a while.

"What can I get you, love?" A middle-aged woman with graying red hair came out from a curtain-covered door opening to her, wiping her hands on her apron before pointing to a free table.

"Black coffee and a piece of apple pie, please," Blue said, as arranged.

"The apple pie comes with complimentary custard," the woman said, her eyes narrowing slightly.

Blue nodded. "Now that's what I call perfection." By this statement, she confirmed she was the contact the woman had been expecting.

The woman smoothed down the apron, poured coffee into a mug, and placed the pie and custard in a bowl. After returning with the coffee and pie, she gave Blue the bill. "Here you go, love."

Casting a quick glance at the small piece of paper, Blue handed over some cash. "Keep the change."

The woman took the money and left. Blue began to eat, and the pie was good, even if the complimentary custard clearly was made from some sort of powder. The coffee was that chicory stuff she loathed, but it would give her energy, nonetheless.

An unbidden thought fleeted through her mind of how she'd grown up in a house that the people residing in the homes in this neighborhood would consider a mansion, with real coffee and, yes, among other things, real, made-from-scratch custard. Kairn AnRaine, her father, wasn't wealthy, but he'd enjoyed perks that came with his high position within the military. He also held a prominent political position, always loyal to President Bowler, who had run Klowdyn for the last thirty years. Growing up with a father who had never let her forget that not only was she not the boy he'd expected, but that she'd killed her mother, had been so hard. For years, Blue had assumed blame for both those things, not understanding the unfairness of her father's accusations. The housekeeper, whose orders were to make sure Blue ate well, studied hard, and obeyed Kairn's every order, and who was the only mother figure in Blue's life, had eventually taken pity on her. She had explained to the then twelve-year-old Blue that her mother had died from preeclampsia and nothing else.

As Blue attended the best schools, always had pocket money, and succeeded in every sport she ever tried, she learned that these attributes made her peers regard her as something of a golden child. They envied her and had no idea how she could have sold her soul to change places with them, if only for a day. She would sometimes be allowed to visit what Kairn called "the right kind of people" and spend time with their children. When she witnessed the interactions between her friends and their parents, she would dread going home to the too-big house, where cold loneliness spread from room to room like smoke. At age sixteen, Kairn decided that Blue was old enough to make her own meals and take care of herself after school. He fired the loyal housekeeper and settled for having a maid clean the house once a week and meals be delivered from a central kitchen service that some of the elite used.

Keeping an eye on her watch, Blue counted down the twenty minutes she was supposed to wait. Having been on countless missions as a bounty hunter, she was taken aback at how antsy she felt. She was seasoned enough not to let her impatience show, but when the twenty minutes had passed, she pocketed the receipt, drank the rest of the now-cold coffee without grimacing, and left the café.

Using the windows as mirrors, which became easier when the sun peeked through the clouds, Blue kept an eye on the sidewalk behind her and the one across the street. Nobody seemed interested in her, and when she turned a corner, she couldn't see anyone at all behind her on her side. The winding street she turned onto, Chellar Lane, had seemingly endless rows of two-story townhouses. The bill the café owner had given her for the pie and coffee had a date stamp on it, and if you knew where to look, the number for the cash register, normally kept for bookkeeping and tax reasons, instead showed which house on a certain street. Blue was on her way to 344 Chellar Lane. Naturally, she couldn't walk up and ring the doorbell, but she planned to pass it and look for the confirmation, which she had to give to the Tallawens. Their methods might be unorthodox, and perhaps even unsophisticated, but their success rate spoke for itself. Using caution was part of their recipe.

Blue walked on the side of the street showing uneven numbers, and when she passed 343, she furtively glanced over to the other side. At first, she thought she had read the bill wrong, but when she raised her gaze to the second floor, she saw a tiny white rectangle in the bottom left corner of a window. The woman, Lorna, and the two children she was going to collect were there. She had made it to the safe house.

As she kept walking, Blue took another right, and now she lengthened her stride. She needed to get back to the car and drive to the pay phone by the park. She made it back to the street where she'd parked and slipped in behind the wheel. As she turned the ignition key, she saw the two agents step out of the café. Gripping the wheel hard, Blue shifted into first gear and leisurely passed them as she drove down the street. In the rearview mirror, she saw them keep walking in the same direction, but they weren't paying any attention to her. Instead, they seemed to shadow someone on the other side of the street. Curious, Blue moved the rearview mirror and saw a young man striding fast, his movements too jerky.

Cursing, Blue realized that the authorities were monitoring the café for other individuals than those in the Tallawen web. The kid on the other pavement was perhaps sixteen or seventeen. He could be a black-market operative, a freedom fighter, or even someone belonging to any of the outlawed political parties. Either way, he was pale, and the men were gaining on him.

Blue couldn't risk her mission to help this boy. She would jeopardize everything and put Lorna and her two children at risk. Still, her chest hurt as she saw the fear on his young face. No matter why the authorities had their eyes on him, he was only a kid. Blue drove on, ready to carry out the next part of the plan, but she doubted she'd forget his expression anytime soon. The irony of that realization didn't escape her. She had successfully caught people like him for years, more than she could count, and she couldn't conjure up any of their faces. How could that one serious concussion and a few weeks in a Tallawen camp change her outlook on life so radically?

The vision her mind conjured of dark, glittering eyes and black hair fluttering in the wind showed her the answer. Of course it had to do with Aurelia. The mere fact that Aurelia would hate Blue when she finally realized who she was—and that was just a matter of time—made this realization even harder to fathom. Aurelia, the children, and the selfless work the Tallawens carried out—perhaps being subjected to those factors while not remembering her childhood and adolescence had functioned like some sort of intervention.

Blue parked in the shade of the large oaks in the north end of the park. Aurelia had been adamant that she should use only the well-shielded pay phone. The authorities kept track of every pay phone in the country, and she'd heard rumors that they had developed a way to listen in on calls. Even Blue didn't have clear information if this was true, but she knew that her own unit had access to surveillance equipment that the Tallawen probably hadn't even heard of. The pay phone at this end of the park had been "dealt with," as Milton had put it and wiggled his fingers in the air. Now Blue added a few coins to the slot and dialed the memorized number. Someone picked up after two rings, and a voice said, "Yes?"

"Hello, it's Daisy," Blue said, making her voice cheery. Even if Milton was certain nobody could listen in, they could still be compromised in other ways. If the person at the other end answered anything else but, "Daisy, you have some nerve calling after what you did to David," Blue was to hang up and dial a back-up number. As it turned out, she received the correct response and could continue. "Sign confirmed."

"Good. Three tonight. Youngest child is nervous. Mother has pills."

"All right. Older child?"

"Should be fine."

Should. Well, Blue would find out when she returned to Chellar Lane. "My ETA at meetup will be at eleven p.m. at the earliest." Blue had memorized three alternative routes to the drop-off site.

"Affirmative. I'll pass that along." The woman at the other end was quiet for a moment. "God's speed."

"Thank you. Bye." After hanging up, Blue returned to the car. There, she checked her watch—two hours to kill before she returned to the townhouse. She knew there was a library at the south end of the park. Parking farther down the street instead of in the parking lot belonging to the library, she slipped the car key into her pocket as she made her way to the large brick building.

Inside, the familiar smell of books, papers, and dust made the place feel familiar, even if she hadn't set foot in it before. Heading for the magazine section, Blue chose one of the issues, not really caring what it was about since she wouldn't be actively reading. She took a seat at one of the tables and began turning pages and pretending to read. A librarian was putting books back into the shelves and didn't pay her any attention. Four teenagers were poring over some book and giggling, which caused stern looks from the librarian.

Blue had changed magazines twice when she heard the large front door open and close. Looking over the edge of the magazine, this one apparently about cooking, she tensed. Two men had entered the library wearing plaid shirts and jeans, far too clean and well pressed. It wasn't the agents from the café, but these men were cut from the same mold. This was a midsize town. What were the odds that the authorities would deploy several teams to the same neighborhood in a generic Klowdynian town? Had they managed to tail the people responsible for getting Lorna and her children here? There was no use in guessing. Blue had to accept that Lorna was now a high-profile dissident by definition. The mere thought that she could hold some information that the Klowdynian authorities were set on keeping on their side of the border made their actions logical. Also, it could explain why they had resorted to sending even the young and inexperienced agents. If she came upon the type of agents she and Aurelia had run into in Jeterson, Blue was still confident she'd be able to identify them.

Folding the magazine, Blue returned it calmly and gave the librarian a friendly smile. "Thank you." She strolled toward the door, and for a moment she thought the men might not be interested in her, but then the taller of the two turned his head and looked right at her.

Blue forced her legs to maintain the easy stroll. She pressed the door open and stepped outside. Checking the time, she saw that she had forty minutes to get to the house on Chellar Lane. She jogged down the stairs and nearly made it in behind the hedge growing below them.

Quick footfalls behind her made Blue turn her head, and she saw the men run toward her. Without hesitation, she rounded the hedge and took off toward the large oaks. She was armed, but she wasn't going to fire her weapon unless her life or, later, Lorna's and her children's, was in danger. Instead, she zigzagged between the thick trunks, staying in the shade. The men would find it took time for their eyes to adjust, which might give her enough time to reach her car. She was glad she hadn't parked in the lot adjacent to the library, or the men could have easily spotted which vehicle she was driving. For now, she could at least hope that nobody had connected her to the scruffy-looking station wagon. Thousands of the same make and model, not to mention the drab beige color, sat on the streets of Klowdyn.

It was impossible to keep up her speed as she ran hunched over behind the hedge surrounding the park, but she had to. She was too tall to run upright; they'd easily spot her. Pulling out a knitted black cap, she pulled it on while hurrying toward her car. She was already unzipping her jacket and hoped the bright blue shirt would look different enough from the black jacket she now shoved under the shirt, making herself look either strangely overweight or pregnant. Aurelia would find this maneuver ridiculous but also clever enough to applaud it.

Upon reaching the car, she was glad it was unlocked. She threw herself into the driver's seat, then felt under the sunscreen for the keys and nearly dropped them on the floor. She pushed the main key into the ignition, and thankfully the car started on the first attempt. Harnessing her desire to floor the pedal, she drove calmly out into traffic, hoping that having five other cars on the street at the same time would confuse the men chasing her.

The two men emerged through the hedge, which suggested they had wasted time looking for her in the park. That meant they had continued running along the path through the oaks, not seeing her when she ran in among them, and then rounded the hedge. She felt their eyes on her but also knew that they were scanning all the cars as well as looking at the ten or so pedestrians with the same interest. Grateful that she'd remembered the black knitted hat, Blue kept pace with traffic and drove in the opposite direction of Chellar Lane.

She would have to circle the residential area and make her way back to the street parallel to Chellar. If her intel was correct, she'd be able to take the mother and children out through the back door. It was already getting darker, and dusk would provide an even better cover than complete darkness. During dusk, they could still see where they were going without flashlights, and the kids were less likely to be afraid. At least that was Blue's game plan. She hoped she really was as good with children as Aurelia claimed.

As she drove along the streets, Blue kept checking the rearview mirrors. She was good at spotting tails and even better at tailing other people. Whoever had trained these agents couldn't be one of her subordinates. They were too green for this type of job and too cocky to realize it. She vowed not to become over-confident. It was important to remember that, for all she knew, the agents she'd trained herself, capable and efficient, could be just around the corner.

Blue didn't want to think about how many times she'd sent agents into the field—well trained, smart, intuitive, and successful. After she had become the chief of the bounty-hunter unit, Blue rarely dealt with any of their prisoners personally. Thinking now that some of them were in the same situation as Lorna and her children, or any of the families back at the camp, made her sick. This was another reason she had made up her mind when it came to her allegiance. Before she let Aurelia know everything, she would keep her promise and help Aurelia carry out her promised mission to help save the Maydorians.

Pinching her thigh hard, Blue forced her brain to stop these unproductive thoughts. If she was going to succeed and reach her goal, she had to focus. Sooner or later her past would catch up with her—but not right now.

CHAPTER EIGHTEEN

"Are you certain?" Aurelia took Tom by the shoulders and nearly shook him. "Three of our newer recruits?" They stood next to Milton and Dacia, and Aurelia had been minutes from climbing onto a bike and heading out for her meetup.

Tom's face was ashen. "And they're good kids. Fast learners and strong. Two boys and one girl, none of them older than twenty-one."

"And they've held hearings with them already?" Aurelia tossed her ponytail back over her shoulder so viciously, it swung around and whipped her across the eyes, causing her to curse. "Did someone rat them out?"

"I don't think so," Milton said. "I listened in on the long-wave radio chatter, and it appears they were simply unlucky. They were picking up a food shipment in one of the smaller villages at the west of us when agents from the BHU moved in."

Aurelia covered her face. She was geared up to go to the primary meet-up location to fetch Ellis and Martha Maydorian and knew she was wasting time. "We have to assume that they've given up everything about this camp."

"I know," Tom said, speaking in a hollow voice.

"Listen, man, I know you feel you just got it running smoothly, but the protocol for something like this is crystal clear." Milton placed a hand on Tom's shoulder, but he merely shrugged it off.

"I know that too. It is just such a damn waste." He wiped at his eyes. "And these kids. There's no chance we can retrieve them. We'd be walking directly into a trap."

Aurelia was certain he was right. "Listen. Get all the bikes and carts ready for a bugout. Those who want to join any of the other satellite camps, or even the main camp, can pair up on the bikes that aren't meant to pull carts. We'll use the rest of the vehicles to transport the last people we have here over the border to Sandslot. We may have to carry a slightly heavier load in the carts, as we might not have enough, but we'll make it work."

"What about you?" Dacia asked. "What if BHU is waiting for you when you reach the meeting point?"

"The five of us, including Blue, are the only ones that know about it. The captured Tallawens have no idea."

"True." Dacia gave Aurelia a hug. "Now you listen. Just focus on getting the Maydorians here. Once you return with them, Blue, and our people, we'll be ready to bug out." She smiled with trembling lips. "This is it, isn't it, Aurelia? This is when we don't return from Sandslot once everyone is safe."

"Yes, Dacia. This is it. Not how I imagined it, but it is. You know what to do. So do the others. Get it set up, and I'll be back in a few hours."

As Aurelia straddled the off-roader, she hoped they wouldn't run into any agents, but as long as she got the Maydorians into their respective carts and headed back to camp and then onward to the border, she would torture the bike enough to take them all to safety, with Blue at her side.

❖

Blue entered through the back door after locating a ladder at a neighbor's house and placing it against the windowpane in case they needed to go out that way—something she prayed they wouldn't.

Inside, she couldn't hear anything, not even movement from the second floor. Holding her sidearm in a two-hand grip, she quickly scanned room after room until she came upon the stairs. They were covered by a red rug, and she tried the first step, which didn't make any sounds. Cautiously she snuck up the stairs, constantly swinging her weapon forward and backward, doing her best to not alert anyone to her presence. Just then, a shadow shifted in the hallway beneath her. Training her gun at it, she pulled back the safety, but the woman, because it was an older, emaciated woman with white hair in an updo, merely shook her head and walked into the room just inside the front door. She was clearly not afraid of Blue or about to call the authorities. And she knew what was going on.

Deciding she had no time to explore what the older woman was up to, Blue crept up the last three steps. Upstairs, she saw two closed doors in a dusty old area. Examining the dust on the floor, she could tell that only the door to the right had been used in a long time. She turned the door handle and carefully pushed it open.

There, on the bed, sat a woman flanked by two children. They were dressed in outdoor clothes, all dark and no bright colors. The children stared at Blue with such fear in their eyes, she immediately tucked the gun back into her pocket. "Hello, Lorna. I'm Blue, and I've come to take you and your children to a safe place, where your parents are waiting for you."

"I can't believe it," Lorna whispered. "When I got the message…Is this really happening?"

"It is, but we need to hurry. How are you doing, Charlotte?" The oldest girl looked afraid but calm.

"I'm fine. Thank you," Charlotte said politely. "Pippa's tired."

That was an understatement. Blue placed two fingers under the chin of the younger girl, whose eyes were half closed. Blue turned back to Lorna. "Can you and Charlotte manage the stairs on your own? I'll carry this one."

"Yes." Lorna stood and buttoned her coat all the way up to her chin, making sure the girls' zippers were closed. "All set."

"Good. Let's go." Blue scooped up Pippa in her arms, and despite the fact that the girl was sedated, her arms still came up around Blue's neck, holding on hard. "I have you, Pippa. Your mother and Charlotte are right behind us. Blue had begun making her way down the stairs, when the sudden outline of the old woman made her stop.

"Someone's at the door," the woman said in a husky whisper. "I don't know who they are or what they want. You can't go out this way."

"Got it. Stall them, please, no matter who they are." Blue didn't wait around for confirmation. Instead she walked into the room next to the one Lorna and the girls had stayed in. Still carrying Pippa, Blue peered out through the window. "I can't see anyone. Lorna, open the window."

Lorna rushed over to the window and managed to open it on the second attempt. Blue knew better than to stress the woman further, but she wanted to yell at her to hurry. "And now?" Lorna asked.

"See the ladder? I'm going to climb down with Pippa on my back. Once I'm down in the backyard, I'll help you and Charlotte. All right?"

"I can't climb that thing!" Lorna paled several shades. "I just can't."

"Yes, you can, Mom." Charlotte grasped her mother's hand. "You can do anything."

"Oh, God, child." Lorna closed her eyes briefly.

"If we don't get out and those people at the door are agents, you and I will be taken into custody and the girls placed at boarding schools and then adopted by strangers." Feeling absolutely rotten for scaring Lorna, Blue knew she had no other choice.

"Mom?" Charlotte yanked at Lorna's coat sleeve. "Come on! I don't want to live with strangers." Her voice was barely audible, but her words seemed to penetrate better than Blue's.

Lorna hugged Charlotte to her. "All right, all right." She was visibly shaking.

"Watch how I do it, then help Charlotte climb onto the ladder once I'm on the ground." Blue let go of Pippa and then grasped her left arm and leg in a different way, tugging them around her own neck. Using this technique, known as a fireman's hold, allowed Blue to have one hand free to grip the ladder. She slipped through the opening and onto the ladder, which just reached the windowpane. Accustomed to this type of maneuver, she quickly descended and soon was on the grass and set Pippa down. The girl curled up on the ground like a wounded animal.

Blue held onto the ladder and checked the windows facing the backyard. No light was on, and Blue hoped that meant the old woman had managed to send whoever had come to the door away.

Charlotte turned out to be a fearless little girl. She climbed down the ladder as if she'd trained for such an undertaking for years. When she was halfway down, Blue signaled to Lorna to follow her. For a frightening moment, Blue thought Lorna would refuse after all, but then she saw the girl's mother ease onto the ladder and hold on with white-knuckled hands.

"Good. Come on down to us. It's not that high. I promise," Blue whispered as loudly as she dared. She heard Lorna whimper, but she began to shift her feet, one after another, though she was going far too slowly.

"There you go. Can you try a little bit faster?" Blue cursed as her words only seemed to slow Lorna down even more.

"Wait." Charlotte climbed up until she was right below her mother. "Mom. I'm here. Just do what I do," the girl said quietly. "One. Two. Three. See? Like a rhythm." She climbed down, counting each step. And miracles could clearly happen in Klowdyn, because Lorna moved at the same pace, and soon, they stood on the grass. Blue lifted Pippa into her arms again and walked ahead of them through the tall hedges, stopping only to make sure no agents were waiting with their weapons drawn. The back alley was empty, and it would be dark very soon.

"Come on. The car isn't far from here." Blue walked heel-to-toe, as she could move much faster and quieter like that. Turning her head, she saw Charlotte mimic her gait perfectly and that Lorna tried to keep up.

The car was where she'd left it, and considering that she still hadn't locked it, that was a miracle. "Get in. Kids in the back, and you in the passenger seat in the front, Lorna. We're going to pass for a married couple, if I can pull off looking male enough."

"Okay. Thank you." Lorna took her seat, and Blue slipped in behind the wheel. She turned the ignition and went through the gears at a good, legal pace. As she drove in the opposite way on Chellar Lane, she hoped they'd look like a family who had been visiting someone and were on their way home. She drove through mostly empty streets for a few minutes, but then merged into denser traffic on the road that would lead them to their meeting place eventually. This was her second backup route, and she hoped it'd work out.

"Where are we going?" Lorna asked, her voice not trembling as much as it had been earlier.

"To a place where your parents will be either waiting for us or come shortly after us. We're on a tight schedule, and so are the people helping them."

"I can't believe we're going to be free," Lorna said and leaned her head back. "Ever since my husband died, our life has been a nightmare."

"I can imagine." It wasn't a lie. Blue's life had turned into a nightmare when her memory returned and she understood she was going to lose Aurelia as soon as she informed her who she really was.

As they drove along the highway leading to the smaller villages west of the mountain chain, Blue allowed her heart to ache and mourn for what would never be. Unless they ran into an impromptu checkpoint, she would at least be part of reuniting the Maydorians with each other.

CHAPTER NINETEEN

Aurelia couldn't have stood still if she tried. She kept walking up to the driveway leading into the old abandoned factory, gazed toward the south, and then returned to the rusty shipping crates where Colin and Lizzy, two of the Tallawens' more seasoned operatives, were waiting with her. She had initially insisted on going alone, with a bike for Blue in her cart, feeling it was her duty to not risk anyone else's life for her promise, but her debt and the new situation with the captured operatives had changed all that. Now they had two extra bikes and carts, which would make the journey into the mountains much less of a hardship for the Maydorians.

"They're not due yet," Lizzy said. "Don't worry. They'll get here."

"So many things can go wrong," Aurelia muttered. "I know, I know." She held up a hand. "I'm usually the resident optimist, but in this case…well, if we've ever pushed the envelope, this is it."

"Your woman is a tremendous resource." Colin lit a cigarette and inhaled deeply. "She looks like she could break me like a twig if she wanted to."

"My woman?" Aurelia sent the flamboyant young man a disapproving look.

"Oh, yeah. That's hardly a secret." Colin grinned.

"Great." Aurelia shook her head and wondered if they were the most popular topic in the camp gossip mill. "Well, either way, don't let her hear you call her that, or you might just take the place of that twig." It pleased Aurelia that Colin actually looked a bit concerned at her words.

"Serves him right. He has no manners." Lizzy chuckled. Then she straightened and peered around the closest crate. "A truck's coming."

Aurelia stood and pulled her sidearm from her coat pocket. She watched the beige truck slow down and turn into the driveway, then stop by the first building, its engine idling. A middle-aged man stepped out though the front passenger door, and he too was armed. The driver remained in the vehicle, no doubt ready to hightail out of there if they'd been compromised.

"Here goes," Aurelia said and stepped around the crate and into the open. "Hello, friend. Any message from Daisy or David?"

The man with the sawed-off shotgun relaxed his stance. "Aurelia? Is that you, girl?" he called out.

"Sure is. Wait…Carl?" Aurelia put her gun back into her pocket and walked toward the man, who was indeed Carl, whom she'd worked with before. "Who's your driver tonight?"

"Same old Margery." Carl grinned and kissed Aurelia's cheek.

"Who are you calling old, you ancient goat?" A husky voice came from the truck, and then a short, stocky woman with slate-gray hair stepped out. "Shouldn't we let the poor people that are tucked in under the floor in the back out?"

"Oh, God." Aurelia rushed to the back of the truck, and now Lizzy and Colin joined her. Aurelia quickly made rudimentary introductions while she tore at the fastenings that held the tarp in place. Inside, Colin and Carl shoved some boxes aside and then unscrewed the corrugated plates that covered the floor. Beneath them were two lids with hinges on one side and a locking mechanism on the other. Carl flipped the lock and pushed open the first lid. On a mattress, and covered with several blankets, lay a pale Martha Maydorian.

"Martha." Kneeling next to the opening, Aurelia helped the older woman sit up and hugged her impulsively. "Are you all right? Was it horrible in there?"

"Well, it wasn't comfortable," Martha said, and even if she sounded shaken, she still smiled and caressed Aurelia's cheek. "You always said you'd come for us."

"Speaking of us," a male voice said from the floor, "may I come out of this casket before I pee myself?"

"Oh, my. Ellis." Martha slapped a hand over her mouth. "Better get him out of there quick. You know old men. They have to go when they have to go."

Lizzy and Colin had already released the second lock and now held the lid open until Martha had moved out of the way so they could flip it over completely. Ellis was wrapped up in blankets as well and looked entirely calm as the two men pulled him up.

Aurelia could feel Martha shiver as they helped her and Ellis off the truck. The temperature was falling, and now it was pitch-black around them. Margery had turned off the headlights, and the only thing making it possible to see was Lizzy's flashlight with red-tinted glass.

"Our daughter? Her children?" Ellis asked after having returned from behind a shed.

"Not here yet." Aurelia patted his arm. "We have plenty of time before we start worrying."

"I worry anyway," Martha said, and now her teeth were clattering.

"Hey, Carl?" Aurelia turned to the man who was fastening the tarp around the back of the truck. "Can we have some of the blankets? It's getting colder than we counted on, and Martha's at risk of going into hypothermia. We have some with us and plenty of padding in the carts, but still."

"Take'em all." Margery had clearly reached this conclusion already, as she handed the rough blankets over. "There's plenty more where they came from."

"Thank you." Martha put one around her, and so did Ellis. The couple stood huddled together, and Aurelia knew that even if it no doubt felt good to move around and stretch their legs after being locked into the hidden boxes for hours, they were also getting cold fast.

"Lizzy, bring the bikes close, please." Aurelia pointed at the nearest structure. "Against that wall. That way, Ellis and Martha can sit down in a cart each and still see what's going on. Well, as much as any of us can see anything. Wasn't there supposed to be a full moon tonight?"

"So we were told, but that didn't happen. On it, Boss." Lizzy motioned for Colin to join her, and soon the three off-roaders and their carts stood lined up against the wall. After some persuading, Aurelia helped Martha sit down in the cart, making sure the heather and tall grass the children in the camp had gathered protected her from any sharp edges. "I know they're not comfortable, but are you all right like this?"

"This is a hundred percent better than the boxes." Martha tugged at Aurelia's hair. "Still got the impossibly long hair, I see."

"Well, it's my signature look, you know." Aurelia kissed Martha's weathered hand. "Now, try to relax. Here are plenty of blankets for you and Ellis. When Lorna and the kids come, I think we'll put them in the same cart, as we saved the biggest one for them. Blue will drive that bike. Colin and Lizzy will be on this one and drive Ellis. I'll pull you."

"How far is it?" Martha asked, plucking at the blanket.

"About three hours from here," Aurelia said, not sure when she should break the news about the changed plans. "If you get hungry or thirsty, you'll find a little bag at your feet with some sandwiches and water. We're big on sandwiches in the Tallawens."

"You're amazing." Martha found the bottle and drank some. "I had water in the box, but I was afraid to drink because I might need to use the bathroom too."

"Wish you'd told me that," Ellis said from behind them. He was installed in his cart with blankets all around him. "I finished my bottle."

"Engine approaching." Margery came up to them. "A smaller vehicle."

Lizzy switched off her flashlight, and Aurelia could hear the rustling and snapping sound as the Tallawens followed her example and took out their weapons. The sound of the engine changed, and Aurelia could hear how the driver changed gears. Soon, it came up behind the truck and stopped. The engine was turned off, as were the headlights. She detected the sound of a door opening and then nothing for a few moments.

"Aurelia?" Blue's low voice called out softly.

Unable to stop herself from sobbing just once, Aurelia was grateful when Lizzy switched on her flashlight again. "Blue." Aurelia hurried toward the woman who looked like she was doused in red gold as Lizzy directed the light toward her.

"Aurelia…" Wrapping Aurelia in her arms, Blue hugged her hard. "God, that was a long day."

"Mom? Dad?" A woman stepped up to Blue and Aurelia. "Are they…?"

"They're fine. They're here." Aurelia didn't care that she'd never met Lorna before. She gave the woman a quick hug. "And the kids?"

"Asleep in the backseat." Blue answered as they took Lorna over to her parents.

Martha cried openly as she hugged her daughter from where she sat in the cart. Lorna knelt on the ground by the cart, and she too sobbed violently. "Mom. It's been so long. Too long."

"It has. Now go hug your father, or he'll break a leg trying to get out of the cart again." Martha wiped at their cheeks.

Lorna knelt next to her father, and now it was Ellis's turn to weep. He kissed his daughter's forehead over and over before finally letting go. "No matter what," he said throatily, "we're together now."

"Yes, we are." Lorna stood and turned to Blue. "Can you help me get the girls?"

"I can." Blue looked around at the others. "Colin, right? Can you take the older girl? They're both exhausted, and I doubt we'll be able to wake them."

"Absolutely." Colin followed Blue and Lorna to the car.

"Remember," Lizzy said in a sing-song voice. "A twig is a fragile thing."

"Excuse me?" Blue looked questioningly at Aurelia and Lizzy.

"Never mind." Aurelia kissed Blue's cheek. "You did really well. Are you all right?"

"I'm fine." Blue's voice was low, and she sounded tired.

"Feeling fine enough to drive the bike pulling Lorna and the kids?" Aurelia waited until Blue had lifted out a sleeping little girl from the backseat of the car.

"Sure thing. Do you have something to eat and drink though? I gave some of my food to the kids when we were halfway here. They were really upset, and I figured it didn't help that they were famished."

Typical of Blue to do something like that. "We have enough to go around, and if I know Carl and his Margery correctly, they have some food in the truck as well."

"Did anyone say food? I have chicken pie. It's cold, but it's still good," Margery said. "I know you have to get going, but you have five minutes to eat, I wager."

"Five minutes well spent," Aurelia said.

Soon they sat on the bikes and in the carts and had some of Margery's pies, which Ellis praised at no end. When it was time to leave, Margery climbed into the truck, and Carl stepped into the driver's seat of the car Blue had used. He was planning to return it to the junkyard, where it was kept among the wrecks when not in use. Aurelia hadn't told them about the captured Tallawens, and it was sad to realize she'd most likely never see the pair again.

After Carl and Margery left, Aurelia stopped Blue as she was about to walk to the bike where Lorna and the kids were tucked into the cart. "Wait. There's a change of plans. We're going back to the camp, but we're moving directly toward the border. I'll explain what happened in detail later, but we're… oh, God, we're leaving the camp and taking everyone with us except the Tallawens who prefer to join any of the other camps in the mountains and continue the fight. She swallowed hard. "It's time for me to go back home. Now that I have the Maydorians with me, I'm going to be selfish and look for my parents. At least that's the plan."

"What…what happened?" Blue asked hoarsely.

"We aren't sure, but the BHU have captured some of our people, and that means the entire camp is compromised. We can't hold it against them that they probably broke under pressure. They're young, and they have their whole life ahead of them."

"And so have you. As for being selfish…" Blue bent and kissed Aurelia. "Nobody could fit that description less. You've more than earned the right to go home."

"But—but you're coming too, right? I mean, once you get your memory back, if you want to return here, you always have that choice…I just can't imagine leaving Klowdyn without you." Aurelia wrapped her arms around Blue's waist. To her surprise, Blue was shaking.

"I can't imagine being without you either. Where you go, I go." Blue spoke lightly, but her voice trembled as badly as her body.

"Okay. Good." Aurelia stepped back. "We better take off. Remember, our headlights are red tinted just like Lizzy's flashlight, so the light isn't great. Stay at a reasonable distance so we don't collide if someone has to slam on the brakes, but not so far that we lose each other in the dark. Colin and Lizzy have a walkie-talkie, and I have one. I'll take the lead, and he'll take the rear. You'll be in the middle with Lorna and the kids."

"Understood." Blue sounded like her usual assertive self again. "Let's get going."

Aurelia stole a kiss and then walked to her off-roader and patted Martha's shoulder. "I'll try to not drive like a madwoman. There are some handles on the inside of the cart if it gets bumpy. The bikes are rather loud, but I'll hear you if you yell."

"I'll be fine. I trust you, Aurelia." Martha patted Aurelia's hand.

As she climbed on the bike, she made sure she didn't kick the rods holding the nets. They needed camouflage in the dark and also if the helicopter searchlights found them. It had happened several times, and on those occasions, only the fact that they had remained still and kept under the nets had saved them and their passengers.

All the bikes started without any problems. Aurelia turned on her headlight, and the terrain around them was lit by a red glow. She pulled out onto the path behind the old factory and headed toward the rolling hills that would eventually turn into mountains. Behind her, Blue drove the bike Lizzy had brought. Colin took up the rear, Lizzy riding behind him on the bike. Aurelia had driven this path several times before and knew which speed was the safest. Tonight, though, she had to disregard that precaution and instead drive as fast as possible. They had no way to know if, or when, the BHU would send helicopters and other vehicles to search for the camp.

If they arrived when the attack was already happening, everyone's life would be in jeopardy, and Aurelia was completely set on getting everyone to safety, no matter where that happened to be. Colin and Lizzy were going to Sandslot, as they were too good at driving with the carts to be allowed to stay and fight. As she flew over roots and smaller rocks, Aurelia estimated how many people they could fit into their twelve available carts and behind the off-road drivers. Thankfully, they'd managed to get a large group across the border two days ago, which meant the camp wasn't as full of refugees and dissidents as it had been known to be.

But Aurelia couldn't allow herself to think about Sandslot and what might be waiting for her there, if anything. If she let those thoughts take hold in her mind, she'd lose her edge and maybe cause an accident or miss early signs of helicopters. Gripping the handlebar harder, she steered toward the mountains in the distance. She intended to keep her promise, and she was determined to take Blue with her to Sandslot.

She refused to consider any other option.

CHAPTER TWENTY

The camp resembled organized mayhem when Blue pulled in behind Aurelia's off-roader. Tallawens were carrying equipment and strapping it to their bikes, and for the first time, Blue noticed mopeds she hadn't seen in the camp before. They were called mokulis, she believed, and were characterized by the flatbeds sitting above two wheels in the front. She could understand they weren't meant for speed, which was probably why nobody transported people on them. Now, the Tallawens were stacking their goods high on them, and Blue wondered dazedly how the drivers would be able to see where they were driving.

Aurelia had jumped off her bike and was helping Martha out. The older woman had just found her bearings when Milton and Dacia came running and threw their arms around her.

"Mrs. M!" Dacia squealed. "You're here." She looked over at Blue and the others. "And you're all here, thank God."

"Oh, goodness, girl. You haven't changed a bit." Martha hugged Dacia and Milton. "Though you have filled out nicely, young man."

Soon, Ellis joined in the greeting, and as Blue didn't want to interfere with the reunion, she busied herself by helping Lorna stir the children. Pippa was drowsy still, but Charlotte stared wide-eyed at the surroundings. "Where are we?" she asked and took a step closer to her mother. "Is…is that Grandma and Grandpa?"

Lorna kissed the top of her oldest daughter's head. "Yes, it is. Let's give them some time to greet old friends." She glanced at Blue. "What's going on? I didn't expect everyone to be asleep here, even in the middle of the night, but this…this has to be all of them. And children are awake too?"

Blue looked around and spotted her students. "Yes, they are. Aurelia will inform you and your parents of recent events."

"This is scaring me," Lorna murmured.

Blue kept her emotions under control. If she gave in to them, the confusion and fear of rejection would overwhelm her. "Here they come now."

Dacia didn't hesitate but hugged Lorna and her children with equal enthusiasm, making even the reserved Lorna smile. "Welcome to the mountains." Crouching in front of the children, Dacia took them by the hand. "I bet both of you are hungry and thirsty. If your mom says it's all right, I can show you where the other kids are, and we can have something to eat."

Charlotte peered up at Lorna, who nodded slowly. "Don't let your sister out of your sight, Charlotte," she said hoarsely. Clearly, she understood that something was up.

"I won't. Come on, Pippa." Charlotte let go of Dacia's hand and took her younger sister's free one. Blue watched her students regard the approaching girls and was proud of how they decided to go meet them as they reached one of the netted areas.

"What's going on here?" Ellis asked as soon as the girls were out of earshot.

Aurelia took a deep breath and then explained the emergency. "It was too late to abort our mission to retrieve you. I'm so sorry for doing this to you after the ordeal you've endured today, but we need to keep going. We have an hour, at the most, before we should have erased the last of the camp and moved out. Those bikes over there will take the remaining Tallawens to other camps. The bikes like ours, with carts, will take you and the rest of the refugees to the border."

"And what about you, Aurelia?" Martha stood close to her husband, but her gaze was calm.

"The Tallawens going to the border will have to cross also and remain in Sandslot until further notice. I know some will go back and fight the good fight, but I won't. I feel selfish for having decided to leave Klowdyn, but—"

"This isn't your country. You need to find out what happened to your parents." Ellis tilted his head. "Something tells me that finally being able to keep your promise has a lot to do with you leaving."

"Yes." Aurelia wiped quickly at her cheeks with jerky movements. "I just wish I could have managed it sooner."

Blue couldn't endure the pain in Aurelia's voice. She stepped closer and wrapped her arm around her shoulders.

"Don't start that again," Martha said. "You're a miracle. All of you are." She looked around the small circle of Tallawens. Tom had joined them and now introduced himself before turning to Aurelia.

"We have to assume that anyone coming after us is mostly out to stop the refugees from leaving, apart from catching us. This means we have to leave now. The rest of the bikes are going in other directions, and they'll have a better chance of getting away. Time isn't our friend here."

"All right. Everyone who needs to use the facilities should do so." Aurelia motioned toward the cave entrance. I take it you've prepared food and drink to be put in all the carts?"

"Already taken care of. We've topped off your carts as well." Tom nodded briskly. "All the children are dressed in as many clothes as it was possible to put on and still be able to move. We've checked and rechecked the camouflage nets. Maintenance is filling up the gas tanks and strapping extra on the bikes as we speak."

Aurelia squeezed Tom's upper arm. "Excellent." She turned to Blue. "We'll be moving very fast through mostly unknown terrain after we've rounded the first mountain. Can you still drive after having been on your feet so long?"

"Yes. And you've been at it for almost as long."

"Not quite true, but I trust that you're being truthful." Aurelia rose on her toes and kissed the corner of Blue's mouth. "Then let's get our passengers loaded again. We're short on seats, so I'm taking both Martha and Ellis this time. It's that or we won't be able to bring everyone."

When Dacia returned with the Maydorian children, Pippa obviously didn't want to ride in the cart again so soon. Charlotte didn't complain, but her eyes were dark with apprehension.

"I don't like this. Mom." Pippa took a step back and folded her arms over her chest. "I don't want to go."

"You can't stay here all by yourself," Charlotte said brusquely.

"Mom won't leave me." Pippa glared at her sister.

"If we stay, people will come to grab us and take us back to that horrible house they made us move into. I hate it there." Charlotte pointed at the cart. "If you get in, you can sit closest to Mom this time."

Pippa's lower lip trembled. "You promise?"

Charlotte softened. "I promise."

"Oh, all right." Pippa watched as Lorna climbed into the cart and arranged one of the blankets around her and yet another across her chest to wrap around the girls. Blue helped the children sit down and strapped the leather belts around them. She had no way of knowing what the paths they were taking were like, but if someone fell out, they could be seriously hurt, or even killed.

Just as Blue straddled the bike, moving her legs even higher than normal to accommodate the extra gas tanks strapped to the bike, a thunderous sound erupted in the distance.

"What's that?" Pippa asked, her voice thin with fear.

"Artillery," Aurelia called out. "We need to go, now!" Her eyes were like black wells as she rushed over to Blue and took her by the waist. "Listen to me, Blue. Ride that bike like the wind. We won't have a second chance to get this part right. We're crossing the border tonight in whatever way we can, and we *will* be successful."

"Yes, we will," Blue said, her heart plummeting.

"Follow me. If you lose me, find Tom or Milton." Aurelia ran to her bike and gave Martha and Ellis a hand getting into the cart. "Here we go." She straddled her bike and kicked the starter. The trimmed machine roared to life. Aurelia turned the bike and cart around, facing north. "Are we ready to leave?"

Blue had moved her bike just behind Aurelia's, and now she gazed behind her. The area lit only by stars, she could make out the outline of twelve off-roaders with accompanying carts. Another rumble rolled toward them, and Blue thought she could hear that its origin was closer. Orange and yellow streaks sliced the blue-black sky, and then explosions erupted as the missiles and mortars hit the mountain chain.

"Let's go!" Aurelia raised her fist and then took off down the path. As she passed the maintenance people and other Tallawens that were going farther into the mountain chain by turning to the west, she stood on the footrests and howled. "Go, Tallawens. Go!"

Blue couldn't see, of course, but she heard the tears in Aurelia's voice as she tore past the people she'd inspired and recruited. New missile tracks in the sky and more explosions drowned out the Tallawens' response, but the raised fists spoke clearly.

Blue was behind Aurelia, keeping the minimum safety distance. She allowed herself to mull over her thoughts of the young recruits that had been captured and forced to betray the camp. Aurelia didn't blame them, and neither did Blue. It was frightening how fast it all had happened, but she wasn't surprised at how efficient the Klowdynian BHU and military were. After all, she had been instrumental in training the lead operatives. Shoving those thoughts aside, Blue focused on the driving.

CHAPTER TWENTY-ONE

Blue pressed her bike to its limit. The engine buzzed like a furious hornet when she turned the handle to the max. She wanted to look up, to see the trails of the missiles that streaked the sky, but she didn't dare take her eyes off the path before her. Behind her, she heard the children scream, and she prayed Lorna would be able to hold them down. The whole problem about keeping the young ones quiet was a moot point by now. The Klowdynian authorities were in pursuit, and the fizzing sound in the sky would soon become something much worse. Blue barely had time to finish the thought before the first missile exploded into the side of a mountain in front of them, lighting up the sky. The boom in Blue's chest happened a second after, and she gripped the handlebars, gasping for air.

Lorna and the children screamed again behind her.

"Just hold on! It's not much farther!" Blue shouted, even if she suspected the wind and the sound of the engine drowned her out. She dared a glance to the parallel path beside her. Aurelia was halfway lying over the handlebar, looking like a warrior queen urging her forces forward. Her long, black hair whipped behind her, and the cart holding the Maydorian couple bounced precariously.

"Careful," Blue whispered into the wind. She was well aware of what would happen to the bikes if any of the carts turned over.

Still, they had no choice. If the missiles hit them, or if the forces hunting them from the south captured them, all would be lost anyway, for them and for the dissidents.

More missiles created fizzing lines in the sky, and only the fact that they seemed to land in a haphazard way made it possible for her to remain cautiously optimistic. It was as if the Klowdynian forces were shooting from the hip, which could mean that they didn't know exactly where the Tallawens were. The thought spurred Blue on, and when she saw the sky in the north begin to look brighter, she knew they were reaching the border. It was always well lit and guarded at the crossing sites.

At this point, Blue knew she had to slow down enough to be able to follow Aurelia, who knew the new path the best. She also was aware of where they had the best chance to cross the dead man's zone, which was the most dangerous part of the escape to Sandslot.

After a few minutes, Aurelia turned a sharp left and drove through what looked like impossibly dense shrubs. The cart jumped, and Blue whimpered slightly as she followed the woman she loved without hesitation. As she drove among the bushes, she was stunned to see a path actually wider than the one she'd left. Behind her, the cart she pulled jumped like Aurelia's had, but a quick glance assured her that all three of her passengers were still in it. Tying the kids to their mother had been a good idea.

Behind Blue, more bikes and carts followed, and as she looked up, she could tell that they were going perpendicular to the missile streaks in the night sky. The covered headlights on the bikes made it possible to keep driving as they headed due west for a while. Blue kept the exact same speed as Aurelia but also a reasonable distance so she wouldn't drive straight into the cart in front of her if Aurelia suddenly stopped.

As they cleared the shrubs, the path wound its way next to a jagged edge of rocks, looming above the Tallawens and their passengers more than twenty feet tall, creating an overhang. If

Blue hadn't been impressed with Aurelia's knowledge of the mountain area earlier, she was now. Not only did the sharp rock formation create protection from being seen by helicopters, but also to a degree from the missiles that hit all around them. Lorna and the children weren't screaming anymore, and Blue wondered if they were in shock or were resigned to the possibility of having one of the missiles hit them.

In front of her, Aurelia gestured to the right, and a few moments later, she turned her bike on what looked like a collision course with the bedrock next to them. Instead, it seemed to swallow her and the cart, and when Blue turned to follow, she saw why. What looked like a cave at first glance turned out to be a natural tunnel leading through the rock formation. It was low enough for Blue to duck over the handlebar, but the ground was even enough to drive on. When they emerged on the other side, Blue saw they were on the other side of the main crossing over to Sandslot, where border guards manned the only road through the dead-man's zone. Squinting, she surmised the distance was about two miles. She turned to Aurelia, who motioned for Blue to place her bike next to hers.

"What are we waiting for?" Blue asked as she lined up her bike and cart.

"I need to talk to everyone at the same time." Aurelia leaned over at Blue and kissed her lightly on the lips. "We're nearing the last leg of the escape. We won't have to worry as much about the missiles this close to the border, but there are other dangers."

Blue cupped Aurelia's cheek. "All right." Her heart ached at how the moment neared when the love she saw in Aurelia's eyes would be snuffed like a blown-out candle.

Aurelia got off her bike but waited until all the twelve bikes and carts were out of the tunnel before she addressed them. "Can all drivers hear me?" She looked around the semicircle and saw them nod. "Keep the bikes idling. We can't risk one of them not starting for any reason." She pointed north. "We're going to drive for as long as we can toward the woods over there. Once we're beyond the tree line, we won't have any clear paths to use the bikes on, so we're going to ditch them."

"What?" Dacia looked down at her off-roader with what appeared to be true mourning.

"We knew this was going to be a one-way trip. The rest of the Tallawens are regrouping and following the protocol we set up if we were ever compromised or detected on a large scale. The ones of us who volunteered on this mission knew we wouldn't be returning to Klowdyn for a long time."

"Yes, I know that, but my *bike.*" Dacia sighed. "All right, all right." She gave Milton a sad smile when he caressed the back of her neck.

"Every biker will be responsible for their passenger or passengers. We will all help carry the smaller children. It's important that we walk in each other footsteps, as the forest has been known to be mined."

Gasps came from Tallawens and the ones in the carts alike.

"Simmer down," Tom said, raising his hands. "That's why I'm along for the ride. Through contacts, albeit a long time ago, I obtained a map of the mined paths, which I memorized. I'll go first, about twenty feet ahead, and if I don't trigger any, you'll walk where I did. All right? It's not a foolproof plan, but it's our only chance—and more importantly, it's *their* only chance." He gestured behind him with his thumb. "It's what we signed up for."

Aurelia felt Blue grasp her hand and squeezed it back. "Tom's right. It's this or run out of gas while trying to escape missiles and helicopters throughout the mountain chain."

"Okay. Let's go before anything like that shows up," Blue said.

Mac dismounted her bike and made a quick round among the carts, accompanied by Aurelia, who helped make sure nobody was in too bad a shape. When even the youngest child wasn't crying, she gave them, and Mac, a thumbs-up and returned to her bike. "Tom will take the lead. Carts with children first after him." She glared at Blue. "No arguments." She could tell Blue wasn't pleased.

Soon the bikes took off with their precious cargo toward the tree line, Aurelia insisting on being last. Blue was three bikes ahead of her. The terrain wasn't too bad from a Tallawen's point of view. Aurelia had ridden on much worse surfaces, still remembering the forest she and Blue had gone through twice only a short while ago. It had taken her a few days to work the kinks out of her back and neck though.

After they reached the trees, they dismounted the bikes and helped their rattled passengers out of the carts. They pulled the bikes in under the trees and covered them with dead branches. The disguise wouldn't fool anyone during daylight, but in the night, and from a distance, they were nearly impossible to see.

"All the work and love," Dacia said sorrowfully. "Oh, well."

Aurelia patted her best friend's shoulder. "You can get a really nice bike after you find work in Sandslot."

"Yeah. I suppose." Dacia had just helped baby Noah and Gill out of her cart. "Can you manage, Gill, or should I carry him for a bit?"

"He's sound asleep, and I've tied him to me with my shawl. If you can find me a branch to use as a walking stick, maybe?" Gill buttoned the large men's coat around her and Noah.

"Here you go," Milton said and gave her one that lay right by his feet. "Just let us know if you need us to take your place."

"I will." Gill walked over to where the other parents stood holding their children close in the cold night air.

Aurelia made sure the Maydorians could join their daughter and her children. Lorna looked her parents over and then smiled at Blue, who had joined them.

"We need to go. Now." Tom came up to Aurelia. "I'll start walking. Once I'm over by that boulder—he pointed at it—I want you to let them walk six feet apart. Parents can walk next to one child, but not three in a row."

"Understood. Be careful, Tom. Please." Aurelia shook his left arm lightly.

"Hey. I plan to return here one day and continue the good fight, okay?" Tom smiled broadly and then began walking. He kept a good pace, probably realizing that children age five and up would have to be able to keep up. Aurelia estimated that once they'd been about a third of a mile, they would enter the dead man's zone. They would have no trees, no cover, but after about three hundred yards, they would be on Sandslot territory.

Highly motivated, they lined up quickly and walked in Tom's footsteps. Each driver remained behind the person or persons they'd driven there, making sure they stayed on the path in the dark forest. Everyone was using the red-tinted flashlights, which weren't invisible up close, but from a distance they were hard to detect. No way could anyone see the paths among the trees without them.

The Maydorians had refused to separate once they were reunited in the woods, which meant Aurelia and Blue walked together at the rear of the group. In front of them, Ellis was holding hands with Charlotte, and Lorna held Pippa's hand. Martha walked behind them, just in front of Aurelia and Blue.

"How far?" Blue murmured.

"A third of a mile or thereabouts. It'll take us a while, as we can't hurry the children too much, but it's not very far. Tom knows." Aurelia glanced over her shoulder at Blue, and at first, she thought she saw anguish on her lover's face. "Hey. We're going to make it. They'd never expect us to go through mined territory with children."

"I can hardly fathom that possibility myself," Blue said. "I feel completely braced for impact, expecting an explosion at any given moment."

"Speaking of explosions…" Aurelia frowned. "Have the Klowdynians given up? I haven't heard many signs of missiles or artillery anymore."

"You're right. Perhaps they've realized how futile it is to shoot randomly like that."

"Yeah." Aurelia wasn't so sure. Ever since they'd received the information about Tom's branch of the Tallawens being compromised, she'd wondered if her and Blue's journey to Jeterson or the haste with which they had collected the Maydorians had revealed enough for the authorities to go after them guns blazing. Ellis and Martha's position at Jeters made them prime targets, as they simply knew too much about what went on at schools like that. The signed witness accounts they were sending to the United Assembly, along with Aurelia's, Dacia's, and Milton's, would have tremendous impact on how the outside world regarded Klowdyn. No doubt it would affect the sanctions already in place against the dictatorship.

Aurelia had turned to Blue to express her opinion when something singed the air next to her head, and then wood splinters pricked her right cheek. Though whatever it was produced no sound, Aurelia identified it.

"Someone's firing at us!" Aurelia tugged at Blue, who still stood behind her. "Get down!"

More bullets hit tree trunks around them, and now the Maydorians noticed and stopped walking.

"Keep going!" Aurelia commanded and pushed at Martha. "Follow the ones in front of you and keep walking." She pulled her sidearm and saw Blue had done the same and was holding it in a two-hand grip. "Blue."

"They're coming. I can hear them." Blue stood very still.

"We need to move as well."

"Or we can wait and take them out."

"We don't know how many they are." Aurelia squinted at the black shadows among the trees. "If we try to wait and fire on them, they'll know exactly where we are. Their shots were too spread out, which means they were simply lucky when one bullet came so close. Blue, please. Come on!"

Blue appeared to hesitate, but then she hurried after Aurelia as they ran faster than advisable in the dark. After a while they caught up with two people, who turned out to be Dacia and Milton.

"Everyone knows and they're running, following Tom. Word traveling back from the ones in the front says they see the end of the forest, which means the dead-man's zone." Milton gasped as they all kept running.

"Yes. Once we're there, we need to spread out. Everyone needs to grab a kid and just run for their life. Once we reach the trees on the other side, we should keep going for another hundred yards and then hunker down." Aurelia had to stop talking to keep up her pace.

"I can hear movement behind us." Blue spoke tightly next to Aurelia. "No matter what happens, promise me you'll keep going. Keep running."

"What?" Aurelia wanted to object, not sure what Blue meant or how her words sounded, but she could see the trees thin out and knew they were at the dead man's zone.

"Aurelia!" Tom hurried toward them. "I've already got the ones carrying children going. We have to be quick." He glanced behind them into the woods they just left. "They're not far behind."

They moved quickly, and Aurelia saw Ellis put Charlotte on his back. Another man, one of the other dissidents, did the same with Pippa. Martha and Lorna held hands as the family began to dash across the field. In the distance Aurelia could hear the all-too-familiar sound of approaching helicopters.

"Now! Hurry!" She dragged at the others, and they began crossing the open field before them. Never had three-hundred-some yards looked so long.

When they were halfway across the zone, a megaphone-enhanced voice echoed from behind. "Stop! Your presence in the dead man's zone is a violation akin to treason!"

Blue began to slow down. "Keep going, Aurelia!" She pushed at Aurelia's back, shoving her.

"Colonel AnRaine! We have you covered." The megaphone voice boomed. "It's time to come in and lead the BHU into victory…to bring these terrorists in. Move away from them and let us get a clear shot."

"What?" Turning her head over her shoulder, Aurelia saw the figures of four individuals against the Klowdynian tree line. Then it dawned on her what one of them had just said. Aurelia stared at Blue. "Colonel AnRaine? They…they know you?"

"Aurelia." Pain flooded Blue's voice as she kept her gun trained on the tree line. "Stay behind me and keep running."

"What's going on?" Milton dragged Aurelia down and pulled Dacia to him, where he crouched.

"It's one of my former subordinates." Blue spoke curtly and remained standing. They're under the impression that I'm still undercover. Just go. I'll hold them off. They won't shoot if they think they might hit their commanding officer." Her voice was bitter but infinitely soft.

"You. Were you the one that compromised the camp and got our young recruits captured? Was it you?" Aurelia's throat hurt. In fact, everything, every cell in her system hurt as if someone had poured acid on her.

"No. Never." Blue spoke with such certainty, Aurelia allowed herself to be fooled for a second.

"Liar," she growled, fury and sorrow filling every cell in her.

"She's right about one thing. We have to move." Milton tugged at Aurelia's sleeve. "Come on, Aurelia."

Aurelia watched Milton grab Dacia around the waist and tug her off the ground as well. Just as she was getting to her feet, firmly gripping her sidearm, Dacia flinched, cried out, and then slumped to the ground.

CHAPTER TWENTY-TWO

Aurelia crawled over to Dacia, her gun still in her right hand while she tore at Dacia's jacket with the other. The large buttons kept it closed, but something dark began to permeate the fabric. Blood.

"Help me!" Crying out, she looked up at Milton, who was on his knees, his arms slumped against his sides. His face glowed white in the moonlight. "Milton! Help me. She's bleeding."

Gravel sprayed against the side of Aurelia's face, and she thought a bullet was the cause, but glancing up in alarm, she saw that Tom had skidded into position next to Blue, who was still firing at the BHU agents. Wait…she was shooting at them? So confused, and so devastated, Aurelia pushed that part of their situation to the back of her mind and tucked the gun into her pocket. Now about to use both hands, she tore Dacia's coat open and shoved the knitted sweater up. Underneath, blood had soaked Dacia's shirt a few inches below her clavicle.

"Milton!" She yelled at the shocked man still kneeling beside Dacia, holding onto her arm. "Take off your shirt and your belt. Now!"

Milton merely blinked—slow movements of his eyelids that looked eerie.

"Milton, she'll die if we don't put pressure on this wound!" Aurelia had the heel of her hand pressed against it. "Come on. Please, Milton, snap out of it."

As if he'd been hit over the head, Milton finally reacted. "Dacia." He groaned and tore off his jacket. Yanking his shirt off too, he ripped off a sleeve and became the old Milton, the one who knew what Aurelia needed from him. He gave her the fabric, and she bunched it up and pressed it against Dacia's wound, which made the girl that was in every respect Aurelia's sister moan. She had life in her. She could feel pain.

"Here. My belt." Milton held it out to Aurelia, but she shook her head. "No. I can't let go. She's lost a lot of blood already. We have to try to roll her and—"

"We'll help." Blue was suddenly at Dacia's head. "Let me see if she has an exit wound." She pushed her hands in under Dacia's shoulder from above. "And she does. Good. But we'll need your other sleeve, Milton."

He was already tearing it off, giving it to Blue, who squeezed it into a ball and pushed it under Dacia. "There. Let's roll her gently onto her good shoulder and wrap the belt around her. We can't tighten it so much she can't breathe, but enough to keep her from hemorrhaging."

Everyone worked together when Tom joined them, throwing himself to the ground. Aurelia's brain finally caught on to the silence. "The agents?" She didn't look up but needed to know.

"Dead." Blue's voice was noncommittal. "There'll be more. I'll help carry Dacia, but when the next wave comes, I'll have to deal with them."

Aurelia's chest constricted, but if she let the pain of everything happening right now surface, she wouldn't be able to function. She pulled at the belt as much as she dared, praying it would keep the fabric in place. As soon as she finished, they buttoned the coat around Dacia to keep her warm. Carefully, they lifted her, Milton with his arms under her back and Blue's under Dacia's hips and the crease of her knees. Aurelia steadied her neck, and Tom was left to monitor the situation that could develop behind them at any given moment.

It was difficult to walk three people in a straight line without anyone tripping on the uneven ground. Aurelia held her arm hooked under Dacia's head and kept her gun in the other. If anyone tried something stupid, she intended to blast them to hell. Her mind was whirling, thoughts swimming in the back of it, trying to make their way to front and center, but she refused to let them. She could think of nothing but one step at a time to get to the trees and be in Sandslot. Keeping her eyes on the ground before them, trying to estimate how long they had left, she counted her steps. Two steps for half a yard, maybe? That would mean a hundred steps. They could do that. A hundred steps for Dacia. Yes. They could.

As they approached the forest beyond the dead man's zone, Aurelia saw someone move among the tree trunks and then come running toward them. "Who's injured?" a female voice called out. Mac.

"Dacia," Milton said starkly. "She's been shot."

"Goddamn it." Mac appeared at their side. "You have only fifteen more yards. Get her in among the trees and over to the clearing farther in. We have everyone sitting there, and two Tallawens have gone to find help."

"We better hurry. I see people running from Klowdyn." Tom sounded calm, but he was nudging them, walking backward.

"Mac. Take her head." Aurelia carefully shifted her grip of Dacia's head and let Mac take over. "Keep going." She turned around, her gun ready. Black figures were racing toward them, and there were many.

"Good. Take her legs. Like that," Blue said behind Aurelia. Someone else must have taken over for her as well. The next second, Blue was at Aurelia's other side, her gun trained on the shadows.

"Ground's more even here," Aurelia said. "Keep walking backward. We don't have far to go to reach the border."

"This is my responsibility." Blue's voice was empty of all emotions. "Run, Aurelia. You too, Tom. I have this."

"Those are your men and women." It hurt to say the words, but Aurelia pushed through the pain. "You can't be expected to keep killing your own."

"I won't, if I can help it, but they're not mine. Not anymore. Not since I woke up in the camp not knowing anything but my name."

Aurelia refused to listen. "I'm not running."

"Me either." Tom lowered his voice. "They're about forty yards away."

"You tell me, Blue. If we turn, all three of us, and run, what will they do? Shoot us in the back?" Aurelia asked.

"Not if I trained them, but I don't know that." A faint tremor pervaded Blue's voice. "I'm going to walk toward them and draw their fire. When they're close enough to recognize me, they'll stop firing."

"They'll have hit you long before then," Tom said calmly.

Aurelia heard a faint pop, and then a projectile passed a few yards to her left. "Fire." She began shooting at the approaching agents, aiming for center mass, hating what they stood for, what they represented. So, this was who Blue was—a bounty-hunter leader. A damn colonel. Yet here was also the other Blue, the one she had trusted, shooting at her own, walking shoulder to shoulder with her and Tom, protecting the Tallawens and the people they'd managed to get across the border tonight. She couldn't process the dilemma.

Some figures in front of them fell, others advancing with frightening speed. Aurelia had to reload and fumbled with her clip. Just as she slammed it into place, she cried out as arms grabbed her from behind. She heard Blue and Tom give startled cries as well, and then they were pulled in among the trees.

At first, Aurelia thought the Tallawens had come out from the woods to grab them, but then she realized that she felt a weapon's harness against her back.

"You're on Sandslot territory. Continue farther in," a brusque male voice said in her ear. He let go of her, and she fell against a trunk, nearly dropping her weapon.

Suddenly the dead man's zone was lit up by strong flashlights that illuminated the agents still standing as well as at least six of them that were down, but they all seemed to be moving as they writhed in pain. Aurelia could only cling to the trunk and stare.

"You are firing ammunition that has crossed the border and entered Sandslot," a male voice boomed over a megaphone. "No military forces are allowed to set foot in the dead man's zone. Your action tonight is a clear violation and an act of war that will be reported to the United Assembly as an international incident. Turn back."

"We have injured!" a female voice called out.

"Either you take them back with you, or you leave them for us to tend to. We will, however, not enter the zone until you have vacated it."

Aurelia watched how the agents managed to take some of the more ambulatory ones with them as they retreated. Two still lay on the ground. The man who had grabbed her earlier gave his subordinates orders to retrieve them as soon as the Klowdynian agents reached the other end of the zone.

"Come, Aurelia," Blue said. "We need to go check on Dacia."

Sobbing now, Aurelia began running toward where she saw lights farther into the woods. As they reached the clearing where the Tallawens and the dissidents sat huddled together, she also saw Mac in the midst of soldiers, with what looked like medical staff, working on Dacia. Milton slumped against a tree, holding his head. Aurelia hurried over to him. "Milton."

"You're here? So many shots were fired." Milton looked up at her, his face chalk white.

"Help arrived. The agents retreated."

"Except for her." Milton looked up at Blue, who stood to the side, her shoulders squared, and her chin raised. She looked like she was staring at a firing squad.

"Yes. Except for her." Aurelia sat down next to Milton and took his arm. "What are they saying about Dacia?" She was afraid to ask.

"Not much. From what I gathered, the soldiers and the medics were already on their way here when our people started for help. They brought them really fast, which is good, right?" He rested his head against the top of hers.

"It is very good." Aurelia sighed. "You love her, don't you?"

Milton shuddered. "It's always been Dacia."

Aurelia could easily envision the little boy Milton had been when she first got to know him at Jeters. He had always been dirty, always ready to defend Dacia and her. But as Aurelia had always been like his sister, Dacia had been more.

"You know what she told me before we left camp?" Milton asked quietly.

"What?"

"She said that we might just get a bit of boring, normal life in Sandslot after all." Milton broke into tears and sobbed helplessly. Wrapping her arms around him, Aurelia wanted to promise him that they would, that they'd all live long, utterly dull lives in Sandslot together like they'd dreamed when they were prisoners at Jeters.

"Milton? Aurelia?" Mac stood before them, and Milton stood so fast, Aurelia fell to the side. She jumped up and took his hand.

"Yes?" Milton asked huskily and wiped at his eyes.

"Dacia is conscious. She's not out of the woods, but the medics had some amazing field dressings and managed to stop the bleeding for now. We have to move out fast though, because we have no way of knowing what internal damage she has. She needs a hospital."

"How far is the nearest one?" Aurelia asked, her heart thundering.

"The major said about half an hour by helicopter. He's already requested one, and they're going to carry her to a place where it can land. You can come along, Milton, but that's it. The rest of us will be put on the busses we've heard about." Mac rubbed at her eyes. "I admit I'm going to like not having to ride a bike or walk."

Milton hugged Aurelia hard. "I'll get word to you guys as soon as I know something. I have to go with her."

"Of course you do." Aurelia walked with him to the stretcher where Dacia lay strapped in. She looked up at them with hazy eyes. Clearly the medics had given her something for the pain.

"Hey. Milton's going with you." Aurelia bent and kissed Dacia's forehead. "I'll see you as soon as I'm allowed to, okay?"

"Okay," Dacia whispered.

"Love you." Aurelia fought back tears but failed miserably.

"Love you too..." Dacia's eyes closed, but the medics assured them she was just exhausted.

Aurelia stood, hugging herself, as Dacia was carried away and Milton received a blanket around his shoulders as he walked next to her stretcher.

"Aurelia?" Blue's voice made Aurelia pivot. "I'm glad Dacia has a chance."

"If you hadn't fired on your own people, they'd have gotten all of us." Aurelia knew she sounded too polite.

"I hear you're being bussed to their closest refugee facility." Blue shoved her hands into her pockets, a gesture Aurelia hadn't seen her make for quite a while. Gone were the blinding smile and the relaxed posture Blue had developed as she became one of the Tallawens.

"Wait," Aurelia said, suddenly alarmed. "What do you mean *we're* getting bussed?" She stepped closer. "What about you?"

"I have to go back. I've betrayed my country and the oath I took. I have to return and face a court martial."

"Return? Are you insane? They'll sentence you to life, or they can even decide to give you the death penalty! They'll accuse you of treason." She was shaking now, from the cold and from all the conflicted emotions, but mostly at the fear of not being able to stop Blue.

"Nothing left for me here now." Blue gazed at Aurelia as if for the last time, and her expression broke through to all the jumbled emotions Aurelia had locked up in the back of her mind.

"When? When did your memory come back?" Aurelia couldn't fathom how Blue had managed to live a lie like this.

"The morning after we made love." Blue pulled her hands out of her pockets and appeared not to know what she should do with them.

"Before you got Lorna and the kids out?" Aurelia gasped.

"Yes."

"And yet...how did you...I mean..." Aurelia was at a loss for words. "Why didn't you report us all? That was why you were with us to begin with? Undercover?"

"Yes. I came up with the plan, in fact." Blue pressed a hand to her stomach.

"Blue?" Blue began to gasp for air now, pressing both fists against her abdomen. "Oh, God. Are you injured?" Had Blue taken a bullet for them after all? Rushing forward, she caught Blue just as she dropped to her knees.

CHAPTER TWENTY-THREE

Blue couldn't breathe. Her world was crumbling around her, and panic rose within her like acid bile. Pine needles pricked her palm, and small pebbles stung her knees as she leaned forward on her hands. Then arms wrapped around her, pulling her off the emotional ledge that threatened to hurl her into the abyss.

"Blue!" Aurelia sobbed. "Please tell me. Are you injured? What can I do?"

Blue had never begged for anything, but she did now. "Don't let go of me. Please, don't…"

Aurelia had run her hands over Blue's body, and now she pulled her right hand back, looking at it. "Whether you know it or not, you've been hit. I-I don't think it's bad, but there's blood."

"I don't think it's mine. It must be Dacia's." Blue had no sense of being physically injured. She'd been shot before, when helping curb riots as a private.

Aurelia pushed her fingers to a spot at Blue's hip, and the pain made her cry out.

"That's not from Dacia." Pulling Blue into her arms, Aurelia called, "We need a medic!"

"Well, I haven't left yet." Mac's voice came from a distance, and then she was there, hovering above Blue and Aurelia. "What have you gotten yourself into now, Blue?"

"I lied. I was afraid you'd all fail without me, so I lied." Blue's tongue felt swollen and uncooperative. "I knew who I was, what my life's been about and what my job entails, and all I could think was to help you stay off the Klowdynian government's radar to keep your refugees safe. They're not criminals, or terrorists, and I never realized that until I became a Tallawen."

"Once a Tallawen, always a Tallawen in my book," Mac said and began cutting into Blue's pants. "Ah, there we go. Not too bad, but you'll need a few stitches." Mac raised her hand and waved one of the Sandslot medics over. "Hey, you got any sutures in that pack? Preferably something to numb this as well?"

Blue knew they were always low on lidocaine in the camp, not to mention regular anesthesia. Now, after feeling them stick her a few times, they cleaned her wound where the bullet had grazed her within minutes, and it didn't hurt at all. "Thank you," Blue said quietly.

"Hey, you're welcome. You did something that had to take a lot of guts, not to mention at great personal cost to everything you were brought up to believe and how you were trained. We owe you, Blue." Mac's voice broke, and she wiped at her weathered cheeks. "I'm just an old fool, so don't mind me. And you shouldn't put any weight on that leg until a doctor clears you. I don't want you to rip any of the stitches." She waved over some other Sandslot soldiers, who came running with a stretcher. "This woman is a hero. Treat her accordingly," Mac said starkly.

"We will. No worries."

Blue found herself being lifted onto the stretcher as if she were feather-light. Aurelia remained by her side, and for some unfathomable reason, she didn't let go of Blue's hand. "This is important," Aurelia said to the soldiers flanking them. "This is Colonel Blue AnRaine of the BHU. She's defecting just as much as any of our other refugees. Ask for asylum, Blue." She spoke the last words with urgency. Blue understood. If she didn't do this formally, she might end up in prison on spy charges.

"I hereby ask for asylum in the sovereign state of Sandslot," she managed to say, and then her voice weakened again. Blue closed her eyes. Aurelia had taken a stance, paving the way for Blue to find a way to live in Sandslot. That didn't mean she still held a place in Aurelia's heart. Just because Aurelia did the decent thing now, Blue found no evidence that Aurelia had forgiven her on a personal level. She doubted the love and trust that had grown between them could be restored. Blue had lied too much. Still, she clung to Aurelia's hand and the miniscule chance that all was not lost. Most important, all the people they'd brought over were safe, together with the Tallawen operatives. Dacia had to pull through. Milton and Aurelia would be crushed if she didn't, and Blue had also come to really like the feisty young woman.

When they reached two large busses, they helped Blue on board through the back door. She was placed on the five back seats and could stretch out. Blue could hardly believe that a Sandslot soldier brought her pillows and blankets. The kindness and acceptance from the Sandslot people staggered her. "Thank you," she said and turned her face away so nobody could see her tears.

Aurelia seemed to understand and squeezed in on her knees by the seats. "You're going to be all right." She spoke quietly into Blue's ear. "You've already taken a stance against the oppressive dictatorship by helping save us all, on several occasions. All you have to do is brief the Sandslot authorities now that we have records and multiple witnesses that heard you ask for asylum."

"Will I be sent somewhere else?" Blue whispered.

"I have no idea. If they intend to do so, I'll fight it. You're in no state to be whisked away somewhere without people you know around you. Mac's right. You did something that went against your grain as a soldier. I can only imagine having to act like that against my people."

"No comparison. The Tallawens are on the right side, with their moral compasses on point. My people are…were good, loyal Klowdynian soldiers, but several in other units weren't… right. BHU operatives trained most of them, and I could always tell, quite easily, which ones would overstep, cause problems, or even hurt someone." Blue's voice began to falter. "But I didn't do anything, not anything *real*, to stop them. To report them."

"Shh. Save your strength. I'll be right here next to you, on the seat in front of you." Aurelia patted the seat right in front. "Just rest."

Blue was certain her agitated state would make sleep impossible, but she was also exhausted and hurt all over. "All right." She rolled onto her good hip and pulled the blanket closer around her. She could see Aurelia from behind, and her presence soothed her nerves somewhat.

And then she slept.

Aurelia regarded the facility for refugees they'd been taken to. She had heard stories about them, which had reached the Tallawens via channels that kept in contact with them after their escape. Now, Aurelia had to settle for how many they'd gotten across the border at once. She also hoped the Tallawens that had left for the main camp made it in time. If the satellite camp had been hard to find in the mountains, the base camp was impossible to penetrate and so much more well stocked. Deeply buried in caves in a mountain, you had to not only know exactly how to find the entrance, but then you had to have the right knowledge to get past their safety system.

"It looks clean, if a bit like a factory." Mac had joined Aurelia on the seat across the aisle from her. "They have a smaller operating room, or so I hear."

"You can reexamine Blue there?" Aurelia swallowed against new tears that threatened to start running again.

"I sure can, but I also know, after pumping the medics for information, that they have an entire operating team on standby. Blue will be taken care of. And what's more, had Dacia's life been jeopardized, they could have performed emergency procedures on her. So, by that logic, if we don't find her or Milton inside, that's good news. That means she was stable enough to go by helicopter to a major hospital."

Aurelia understood that Mac was trying to cheer her up. "Thanks, my friend." The news did help her regain some of her strength. They might be on Sandslot territory, but she was still the Tallawen leader, the one ultimately responsible for all their actions over the years.

As the bus halted by a cordoned-off area, more soldiers met them, but unlike the Klowdynians, these looked friendly enough. A tall woman stepped aboard the bus and spoke quietly to the bus driver, who indicated with his thumb toward the back. The female soldier, who, judging from her insignia, turned out to be a major, came down the aisle and scrutinized the Tallawens and refugees sitting very quietly in their seats. She stopped by Mac and raised a questioning eyebrow. "Aurelia?"

Mac shook her head and pointed behind the major. "Nope."

The woman turned around and stared in disbelief at Aurelia. "You're the Tallawen leader?"

"I am, yes. Aurelia DeCallum." Aurelia stood and extended her hand, well aware that she was dirty and bloody after helping first Dacia and then Blue.

"Major Sarah Moyar." The major shook Aurelia's hand, clearly not bothered that it wasn't clean. "Welcome to Sandslot. Your reputation precedes you."

"I can only imagine." Shrugging and feeling strangely self-conscious, Aurelia wondered if it was a prerequisite for all soldiers, female or male, to be so damn tall. "I'm happy to answer any questions you may have, but I also have a wounded woman here." Aurelia pointed to Blue, who hadn't woken up yet, which was worrisome. "She's been treated in the field after being grazed by a bullet, but if your people could tend to her?"

"I'm sure you're used to rougher treatment where you come from, but we don't interrogate refugees before they're tended to by our medical staff, fed, and had a good night's sleep." Smiling now, Major Moyar waved at some of her people to step inside. "Get a stretcher for…what's her name?"

"Colonel Blue AnRaine, BHU." Aurelia could see the major tense. "She's been instrumental in our escape and is seeking asylum." As soon as she uttered the magic word on Blue's behalf, Moyar's demeanor changed from tension to the realization of what this could do for her career in two seconds flat. Aurelia didn't care, as long as they took good care of Blue.

Moyar turned to the two men carrying a stretcher behind her. "Take this woman to the infirmary. She's to be kept in isolation, but mainly for her protection. Nobody talks to her but me or Ms. DeCallum here." She indicated Aurelia.

"Yes, ma'am." The men stepped around their commanding officer and began moving Blue onto the stretcher. She stirred and moaned but didn't open her eyes. Aurelia wanted to elbow her way over to her and make sure she was all right, but these people had the resources to take care of her, while she didn't.

After everyone had exited the bus, the families stood huddled together and looked up at the tall, modern building. Aurelia did too and knew that outside of the Klowdynian capital, there were no structures like this in Klowdyn.

"All right." Moyar waved them over. "Come with me. We'll get you sorted once we're inside."

Aurelia stepped through the doors and found herself in a surprisingly welcoming environment. As much as the outside of this building looked like some modern factory, the foyer had a reception area, wooden panels, a blue carpet, and fabric-covered ceiling lights. Behind the counter stood two civilian women stacking small binders.

"If all adults would take a binder each, that'd be great." Moyar pointed at them. "There are sections in the binders meant for children as well."

"Are they interview forms?" Martha asked from where she stood right behind Aurelia.

"Forms? No, no. These are information binders for your convenience, ma'am." Moyar came over and handed Martha and Ellis a binder each. "They'll help you find out most things on your own, both about this building, what you can expect during your time here, and some about Sandslot as a country. Most Klowdynians who manage to cross the border have a very skewed image of our country, even if they hope it's better than where they came from."

"Does it say anything about ice cream?" a small voice asked Aurelia. A little girl, Aurelia thought her name was Jade, pointed at her mother's binder. "Blue said we would have ice cream in Sandslot." Jade then turned to the major. "And is it true I don't have to hide in a box in the basement when someone comes for a visit?"

Major Moyar swallowed spasmodically as she crouched in front of the girl. "I can promise that you don't have to hide here. And we have lots of ice cream in Sandslot, in lots of different flavors."

Jade nodded thoughtfully. "Then, may my family and I stay, please?"

"That's not up to the major, darling," Jade's mother said.

"Actually, when it comes to families with children, it's a quite easy process," Moyar said after clearing her throat. "After the relationship between the family members is investigated, we consider Klowdyn's treatment of families a crime against the International Children's Act, which makes for a blanket approval for citizenship. You can read more about it on page—"

"Page twelve, mom," Jade's older sister said. "I found it on page twelve." She was clutching her father's binder.

"Clever girl," Moyar said and then turned to Aurelia. "Let me show you to your quarters, Ms. DeCallum—"

"Aurelia, please."

"All right. I'm Sarah. Once you've had a chance to clean up and eat, you can either get some sleep, or I can take you to your friend the colonel."

Aurelia pressed a hand to her stomach. "Sounds good." She couldn't quite grasp that she didn't have to fight them to be allowed to sit with Blue. Still, a lot of things could go wrong, which she was fully prepared for. "When will I hear about my operatives that were helicoptered to a hospital?"

Sarah motioned for Aurelia and the Maydorian family to follow her. "I'll take you to the first floor in the north wing. It's the closest to the infirmary." She eyed the children. "Does a physician need to see them tonight?"

"No, thank you, Major," Lorna said. "It's been a long day for them. We've been traveling for eighteen hours straight."

"All rooms have telephones. Don't hesitate to call the switchboard if you need help. You'll find all the information in the binder." Sarah stopped at the first door in a long corridor. "This is your room, Aurelia. I'll be back in an hour to take you to the infirmary, if that's all right?"

Aurelia nodded. "Thank you. You've been very kind, and you've made this part of our escape so much easier than we ever could have dreamed of."

"Not the first time I've heard that, but it's good to know." Sarah kept walking, the Maydorians in tow.

Aurelia's room was so unlike her cordoned-off area with a cot in the cave dormitory, it was ridiculous. Two single beds stood against one wall, and opposite them was a small table and two chairs. A door caught her interest, and she carefully felt the door handle. It was unlocked, and she opened it a crack and peered inside. It was dark, and after fumbling on the wall to the left, she found a light switch. And stared. White tiles covered the walls, a bathtub sat to the right, and on the other side were a toilet and a sink with a mirror above it. Aurelia had thought she would have to read the binder to find the closest latrine, but this was clearly her bathroom for as long as she stayed in this room. As if her bladder had caught up with her with a vengeance, she used the toilet and flushed it afterward. She couldn't remember the last time she'd had access to a modern bathroom. The boarding school had, of course, had all the comforts that way, but after their escape, they had been used to roughing it.

Aurelia was dying to fill the tub and soak for a very long time but opted to pull the curtain that hung on a ring in the ceiling and use the shower instead. She nearly scalded herself before she managed to set the water to warm rather than boiling. Being used to lukewarm showers—at best—she shivered from the pleasure of a warm one. When she stepped out of the tub, she swept one of the white terrycloth bath sheets around her and realized she couldn't put on her dirty clothes again. Not sure what to do, she then figured that the binder might contain something about this subject. She opened it and soon found a section about clothes. Apparently, she would find what she needed in the closet by the door.

Opening the closet, she saw it was filled with clothes, linens, towels, toilet paper, toiletries, and so on. The shelves holding the clothes were marked with gender and sizes, and she pulled out a pair of briefs, socks, a T-shirt, a cardigan, and a pair of soft pants that resembled what she used to sleep in, in the cave. They were all off-white, which made them look like pajamas, but they were clean and appeared new. After pulling them on, she folded up the cardigan sleeves and then spotted several pairs of slippers on the bottom shelf. Finding her size was easy, so she put them on and regarded herself in the mirror. Unwinding the towel she had wrapped around her hair, she brushed it out and looked in the toiletry shelf for some hair ties. After putting her damp hair in a ponytail, she checked the binder and read about the food dispensers farther down the hallway. As she walked outside, she saw several of the Tallawen and the refugees milling about, some even staggering from sheer fatigue, but also wanting something to eat.

When it was Aurelia's turn at the dispensers, she had made up her mind what she wanted to eat. That decision was easy. Anything, as long as it wasn't a sandwich.

CHAPTER TWENTY-FOUR

Blue had only vague memories of being treated a second time. When she stirred, she found herself in a bed, and after a quick glance around the room, she surmised it was a hospital room. Or maybe an infirmary, with light-gray walls, a white ceiling, and one wall that boasted white cabinets. The bed was quite comfortable, but she still ached everywhere, and her hip was throbbing.

"I turn my back for two seconds, and you're awake. Go figure."

Aurelia's voice made Blue snap her head to the right and stare toward the door. There she was, not smiling exactly, but not looking furious either. Or as if she was about to start screaming at Blue again.

"Are you in pain?" Aurelia set down two mugs on the nightstand next to the bed.

"Not too bad." Blue attempted to sit up but found herself annoyingly weak.

"Liar." Reaching under the head of the bed, Aurelia pulled at something and tugged it toward her, bringing Blue into a half-sitting position. "That okay?"

"Yes. Thank you." Blue had a strange feeling of déjà vu, or not so strange, as it really had been only a few weeks since she'd been injured and Aurelia had hovered over her in the Tallawen cave. "And here we are again."

"What?" Aurelia frowned but then nodded. "Yes, here we are. This time, at least, your head's intact."

Blue wanted to say something but didn't even know where to begin. She glanced at the second mug. "That for me?"

"Yes. Yes, of course." Aurelia gave Blue the mug. "I asked the nurse if I could try to rouse you with coffee since you've slept for twelve hours, if you count from when you fell asleep on the bus."

Twelve hours? It didn't seem possible. Blue remembered hardly anything from the bus ride, which meant it was true. She sipped the coffee. "Wow."

"Right? They have big pots in the dayroom with real coffee, and when they're empty, they make a new pot. Just like that." Aurelia snapped her fingers. "It's even tons better than what we had stashed away in the cave."

"It's amazing." Blue sipped the hot coffee and felt it permeate her entire system. After a few minutes of silence between them, she couldn't stall any longer. "How is it I'm not under arrest, or if I am, why am I not in handcuffs or in a guarded ward?"

"Because I told them exactly who you are and that you're seeking asylum. They're pretty psyched about you." Aurelia pointed at the side of the bed, even if a visitor's chair sat right next to her. "May I?"

"Sure." Blue's breath caught as Aurelia eased down close to her. She wore off-white clothes, and her hair flowed around her like black water. Whatever Aurelia had washed it with was clearly a much better product than the cheap soaps the Tallawen used in their showers. The waist-long hair looked like a shiny entity with a life of its own. "They know my rank?"

"Yes. I saw no reason to lie, and I was right. You'll meet Major Sarah Moyar and her commanding officer later today, and of course you can take any approach to their questions you deem fit, but they will have lots of them, judging from everything they asked me this morning."

"They let you get some sleep before that, I hope." Blue scanned Aurelia's face and saw the blue circles under her eyes.

"I was in here with you most of the night," Aurelia said and plucked at the blanket. "Once you got back from having your wound and some other cuts and bruises checked, I cleaned up and ate. They were nice and brought me a cot so I could sleep some, but I was so…s-so worried…" Aurelia didn't look up, but Blue could see large tears dislodge from her eyelashes and splash down on her hands that were still busy with the pattern on the blanket.

"I'm sorry I worried you," Blue whispered and dared to take one of Aurelia's hands in hers. "I'm sorry I lied to you, but I swear, it was only the last few days, just before I left for Cerdynia to fetch Lorna and the kids. Before then, I had no idea who I was."

"You should have told me." Aurelia lifted her gaze, and a fire burned in the center of her black eyes. "You know that, right?"

"I do. I mean, I do now. I can try to explain my decision not to, but I don't have a good excuse." Blue clung to Aurelia's hand, grateful she didn't yank it free.

"Then explain why you lied by omission." Aurelia shifted their grip of each other and laced their fingers together.

"Pure selfishness, to be brutally honest." Blue pushed herself farther up against the head of the bed with her free hand. Her movement didn't create much more distance between them, but she needed a few extra inches for some reason. "I was afraid of losing you. The night before, we'd made love, we'd talked about feelings, and we'd survived together and…I'd never been happier. Never." Blue tried to read Aurelia's expression, but now those black eyes were opaque and didn't give anything away.

"Go on," Aurelia said softly.

"I woke up, and it was as if my memory had been there all along. My entire life was simply back. I remembered my father, my upbringing, of feeling less-than all my life because I wasn't the son my father anticipated. I pushed myself so hard from a young age to be what he wanted, what he needed me to be, and that's why I became a soldier like him, a BHU officer, always struggling to be the best at whatever I did. I was so set on succeeding on every mission, I nearly got myself killed after I ordered several of my subordinates to make the assault look credible and authentic. When they were telling me it was enough, I became my father," Blue said, her voice nearly betraying her at the memory.

"I roared at them. I told them that if they couldn't follow orders, I'd lower their marks in their next evaluation. That did the trick. I remember one of them picking up a rock, and then I must've blacked out. I'm not sure if my unit and I misjudged when we estimated your return, or if any of my people came back to check on me."

Blue pulled free and covered her face with both her hands. "I was supposed to infiltrate one of your camps and get as much information about the leadership among the Tallawen as I could. Instead, I found all the information about you that not a single person in the Klowdynian military or law enforcement has ever been taught. I learned how you operate, how you risk your lives for others, how you don't take any money, and how incredibly brave and intelligent you are. It starts with you and filters down through people like Dacia and Mil—" Blue flinched. "Dacia? What happened to Dacia? Is she…?"

Aurelia took Blue's hand again, this time squeezing it firmly. "Dacia is going to make it, but she has a long recovery ahead of her. Fortunately, Milton isn't leaving her side, and he keeps ringing this facility to give us updates. No doubt he'll start driving her crazy as she gets better."

"He loves her." Blue was certain of it.

"I know. He always has. This last turn of events might just prove to Dacia that he's never going to leave her and that she can allow herself some happiness." Aurelia bit her lower lip and sucked it in between her teeth for a moment. "Can I?"

"What?" Blue looked at Aurelia in confusion. "Can you what?"

"Will I be able to allow myself some happiness?"

Her heart beating wildly now, Blue took Aurelia's free hand and tugged her gently toward her. "Are you asking me if I'll betray you again? If you are, the answer is never, but I'm not delusional. I realize you have very few reasons to trust me."

"I don't trust easily, but I did eventually put faith in you to such a degree that I risked my own life and those of all the Tallawens in the camp, not to mention the refugees." Sighing, Aurelia leaned forward and pressed her forehead to Blue's. "And you came through for us."

Blue placed a hand at the back of Aurelia's neck and felt the tension there. "I hated lying to you, and on my way back from Cerdynia, I had vowed to tell you everything up front, even if it meant losing you. I just wanted the chance to see you through across the border. When we were attacked, I thought if the BHU crews recognized me, I'd be able to stall them, which I did. And even if I was certain I'd lose you, it still brought me hope that you'd be back in your own country. I miscalculated how many BHU operatives were in those woods."

Aurelia pulled back enough to meet Blue's eyes. "A lot. And you shot several of them. Even after realizing who you were, your former duties, and your ultimate mission…was that to bring me in, once you'd gathered your intel?"

"Yes. You, Dacia, Milton, Mac, and Tom. I didn't know any name but yours before I went undercover. Everyone in the BHU has heard of Aurelia, the Tallawen leader, but very little about the command structure and strategies among you." Blue sat up and grimaced. "And then I knew my own name, and that was it. I had learned about the Tallawen, the camp, and met so many of the Tallawen without any prejudice or preconceived ideas."

"And then we went on our mission." Aurelia raised her right hand and ran it across Blue's forehead. "We saved each other a few times. We slept very close together. We risked our lives together several times."

"We did." Blue closed her eyes briefly. "And I'd do it again, in a heartbeat."

Aurelia studied her gently. "I realize that. I got to know the real you. That's how I feel, at least. Unfiltered. You're protective, loyal, and very good at your job, obviously."

"And now I'm a refugee, much like the ones you've helped over the years."

Aurelia nodded. "Yes. And so am I. They have just as many questions for me, as the Tallawen leader, I think, as they'll have for you."

"Do they know your history yet? I mean, that you were abducted as a little girl?"

"No. I'm not sure how common my name is. At least Major Moyar hasn't said anything. After all, I have a Klowdynian accent after all these years."

Blue nudged Aurelia, silently asking her to move, and swung her legs over the side of the bed. She was a bit light-headed, but the room soon righted itself as she found her bearings. She put her arm around Aurelia and held her close. "We'll find someone who knows about what happened to your family."

"I like how you say 'we.'" Aurelia rested her head against Blue's shoulder. "It's overwhelming to think about it. I mean, Sandslot is three times as big as Klowdyn."

"No matter how long it takes," Blue said. "And that's an absolute promise."

"That goes for both of us, Blue. We'll do this together. Don't forget that." Throwing her arms around Blue's neck, Aurelia clung to her, and Blue swore to never let this woman down again if she could help it. No more lies. No looking back.

"Okay," Blue whispered.

"Okay, what?" Aurelia pressed her lips against Blue's neck.

"What you just said." Blue tipped Aurelia's head back and gazed into the depths of her black eyes. "I won't forget."

EPILOGUE

Aurelia gripped Blue's hand so hard she knew it must hurt, but it was the only thing grounding her at the sight of the house. They were standing on a street in a well-to-do residential area in the outskirts of Endinslot, the capital of Sandslot. Having learned the address through the federal agents that had interviewed them, Aurelia now stared at an image that had followed her since she was four. This was her house. At least it used to be her house.

"This it?" Blue asked and put an arm around Aurelia. "God, you're as white as a wraith."

"I used to live here." Aurelia drew a trembling breath. "I was very little, but I remember so much from just looking at it."

"Take your time." Blue pulled Aurelia with her and pointed at the green mailbox. "Recognize the name?"

"Lisette DeCallum." Snapping her head up to meet Blue's gaze, she began to tremble. "My surname. Remember?"

"I remember." Blue stroked her back. "Any idea how you might be related?"

"Lisette? No. I was only four. If this is a relative, I probably didn't know her first name. I may have called her auntie or nana. I have no idea."

"Want to come back later or—"

"No!" Aurelia tugged Blue's hand. They walked up the gravel path lined with rose bushes, where one single rose clung to a twig. "Look." Aurelia stopped and studied the pink, slightly frazzled flower. "It's still alive, among all the thorns."

"Oh, Aurelia." Blue stroked the back of Aurelia's hand with her thumb. "Just like you among the enemies that took you."

They continued along the path until they reached the front door. Aurelia didn't recognize everything, but more than twenty years had passed, and that was a long time. These thoughts made her nauseous, but she raised her hand and rang the doorbell.

After several heartbreaking moments, the dark wooden door opened and revealed an elegant, gray-haired woman in her fifties. "Yes? Can I help you?" Her face wasn't familiar, but her voice was. Aurelia merely stood there, gasping for air. "Are you all right, dear?" the woman asked.

"Are you Lisette DeCallum?" Blue asked politely.

"I am. And you are?" The woman folded her arms over her chest as she scrutinized Aurelia and Blue carefully, but then focused on Aurelia, who just stared at the woman.

"My name's Blue AnRaine." Blue spoke distinctly. "This is Aurelia DeCallum. She's looking for information about her parents. She grew up in this house."

"What? Aurelia?" Lisette gripped the doorpost, and her blanched knuckles showed how hard she clutched it. "What nonsense is this?" Her words would have been harsh if she hadn't sounded so breathless…and hopeful.

"You used to sing to me." Aurelia finally found her voice. "You sang lullabies."

Lisette gasped. "I did." She stepped out on the deck that ran the entire length of the house. "I babysat a lot."

"Your hair. It was red." Aurelia could picture it, the same curly texture she remembered. "I used to push my fingers into your long curls."

"Yes…you did. You loved giving me new hairdos all the time."

"You didn't let me cut it though." They were talking about insignificant things, but they felt important. Personal. Like reclaiming a piece of her childhood. Aurelia glanced into the hallway behind Lisette, and even if she couldn't remember the entire layout of the house, she could tell the staircase leading up to the next floor had the same ornate railing.

"You're really Aurelia?" Lisette stepped closer and cautiously took Aurelia by the shoulders. Squinting, she gazed into Aurelia's eyes and then appeared to examine all her features at once. "Yes. You have my big brother's eyes. Oh, God." Tears streamed down Lisette's cheeks.

"Where are they?" Aurelia asked, her heart sinking in fear of the answer. She took Blue's hand again. "Please."

Lisette shook her head and wiped at her tears. "I don't know, my girl. But, please, come in. We have so much to talk about."

Aurelia hesitated, her emotions so raw she was afraid to step into her childhood home. "What do you mean, you don't know?" At least Lisette hadn't said they were dead.

Lisette led them into a large, bright kitchen, where yellow wallpaper and pine cabinets made it look sunny. "Have a seat." She pointed at the round kitchen table. "I'll put some coffee on." Lisette began answering Aurelia's question while busying herself with the coffee machine. "Your parents went underground after the Klowdynians almost assassinated your father. We kept looking for you in their place but didn't find a trace of you, and neither did the people we paid to look in Klowdyn."

Aurelia began to tremble. Assassinated? It had always been her greatest fear.

"Does Aurelia have any other relatives than you, Ms. DeCallum?" Blue asked and placed her arm around Aurelia's back.

"Yes, of course. My mother, Bethany, is still alive. She lives not far from here." Lisette sat down at the kitchen table as well. "You have aunts, uncles, and cousins on both sides. Your parents had many friends who will be thrilled to find out you've come home. Not to mention that your kidnapping case was quite well-known at the time." Lisette looked startled. "You can't talk to the press until we try to contact your parents."

Aurelia blinked. "What? But you said you don't know where they are."

Lisette took Aurelia's hand, blinking at new tears. "I'm an idiot. I should have explained better. I have no idea where your parents are, but we do have a way of contacting them. We've used it only four or five times since they left, as it's dangerous for them, but now everything's changed."

Yes. Everything had changed. Aurelia rested her head against Blue's shoulder, closing her eyes briefly. "I can't believe I'm here. In this house. With you. With my Aunt Lisette."

Blue squeezed her gently. "But you are. You're home."

"And you had to leave your home. Because of me." Aurelia cupped Blue's cheek.

"There was nothing left for me there, and the way I see it, wherever you are, Aurelia, that's my home. Whether it's under a tarp in the woods, in a cave, or in a nice house like this one."

"Sounds like you've found a good one there," Lisette said kindly. "I'll go get us some coffee, and in the meantime…" She opened a drawer and pulled out a writing pad and a pen. "I think you should write your parents a note. I'll make sure it's sent later today."

Aurelia took the pen in her hand and opened the pad to an unused page. Flipping her hair back over her shoulders, she began to write.

❖

Glancing in the mirror as she passed it, something she normally didn't bother with, Guinevere saw that her long, formerly jet-black hair had fallen out of the low bun she automatically formed it into every morning. As she was going to work in the vegetable garden, she reached for some extra hairpins from the blue ceramic bowl on the dresser. She deftly pinned up the errant tresses and then exited the house.

On the porch, a basket holding her garden tools and gloves waited for her, and she picked it up and looked over at the man sitting in a recliner only a few feet away. Next to him stood an empty wheelchair, and he was busy reading the morning paper.

"Anything good, Peter?" the woman asked, as she did every morning.

"I'll say," the man that was her husband of thirty years said, which wasn't his usual response. "A lot going on at the border. The refugees are apparently coming over in droves. Isn't that something, Ginny?"

A sudden weakness in her knees made Guinevere grab hold of the railing. "It sure sounds like something. This weakens Bowler's position in the United Assembly. Or, it should, at least." She spoke calmly, but her gaze was drawn to the south end of their large property. Around them the forest went on for miles toward the northwest and billowing fields in the southeast.

Peter pulled off his reading glasses. "Why don't you take a walk down to the tree, darling?"

"I was there yesterday." Guinevere bit her lip and tried to sound dismissive, but her heart was pounding so hard, she could barely breathe.

"I'd go myself if I could," Peter said and smiled gently. Reaching out, he took the basket from her. "I'll just mind these for you until you come back. When you have that look in your eyes, you won't settle down until you've been to the tree."

"Okay." He was right.

Guinevere kissed her husband on the lips and pushed her naked feet into some rubber boots. Walking through the garden toward the tree line, she slowed her steps as she neared the woods. She knew every inch of this place. They had lived in the cottage for more than twenty years. Before, when they lived in the capital, Peter had been a physically broken man after surviving a stealth attack by Klowdynian agents operating in Sandslot. The attack had been the catalyst that started the uproar against Klowdyn in the United Assembly.

She and Peter had used to be well known for being politically active and raising awareness about Klowdyn's oppressive regime and blatant disregard for human rights. The abduction of their daughter more than twenty years ago had catapulted them into a cult phenomenon. When Klowdynian agents had tried to assassinate Peter, leaving him a physically broken man for several years, the outrage around the world and in the United Assembly had created such a backlash and sanctions against Klowdyn that letters from their daughter's kidnappers containing threats against her life had increased exponentially.

So, Peter and Guinevere had decided to go underground. If no one could find or blackmail them, they wouldn't gain anything by harming Aurelia. Despite the efforts of the Sandslot law-enforcement agencies, no one ever found their child or brought the people who took her to justice.

Only two people knew of their whereabouts. Through a chain, they sent messages with news, yet so far they contained news only about their relatives and friends throughout Sandslot, and never about Aurelia. Nobody knew if their child was still alive or where she might be. Klowdyn had two colonies in the southern hemisphere, and for all they knew, she could have been placed in one of them twenty-one years ago.

Guinevere walked in among the trees, and the shade chilled her bare arms, making her wish she'd put on her cardigan. She rubbed her palms up and down her arms as she walked. When she grew close enough to see the old tree with a hole in the trunk, perfect for clandestine notes as it was protected from the elements, her heart began to ache. She gave a muted sob and began to run.

Their secret mailman, or woman, had never revealed themselves, but Guinevere and Peter realized it had to be a local who received their notes in letters delivered to them. She hoped she one day could thank this person.

Guinevere reached the tree and climbed up on the boulder right next to it. She drew a deep breath and pushed her hand into the hole. At first, nothing. She turned her wrist and tried from another angle. And there. Something. She closed her fingers around the small envelope and pulled it out. Slowly she sank onto the boulder and stared at the envelope with blurred vision. Wiping impatiently at her tears, she opened it.

The note wasn't long, but the letters seemed to move, dance, even, across the paper, and it took Guinevere a moment to calm herself enough to read.

Mom and Dad,

It is safe for you to return home since the threat to me is gone. Or, I can come to you. You can verify with Aunt Lisette. I have missed you every day since I was taken, and I never forgot.

I love you both.

Aurelia

Guinevere gripped the note so hard after rereading it three times, she feared she might have torn it. She jumped to her feet and ran back toward the house. The bun she had just reinforced with more hair pins began to shift, and soon her hair fluttered behind her. When she was within sight of the cottage, she waved, holding the note high above her head.

Over on the porch, she saw Peter pull himself onto his feet, clutching the railing with both hands. Guinevere raced through the garden and stopped just below, where her husband stood staring at her, tears streaming down his face.

Guinevere held out the note to him, but he only shook his head and clung to the railing.

"Ginny?"

"It's her. She's alive. She's in the capital." Guinevere took another deep breath and hurried up to Peter, wrapping her arms around him. He clung to her, and she lowered him back into the recliner. Falling to her knees, she hid her face in his lap as he stroked her hair with trembling hands. "Aurelia's home."

About the Author

Gun Brooke, author of more than twenty novels, resides in Sweden, surrounded by a loving family and two affectionate dogs. When she isn't writing on her novels for Bold Strokes Books, she works on her arts and crafts whenever possible—certain that practice pays off. Gun loves creating cover art for her own books and for others using digital art software.

Web site: http://www.gbrooke-fiction.com
Facebook: http://www.facebook.com/gunbach
Twitter: http://twitter.com/redheadgrrl1960
Tumblr: http://gunbrooke.tumblr.com/

Books Available from Bold Strokes Books

Best Practice by Carsen Taite. When attorney Grace Maldonado agrees to mentor her best friend's little sister, she's prepared to confront Perry's rebellious nature, but she isn't prepared to fall in love. Legal Affairs: one law firm, three best friends, three chances to fall in love. (978-1-63555-361-1)

Home by Kris Bryant. Natalie and Sarah discover that anything is possible when love takes the long way home. (978-1-63555-853-1)

Keeper by Sydney Quinne. With a new charge under her reluctant wing—feisty, highly intelligent math wizard Isabelle Templeton—Keeper Andy Bouchard has to prevent a murder or die trying. (978-1-63555-852-4)

One More Chance by Ali Vali. Harry Bastantes planned a future with Desi Thompson until the day Desi disappeared without a word, only to walk back into her life sixteen years later. (978-1-63555-536-3)

Renegade's War by Gun Brooke. Freedom fighter Aurelia DeCallum regrets saving the woman called Blue. She fears it will jeopardize her mission, and secretly, Blue might end up breaking Aurelia's heart. (978-1-63555-484-7)

The Other Women by Erin Zak. What happens in Vegas should stay in Vegas, but what do you do when the love you find in Vegas changes your life forever? (978-1-63555-741-1)

The Sea Within by Missouri Vaun. Time is running out for Dr. Elle Graham to convince Captain Jackson Drake that the only thing that can save future Earth resides in the past, and rescue her broken heart in the process. (978-1-63555-568-4)

To Sleep With Reindeer by Justine Saracen. In Norway under Nazi occupation, Marrit, an Indigenous woman; and Kirsten, a Norwegian resister, join forces to stop the development of an atomic weapon. (978-1-63555-735-0)

Twice Shy by Aurora Rey. Having an ex with benefits isn't all it's cracked up to be. Will Amanda Russo learn that lesson in time to take a chance on love with Quinn Sullivan? (978-1-63555-737-4)

Z-Town by Eden Darry. Forced to work together to stay alive, Meg and Lane must find the centuries-old treasure before the zombies find them first. (978-1-63555-743-5)

Bet Against Me by Fiona Riley. In the high stakes luxury real estate market, everything has a price, and as rival Realtors Trina Lee and Kendall Yates find out, that means their hearts and souls, too. (978-1-63555-729-9)

Broken Reign by Sam Ledel. Together on an epic journey in search of a mysterious cure, a princess and a village outcast must overcome life-threatening challenges and their own prejudice if they want to survive. (978-1-63555-739-8)

Just One Taste by CJ Birch. For Lauren, it only took one taste to start trusting in love again. (978-1-63555-772-5)

Lady of Stone by Barbara Ann Wright. Sparks fly as a magical emergency forces a noble embarrassed by her ability to submit to a low-born teacher who resents everything about her. (978-1-63555-607-0)

Last Resort by Angie Williams. Katie and Rhys are about to find out what happens when you meet the girl of your dreams but you aren't looking for a happily ever after. (978-1-63555-774-9)

Longing for You by Jenny Frame. When Debrek housekeeper Katie Brekman is attacked amid a burgeoning vampire-witch war, Alexis Villiers must go against everything her clan believes in to save her. (978-1-63555-658-2)

Money Creek by Anne Laughlin. Clare Lehane is a troubled lawyer from Chicago who tries to make her way in a rural town full of secrets and deceptions. (978-1-63555-795-4)

Passion's Sweet Surrender by Ronica Black. Cam and Blake are unable to deny their passion for each other, but surrendering to love is a whole different matter. (978-1-63555-703-9)

The Holiday Detour by Jane Kolven. It will take everything going wrong to make Dana and Charlie see how right they are for each other. (978-1-63555-720-6)

Too Hot to Ride by Andrews & Austin. World famous cutting horse champion and industry legend Jane Barrow is knockdown sexy in the way she moves, talks, and rides, and Rae Starr is determined not to get involved with this womanizing gambler. (978-1-63555-776-3)

A Love that Leads to Home by Ronica Black. For Carla Sims and Janice Carpenter, home isn't about location, it's where your heart is. (978-1-63555-675-9)

Blades of Bluegrass by D. Jackson Leigh. A US Army occupational therapist must rehab a bitter veteran who is a ticking political time bomb the military is desperate to disarm. (978-1-63555-637-7)

Guarding Hearts by Jaycie Morrison. As treachery and temptation threaten the women of the Women's Army Corps, who will risk it all for love? (978-1-63555-806-7)

Hopeless Romantic by Georgia Beers. Can a jaded wedding planner and an optimistic divorce attorney possibly find a future together? (978-1-63555-650-6)

Hopes and Dreams by PJ Trebelhorn. Movie theater manager Riley Warren is forced to face her high school crush and tormentor, wealthy socialite Victoria Thayer, at their twentieth reunion. (978-1-63555-670-4)

In the Cards by Kimberly Cooper Griffin. Daria and Phaedra are about to discover that love finds a way, especially when powers outside their control are at play. (978-1-63555-717-6)

Moon Fever by Ileandra Young. SPEAR agent Danika Karson must clear her werewolf friend of multiple false charges while teaching her vampire girlfriend to resist the blood mania brought on by a full moon. (978-1-63555-603-2)

Quake City by St John Karp. Can Andre find his best friend Amy before the night devolves into a nightmare of broken hearts, malevolent drag queens, and spontaneous human combustion? Or has it always happened this way, every night, at Aunty Bob's Quake City Club? (978-1-63555-723-7)

Serenity by Jesse J. Thoma. For Kit Marsden, there are many things in life she cannot change. Serenity is in the acceptance. (978-1-63555-713-8)

Sylver and Gold by Michelle Larkin. Working feverishly to find a killer before he strikes again, Boston Homicide Detective Reid Sylver and rookie cop London Gold are blindsided by their chemistry and developing attraction. (978-1-63555-611-7)

Trade Secrets by Kathleen Knowles. In Silicon Valley, love and business are a volatile mix for clinical lab scientist Tony Leung and venture capitalist Sheila Graham. (978-1-63555-642-1)

Death Overdue by David S. Pederson. Did Heath turn to murder in an alcohol induced haze to solve the problem of his blackmailer, or was it someone else who brought about a death overdue? (978-1-63555-711-4)

Entangled by Melissa Brayden. Becca Crawford is the perfect person to head up the Jade Hotel, if only the captivating owner of the local vineyard would get on board with her plan and stop badmouthing the hotel to everyone in town. (978-1-63555-709-1)

First Do No Harm by Emily Smith. Pierce and Cassidy are about to discover that when it comes to love, sometimes you have to risk it all to have it all. (978-1-63555-699-5)

Kiss Me Every Day by Dena Blake. For Wynn Evans, wishing for a do-over with Carly Jamison was a long shot, actually getting one was a game changer. (978-1-63555-551-6)

Olivia by Genevieve McCluer. In this lesbian Shakespeare adaptation with vampires, Olivia is a centuries old vampire who must fight a strange figure from her past if she wants a chance at happiness. (978-1-63555-701-5)

One Woman's Treasure by Jean Copeland. Daphne's search for discarded antiques and treasures leads to an embarrassing misunderstanding, and ultimately, the opportunity for the romance of a lifetime with Nina. (978-1-63555-652-0)

Silver Ravens by Jane Fletcher. Lori has lost her girlfriend, her home, and her job. Things don't improve when she's kidnapped and taken to fairyland. (978-1-63555-631-5)

Still Not Over You by Jenny Frame, Carsen Taite, Ali Vali. Old flames die hard in these tales of a second chance at love with the ex you're still not over. Stories by award winning authors Jenny Frame, Carsen Taite, and Ali Vali. (978-1-63555-516-5)

Storm Lines by Jessica L. Webb. Devon is a psychologist who likes rules. Marley is a cop who doesn't. They don't always agree, but both fight to protect a girl immersed in a street drug ring. (978-1-63555-626-1)

The Politics of Love by Jen Jensen. Is it possible to love across the political divide in a hostile world? Conservative Shelley Whitmore and liberal Rand Thomas are about to find out. (978-1-63555-693-3)

All the Paths to You by Morgan Lee Miller. High school sweethearts Quinn Hughes and Kennedy Reed reconnect five years after they break up and realize that their chemistry is all but over. (978-1-63555-662-9)

Arrested Pleasures by Nanisi Barrett D'Arnuck. When charged with a crime she didn't commit, Katherine Lowe faces the question: Which is harder, going to prison or falling in love? (978-1-63555-684-1)

Bonded Love by Renee Roman. Carpenter Blaze Carter suffers an injury that shatters her dreams, and ER nurse Trinity Greene hopes to show her that sometimes love is worth fighting for. (978-1-63555-530-1)

Convergence by Jane C. Esther. With life as they know it on the line, can Aerin McLeary and Olivia Ando's love survive an otherworldly threat to humankind? (978-1-63555-488-5)

Coyote Blues by Karen F. Williams. Riley Dawson, psychotherapist and shape-shifter, has her world turned upside down when Fiona Bell, her one true love, returns. (978-1-63555-558-5)

Drawn by Carsen Taite. Will the clues lead Detective Claire Hanlon to the killer terrorizing Dallas, or will she merely lose her heart to person of interest, urban artist Riley Flynn? (978-1-63555-644-5)

Every Summer Day by Lee Patton. Meant to celebrate every summer day, Luke's journal instead chronicles a love affair as fast-moving and possibly as fatal as his brother's brain tumor. (978-1-63555-706-0)

Lucky by Kris Bryant. Was Serena Evans's luck really about winning the lottery, or is she about to get even luckier in love? (978-1-63555-510-3)

The Last Days of Autumn by Donna K. Ford. Autumn and Caroline question the fairness of life, the cruelty of loss, and what it means to love as they navigate the complicated minefield of relationships, grief, and life-altering illness. (978-1-63555-672-8)

Three Alarm Response by Erin Dutton. In the midst of tragedy, can these first responders find love and healing? Three stories of courage, bravery, and passion. (978-1-63555-592-9)

Veterinary Partner by Nancy Wheelton. Callie and Lauren are determined to keep their hearts safe but find that taking a chance on love is the safest option of all. (978-1-63555-666-7)